Anonymous

Aristocracy

A Novel

Anonymous

Aristocracy
A Novel

ISBN/EAN: 9783337002428

Printed in Europe, USA, Canada, Australia, Japan

Cover: Foto ©Andreas Hilbeck / pixelio.de

More available books at **www.hansebooks.com**

A NOVEL

NEW YORK
D. APPLETON AND COMPANY
1888.

ARISTOCRACY.

CHAPTER I.

It is half-past ten on a dull November morning at Ashwynwick* Park, the seat of the Marquis of Oaktorrington,† in Hertfordshire.‡

Ashwynwick is one of the show-places of the county—if, indeed, not of England—and shares fairly the local position of honor with Hatfield. The estate, some twenty-odd thousand acres in extent, has been in Lord Oaktorrington's family since the Conquest. An ancestor, the first of the English line, one Brian de Vesci, came over with William of Normandy, and thereafter faithfully attending him " in his wars," as the family chronicle put forth by Burke, that obliging servant of the British aristocracy, hath it, was granted the property by his royal master " in recognition of his services."

There are some ill-natured rumors current that these services consisted of those of valet and body-servant to the conqueror, combined on occasion with the

---

* Pronounced *Azzick*.   † Pronounced *Otton*.
‡ Pronounced *Harfudsheer*.

duties of cook. It was all, however, so long ago that the family has had time to considerably improve its condition. The house was built in the time of Queen Elizabeth, during whose reign the head of the family became a court favorite, and in due time was created a baron by the Virgin Queen. Its massive gray, moss-grown walls and ivy-covered gables of ancient days are relieved by the plate-glass windows and gas-lamps of modern times. It is a combination of past and present both in its exterior and interior. It has a picture-gallery, from whose walls scores of pointed-bearded and villainous-countenanced men, and pink-cheeked, immodestly *décolleté* women, look down upon you ; a banqueting-hall whose carved-oak wainscot is lined with the armor of every knightly De Vesci who fought under his sovereign's banner from Cressy to Agincourt ; and a haunted room, in which the ghost of the Sir Roderick de, Vesci who was beheaded by Charles II on Tower Hill for treason, is wont to hold high jinks as the fit seizes him—just as it has a billiard room, a sanitary system of drainage, and a gasometer. The gardens, conservatories, and greenhouses cover ten acres of ground, and the pleasure-grounds twice as much more. The establishment is one of the grand-est in the kingdom. There are between thirty and forty servants, irrespective of gardeners and game-keepers who, together, number as many more. In the stables and coach-houses which form a quadrangle round a paved yard, and resemble in their exterior a pretentious human residence more than an equine abode, are upward of thirty horses and a dozen car-riages. And Ashwynwick is not Lord Oaktorrington's only residence. He has, besides, two other country-houses : Campsottin * Court in Bedfordshire; and Tewtorlock † Towers in Devonshire; as well as a town-house in Eaton Square. He is the fourteenth baron (creation of Elizabeth, 1565), eighth viscount and earl (creation of Charles I, 1642), and fifth marquis (creation of William III, 1701) of his line, and from rent-roll, coal-mines, pensions, and invested money in the funds, is in receipt of the reputed income of one hundred and twenty thousand pounds per annum. So far as exalted rank, long line of ancestry, and the possession of large estates and this world's goods are concerned, he is as fair a sample of the five hundred and thirty-odd gentlemen who compose the peerage of Great Britain as one could pick out.

Breakfast has been over about a quarter of an hour, and the Marchioness of Oaktorrington is seated at her writing-table in her boudoir, reading again the letters she had but hastily glanced over at the breakfast-table. There is an air of solid comfort about the apartment, rather than gilded decoration and display. The walls and ceiling are not frescoed, and the furniture is plain, unvarnished oak like that of the rest of the house, and has—with the title, jewels, plate, pictures, and wine in the cellars—been in the family a very long time. A bright fire burns in the grate, and sheds a look as well as a sense of warmth over the room. Without, a chill November fog hangs about and clings to the leafless trees and sodden turf, and dims the window-panes into the resemblance of ground glass. The Marchioness has taken one letter from an envelope with a foreign stamp and postmark, and holds it long before her with

---

* Pronounced *Capston*.   † Pronounced *Tellick*.

a look which began by one of vexation but has ended in one of satisfaction.

While she thus sits let us have a look at her and see what she is like.

Fat, red-faced, and waddling—that doom of nine tenths of British highborn matronhood, the other tenth being thin, bony, and pinched—she yet shows in her arched eyebrows, thin nostrils, short, curled upper lip, white, smooth forehead, small ears, and delicately poised head on a neck which refuses to grow short and fat with the rest of her body, those indices of noble birth which are supposed to belong exclusively and of natural right to the nobility, but which as a matter of obstinate fact are found quite as often, if not indeed oftener, among the so-called " middle " classes. Did you have a real, personal knowledge of all classes in England you would say she had the body of a peeress and the face and head of a had-been pretty woman of no class in particular. Did you depend upon Bulwer Lytton, Disraeli, "Ouida," "The Duchess," and Miss Braddon for the formation of your ideal you would think her face a model of British high-born femininity, while her body you would regard as a painful exception to the general rule. However, though she may not satisfactorily look it, the Marchioness of Oaktorrington is a representative of the English aristocracy, and a pretty fair one at that. Not only is she the wife of the Marquis of Oaktorrington (which any costermonger's daughter might be), and therefore an aristocrat by marriage and position ; but she is the daughter of the Duke of Tallyforward,* one of England's most ancient *duces,*

---

* Pronounced *Telford.*

and therefore an aristocrat by birth. She is verging close upon fifty, and has been married to Lord Oaktorrington since she was sold to him for a jointure of six thousand a year, a dower-house in Kent, an annual pin-money allowance of a thousand pounds, the life-use of the Oaktorrington diamonds, and a marchioness's coronet and title—just eight and twenty years ago. The Duke of Tallyforward, though of as ancient a family and title as Burke or De Britt can produce, was yet what is known in aristocratic parlance as a "poor duke," the meaning of which was not that he was not a good specimen of England's first grade of nobility (mutual doubts as to fitness never arising in the aristocratic breast) but that he was the reverse of a rich one. His daughter's dowry was not consequently large. Ten thousand pounds it was—("Fancy! and a duke's daughter," was the comment of the day) so, though Englishmen of Lord Oaktorrington's class seldom, if ever, are known to marry where there is no money, his lordship, who was then a youth of two and twenty in the Grenadiers, had special reasons for taking to himself a wife, and therefore was pleased to let it be thought that he presented the marvelous spectacle of an English peer marrying for beauty's sake alone. Lady Julia Talbot's beauty was of the sort which in its mere symmetry more than regularity of feature was of a piece with two thirds of the other girls out that season. There was the same small head, the same straight nose, the same white forehead, the same curled upper lip, the same pink ears, the same half-closed eyes, the same square shoulders, the same swelling bust, the same small, round waist, the same vacant expression, and the same frigid repellant manner in every girl he saw whether in ball-dress or habit, in Belgravian drawing-room at night or in the Row of an afternoon. It didn't matter which he chose. One would suit his purpose as well as the other. " They are as like as peas, all of 'em," he said to his friend Percy Van Sittart of the Scots Fusiliers (the Duke of Cambridge hadn't played the fool with regimental titles then). " Don't seem to matter which I pick out, but marry I must. The title and property must have an heir, so one's as good as another for that, don't you know. It's a bore to make up one's mind, though."

" Care for any of 'em ?"

"No. Not really. Must marry *some* girl, don't you see ? "

"Toss up, why don't you?" said Percy, producing his tossing guinea from a waistcoat-pocket. " Now, then ; name two of the lot. Quick, don't think.

"Julia Talbot, Emily Walsingham !"

"All right. Talbot heads, Walsingham tails. Here goes. Hi! It's Talbot. That settles it. Now, go this very afternoon and propose, old chap."

And that's how it came about that Lady Julia Talbot became the Marchioness of Oaktorrington.

In her eight and twenty years of wedded bliss, if the artificial mechanical existence of a woman so married can be denominated such, she has dutifully fulfilled the function of maternity for which she was selected, and has presented her liege lord with the following seven offspring:

(*Place aux gentilhommes en Angleterre.*)

Viscount Beyndour,* a lieutenant in the Life Guards; aged twenty-five.

---

* Pronounced Banner.

.Lord Frederick-Fitzwhistle-Adelbert-James-De-la-Crash-Vesey (the latter being the moderized family name of the Oaktorrington marquisate), out upon a Colorado cattle-ranch ; aged twenty-two.

Lord Bertie-Cornwallis - Boscawen - Berkeley-John-Jervise - William - Vesey, an undergraduate at Christ Church College, Oxford ; aged nineteen.

Lord Cecil-Somerset-Frederick-James-John-Spencer-Digby-Henry-Vesey, a boy at Eton ; aged twelve.

Lady Mary-Victoria-Caroline-Frances-Vesey, plain and *passée*, having passed through four London seasons unasked ; aged twenty-seven.

Lady Edith-Maud-Alexandra-Emily-Vesey, a reproduction of her mother at the same age and, therefore, a beauty ; presented last season ; aged eighteen.

Lady Maud-Mabel-Hilda-Mary-Edith-Ponsonby-Eliza-Vesey, a girl still in the school-room ; aged ten.

The marchioness still holds the open letter in her hand when the marquis opens the door abruptly, and walks in with a heavy, striding step.

George-Rupert-Cecil-Frederick, Baron Ashwyn-wick, Viscount Beyndour, Earl of Campsottin, and Marquis of Oaktorrington, is a tall, raw-boned man, five years his wife's senior. He has short, red hair, moustache and beard considerably shot with gray ; cold, steely-blue eyes ; a large, sensual, and weak mouth ; uneven yellow teeth ; a pug nose ; a receding chin, which his beard is too close-cropped to conceal ; a bright-red face and neck ; large, bony hands ; and immense feet. In short, to look at him, he is about the last man in the world that an uninitiated person would expect to find a " lord." He wears a scarlet

hunting-coat, denominated "pink" in sporting parlance; a white scarf, with a silver horse-shoe pin stuck
in it; a white, ribbed waistcoat; white cord breeches
and top boots. On his head is a tall, black hat; in
his left eye a rimless eyeglass; and in his hand a
hunting-crop.

"Look here, Polly," he says, as he strides up to the
chimney-piece, and spreading his coat-tails, stands with
his back to the fire; "I'm rather up a tree. Here's a
letter from Harborough, proposing himself for next
week; says he'll fetch down a couple of hunters, and
evidently means to stay when he gets here. It's deuced
awkward, you know."

"Why?" asks his wife, putting down her letter on
her lap, and looking at him impatiently.

"Why? That's a pretty question for you to ask.
Aren't the Bouveries coming on Tuesday? You keep
a nice run of your guests, I must say. Well, you can't
have a man like that to meet them. They'd book it
the minute they saw him, and a delightful scandal we
should have. Humph! As usual, not a word. You
irritate me."

"Isn't his Grace swell enough for the Bouveries?
I should have thought so," and Lady Oaktorrington
shrugs her fat shoulders with a little more curl than
ever on her lip.

"No, he's not. I don't care if he is a duke; he's an
out and out blackguard, as every one knows, and you
too."

"I? I *know* nothing. I dare say the stories about
him are shamefully exaggerated."

"Exaggerated? They're not half bad enough, as *I*
happen to know. Why he's to be made a co-respond-

ent·for the sixth time in a day or two.   It's all over the clubs.   Chandos-Peele is—"

"So Lord Chandos has actually taken notice of her ladyship and Harborough at last, has he?   Ha-ha! His obliquity of vision has been astounding."

"I tell you there isn't a greater scoundrel in the kingdom."

"What, than Chandos Peele?   I thought he was only a fool."

"You know quite well I mean Harborough."

"You seem to be on rather intimate terms with the greatest scoundrel in the kingdom," her ladyship says, with another little shrug.   "Fancy your knowing a scoundrel well enough to have him write and propose a visit to you!"

"I like that.   You know as well as I do that I can't cut a man in his position.   I have to know him and be civil to him, no matter what my private opinion may be.   And you know I want him to give Bertie a living one of these days.   He's got over twenty in his gift."

"Yes, and eighty thousand a year, half a dozen places, and a ducal coronet on his head.   You seem to forget Mary and Edith, my dear."

Whenever Lady Oaktorrington wishes to be very impressive to her husband, or to give particular point to her words, she always ends up with "my dear."

His lordship looks at her quickly.   His eye-glass drops like a shot, and his left eyelid quivers.   It is his sign of weakening.

"I see what you mean," he says, in a subdued voice. "One forgets one's tiresome gals sometimes.   Yes, yes, you're right.   I suppose we must have him."

His wife relents, woman-like, the moment she has won, and veers round like a weather-cock in a whirl-wind.

"Oh, you needn't cry about it," she says. "If you feel so awfully cut up about his meeting the Bouveries, why, perhaps—let me see his letter."

The marquis tosses it absently over to her. It falls at her feet, and she stoops and picks it up, and reads :

> "*Marlborough Club*
> "*Pall Mall, S. W.,*
> "*Wednesday.*
>
> "*My dear Otty :*
> "*In response to your many pressing invitations expect your humble servant, two nags, a groom, and valet by* 4.16 *train Tuesday. By-the-by, I saw—* ·What's this ?"

"Oh, I say !" shouts the marquis, suddenly waking up, and making a spring for the letter which his wife puts quickly out of his reach, behind her back. "You needn't mind reading that. It's only some chaff about —about a—a horse at Tattersall's I didn't buy. Give it to me."

"I mean to read this letter through, my dear," Lady Oaktorrington says, in a self-possessed, deter-mined voice.

The marquis turns with a smothered oath and strides back to the hearth-rug like a sulky dog. "Read it to yourself, then," he mutters between his teeth.

"*By-the-by,*" continues the marchioness aloud, "*I saw Val last night and she inquired most affectionately after you, and said you were no end of fun on Saturday.*
> "*Yours ever,*
> "*Harborough.*"

"Hum ! Horse—Tattersall's ! Wasn't it Saturday that you had to go up to town in response to an urgent whip from Lord Salisbury to be in your seat in the Lords for an important division on the Irish Land Bill. Parliament never sits on Saturday, does it?"

Lord Oaktorrington does not answer. He gnaws at his moustache, lets his eyeglass drop, puts it in his eye again, and cracks the knuckles of each finger in rotation. He tries to carry it off at last by whistling a bar of "Oh, What a Surprise!" without seeming to notice the peculiar applicability of the song, but signally fails.

"Oh, don't worry about it," Lady Oaktorrington says at last, after watching his discomfiture with malicious composure. "It doesn't matter in the very least. *I* don't care, I assure you. Here's the letter."

The marquis snatches it, tosses it into the fire, and turns to go.

"Stay a moment."

"I can't. I shall be late," he answers, without halting.

"Oh, come. I know better than that. I happen to know where the hounds meet. I have the fixtures in my looking-glass, there. If you look you'll see under Tedworth 'Shernfold Gate, 11.30.' It's less than a mile from the park gates, and you have an hour now. Do you hear, my dear?"

He comes back resignedly and, throwing himself into a chair, says :

"Well ? "

"Oh, I haven't a word to say about that letter. It's about this, I'd like to speak to you. It's from Freddy."

"More money, I dare say."

"No.   He's coming home."

"Coming home ?   What the deuce does he mean ?"

"I thought you'd be angry about it.   But that's not the worst, you'll think," and her ladyship smiles grimly to herself as she thinks of the bombshell she is going to explode in her husband's ears.   "He's bringing an American friend—"

"What, here ?   An American ? " and the marquis jumps to his feet and walks up and down the hearthrug like a caged tiger at the Zoo.   "No fear."

"I thought you'd say that.   But unfortunately it's not so easy as you think."

"And why, pray?   Am I obliged to turn my house into a bear-garden to suit the whim of a younger son ? By Jove, I rather fancy not ! "

"Don't go on striding up and down that rug. You'll wear it out."

The marquis pays no heed.   "Do you hear, my dear ? "

He stops like a shot.

"Shall I tell you why," she asks, presently.

"Yes.   Out with it."

"In the first place its quite absurd the hatred you have for Americans.   The prince has the greatest admiration for them.   You certainly can't set yourself above him in that."

"Yes, I can.   Why shouldn't I ?   I don't care two straws what Tummy does.   I know he makes an ass of himself over every Yankee girl with a pretty face and a loud voice that comes to London.   Their free and easy manners suit his fastidious taste, I dessay. It's only Yankee *women*, at all events, that he has any thing to do with. He takes devilish good care to give the *men* a wide birth."

"Really, I rather fancy he was especially civil to a Dr. Holmes last year."

"And who's that? Fancy, too, having a doctor to meet our friends on equal terms! You'll be wanting me to ask my dentist down here next. People blame Chamberlain and Bright and Bradlaugh and Labouchere for trying to pull down the throne and upset society, but its my opinion that Tummy's the worst of the lot. Talk of Radicals—"

"I have no wish to do that," interrupts Lady Oaktorrington, with her Primrose Dame's nose in the air. "One gets quite enough of that at every League meeting. What I wish to say is : You can't refuse to do what the prince does."

"Haw — haw!" laughs the marquis. "Really? I dessay now you'd like me to have a lot of Gaiety charmers down from a Saturday to Monday?"

"Gaiety charmers? I don't quite understand."

"Oh, no, I dessay not. You never heard of Millie Montague and Fanny Barron and Val—ahem—er—er, and—and—"

"Go on," says the marchioness as cool as you please, but with a vindictive glitter under her half-shut eyelids.

"And — er —" flounders his lordship, "Maudie Verschoyle, and—and—Hyacinthe Dameron. Better have *her* down to meet Swansdale next time he comes."

"Are you quite done?" asks his wife, haughtily. "If so, don't you think we had better change the subject, and go back to Freddy's letter? I'll read it, and then you'll see why I think we must have his friend

2

come here." It was Lady Oaktorrington's invariable custom to go through the form of consulting her husband in everything, just as it was to act upon her own sole judgement afterward.

> "*Hotel Brunswick,*
>> "*New York, Oct.* 30.

"*My dearest Mother :—*" she begins.

"Oh, cut all that," his lordship mutters, giving the fire a vigorous poke to emphasize his words ; the result being that his wife repeats even the date.

"*I haven't written for an age because I didn't like to tell you I'd left the ranch. Fact is, I couldn't stand it. It's all very well you know eating pork and beans every day for every meal, but when it comes to having to bunk it with a cowboy—* ' Bunk it with a cowboy '? " repeats the marchioness. "What on earth can he mean ?"

The marquis belongs to the Royal Yacht Squadron and says, authoritatively : "A bunk is where you sleep aboard ship, don't you know. I dessay he means he had to sleep with a—what did you say ?"

"Cowboy."

"I'm blessed if I know what that is. Some atrocious Yankee slang, no doubt, that Freddy has picked up. What a bore he'll be with it when he comes back. But, never mind. Go on."

"*But when one comes to having to bunk it with a cowboy, why then, one seems suddenly to remember who one is, don't you know. I was sure you and father would agree with me when you thought it over, and so I let the time go over without writing. I walked three and twenty miles to Medicine Bow on the Union Pacific, and had just money enough to take an emigrant ticket for New York.*

The emigrant train didn't pass through till night, so I had several hours to wait at the station. While I waited the East bound express from California stopped for dinner, and most of the passengers got out. Several stayed in the train and had their dinner from their lunch-baskets, which all overland passengers carry."

"What a bore Freddy is?" growls the marquis. "Who the deuce cares a penny farthing what the traveling Yankees do? Can't you cut all that rot?"

Lady Oaktorrington makes no reply, but goes on: *"I was walking up and down, feeling painfully hungry, when I saw a young man stick his head out of the window of one of the cars and signal to me. 'Look here,' he said, 'would you mind getting me a couple of bottles of lager in the saloon? Here's a dollar. You can keep the change.' Fancy our Freddy!"*

"Fancy indeed!"

"Of course I was only too glad to go. The change was thirty-five cents—about eighteen pence—and I was just upon the point of getting myself a glass of beer with it when I thought—no, I won't."

"Bosh!" from the marquis.

"It's not in accord with the American idea of my class. No American would accept a tip like that for a neighborly service, and while I'm here I'll be as good as they are—
'As good as they are'? I don't quite comprehend."

"No more do I," says the marquis. "It's some republican, democratic rubbish he's picked up among the Yankees. If he goes on airing such balderdash here, I'll turn him out neck and crop."

"So I brought back the lager beer and handed him the change with it. 'What, won't take it?' 'No, thanks,' I said. 'I think I'd rather not.' I was starving, too."

"Ass! Idiot!" breaks in the marquis. "There's universal equality for you! Universal rot!"

"'*Well, then, come in and have a glass of beer with me,' he said. I couldn't refuse that, so in I got. He had that part of the Pullman car called the drawing-room—*"

"More Greek," mutters the marquis.

"*All to himself, and after the beer he asked me to have something to eat, and the first thing I knew the train started and carried me off. It was twelve miles to the next station, which meant over half an hour, and by that time we were such friends that he wouldn't let me go. I told him the hole I was in, and he said not to mind, he'd stake me till I got home. And so I've been with him ever since. He has paid for everything for me, and actually made me take money to spend for anything I wanted, and, in short, has acted like a real prince to me.*"

"Sharp Yankee trick that. Of course I shall have to pay up."

"You won't have to do anything of the sort, as you'll see. Don't interrupt again. *He is on his way to Europe and has paid my passage in the 'Etruria' with him on Saturday when we sail. So what could I do? I told him then who I really was. He had thought all along that I was some commercial chap or other in distress—*"

"Likely," sneers the Marquis. "Trust those Yankees to smell out a title."

"*And I've asked him to come and stay with us. I felt sure you and father wouldn't object when you heard how kind he was to me and who he is. He's the only son of a 'Frisco millionaire, one of the solid men, they call it here, and he's such an awfully nice fellow, so good looking and*

good mannered, and well educated—in fact, he's fit for any
society. He is very shy and modest—"

"Haw—haw!" laughs the marquis. "Fancy a Yankee that!"

"*—and I have persuaded him to come and see us at
once. He intended to go to Italy, but he'll come down with
me, and you may look out for us about Monday or Tuesday week, and you must be sure to give him a warm reception. I must now stop. My best love to all.*

"*Your most affectionate*
"*Fred'k F. J. Vesey."*

Lady Oaktorrington puts down the letter, and, looking up at her husband, says, "Well?"

She has already quite settled in her mind about it,
but nevertheless goes through the usual form.

"Not to be heard of," answers the marquis. "Not
for a moment. Fancy a Yankee in my house! A Yankee adventurer from an outlandish place called 'Frisco!
The name's enough to show what he is. I never heard
the like," he goes on, waxing more indignant; "I shall
wire Freddy at Queenstown to say so."

"No, you won't. We shall have to let him come."

"Polly!"

"Yes, I've thought it all over, and though I confess
I wasn't very keen about it at first, I've decided that
we must make some return for the young man's kindness."

"Oh, let Freddy stand him a dinner at the Cri or
Metopole. That'll be enough. I'll pay for it. Tom
Fielding told me the other day he had a Yankee, who'd
done the civil to him in New York last year, come over
and hunt him up at his club. Fancy the cheek of that!

So he asked him to dine at the Cri, or Gatti's, or the
Grosvenor Gallery, I forget which, and that quite satisfied the fellow, whom he's managed to dodge ever
since."

"But that won't do for us. We are not Tom Fielding. He hasn't any daughters, and we have."

"The gals again," sighs the marquis.

"If he's all Freddy says he is, we might do worse
for Mary."

"All Freddy says he is? Are you quite so green
as that? And even if he is, do you think I'd consent
to a daughter of mine marrying a Yankee? No fear."

"Oh, yes, you would—if he had lots of money.
What do you call Lord Rudolph Campbell's wife, and
Lord Sanduval's, and Sir George Castor-Paye's, and
Sir Henry Haskell's, and Captain Dodget's, and Colonel
Hayes-Wallet's? All Americans, every one, and all
heiresses into the bargain."

"Ah, yes; true. They are wives. That's different. But who ever heard of an English lady of our
class taking a Yankee husband?"

Lady Oaktorrington is stumped for a moment, but
only for a moment.

"I see what you mean," she answers; "but there's
nothing in it, all the same. It doesn't in the least signify that we've no one else's example to follow. We
can afford to set the fashion. I'm quite willing that
Mary or Edith should marry an American gentleman
—if he has plenty of money."

"An American gentleman!" exclaims the marquis,
derisively. "Whoever saw one? Not I. There isn't
one of 'em that I've met abroad on the Continent that
isn't either a loud-voiced, inquisitive, bumptuous, self-

asserting auctioneer, or a supercilious, effeminate, mincing barber."

"Well, we shall see what this one is like; it's worth having him down if only to satisfy one's curiosity; and if, as I say, he is all that Freddy says, and has lots of money, I shall be willing to let either of the girls marry him, and so shall you, my dear."

The marquis strikes his colors at once.

"By Jove! I shall be late!"' he exclaims, as the stable-clock distantly chimes the quarter past, and, without another word or further hindrance from his wife, he strides from the room.

"Two large fish in sight," muses Lady Oaktorrington, spreading note-paper before her. "Not exactly what one might wish, perhaps, either of them. But one can't pick and choose in these days, and, with girls to settle, one mustn't forget the money. Yes, I shall write to the duke to come, and Freddy shall have a telegram of welcome for his friend awaiting him at Queenstown."

CHAPTER II.

HERBERT-Charles-Spencer-Henry-William-Colville, Baron Bouverie, of the United Kingdom, and a baronet, sits at breakfast in the breakfast-room of the Army and Navy Club, euphoniously termed among the aristocracy of the Army and Navy, who by a concatenation of fortuitous circumstances are enabled to become its members (and by those who delight to imitate them), "the Rag."

Lord Bouverie is an ex-officer of the Guards, hav-

ing served for six months in a battalion of the Cold-
streams, just before the breaking out of the Crimean
War. He had fairly begun to like the perils and hardships of a soldier's existence as they are typified in an
ensign's barrack life at the Tower, Windsor, and Chel-
sea, when his military career was terminated by his
having to sell out upon unexpectedly succeeding a
distant kinsman in the Bouverie title and estates.

"If it hadn't been for old Jack Bouverie coming a
cropper when out with the Pythcley at ninety-one, sir "
(to use his own words so expressed at least three
hundred and sixty-five times a year), "I should have
marched up the hill at Alma with the old regiment,
sir."

His friends know by this time that he then expects
some one to say:

"And marched down again, I hope?"

Whereupon he will shrug his shoulders, and say
with a look of much consequence: "Ah, can't tell
you *that*, sir." If he doesn't get a chance to say this,
it puts him in a sulk for the rest of the day.

He is a short, stout, man with a red pudding face
adorned with mutton-chop whiskers cut in a straight
horizontal line from ear to mouth corner; a bald head
on the crown, and longish dark hair at the back and
sides. He affects the military style as it prevailed in
the British army from Waterloo to the Crimea, and
wears a high pointed shirt-collar and black satin
stock; a tightly buttoned blue frock-coat, with short
waist, long skirts, and tight sleeves buttoned at the
wrists; buff trousers and straps, and a wide-brimmed
bell-crowned hat. In the street he never appears
without yellow chamois gloves, and a walking-stick

with a tassel. This gives him, he intends and thinks, an air of the great Duke of Wellington. There is, however, in him a deficiency of nose and chin, which (were there not one or two other essential qualities of Napoleon's conqueror unnecessary to mention also lacking) considerably mars the resemblance to the Iron Duke, and ruthlessly prevents it from being the startling success it otherwise might be.

When Lord Bouverie parted with his ensign's commission in consideration of the sum of six hundred and fifty pounds, upon succeeding to the title, he made in due course the orthodox, stereotyped, English "marriage in high life." In short, he bought and paid for an earl's daughter of the most approved pattern. Tall, long-necked, small-eyed, haughty, cold, proud, silent, and utterly indifferent to him, she had met him at two balls and while staying at the Duke of North-acres* for a week's hunting; and upon his declaring his intentions in due form her father and mother had told her she must marry him, and that was all there was about it. The following week the formal announcement that "A marriage is arranged and will shortly take place between," etc., appeared in the "Court Journal" and "Morning Post," and thereupon congratulations from relatives and friends poured in. The world knew not that *he* had thrown over a pretty brown-eyed girl, a clergyman's daughter down in Devonshire, with whom marriage had now become practically impossible ; and that *she* lavished all the love of which her rule-curbed nature was capable upon a certain handsome-faced curate of her father's

---

* Pronounced *Nakes.*

rector. It would not have mattered if it did know. That was thirty-odd years ago, and now "the Bouveries" as they are called—the name of family and title being the same—consist, with father and mother, of two sons and two daughters.

The eldest, the Honorable Percy, is keeping up the military spirit of his father as a subaltern in the Tenth Hussars, of which the Prince of Wales is colonel, and at the present moment is stationed with the regiment in India.

The second, the honorable John (called Jack), is a young man of twenty-two who hopes to get into the army, too. He has been up for his preliminary "exam" three times and egregiously failed, notwithstanding the fact that his father has paid a hatful of money to "crammers." Jack is still with a tutor preparing for another shy. The girls are the Honorables Emily and Augusta. They are twins, but no more alike than if they were not even sisters. Emily is dark, rapid, slangy, horsey, and plain. Augusta is fair, quiet, prim, and pretty. Both have perfect figures. Their age is twenty-four. *Voila les Bouveries!*

Lord Bouverie has drank his last mouthful of tea and swallowed his last bit of sausage, and does not know it, so busy has he been in reading his letters.

"What! By Jove, I can't have breakfasted, can I?" he exclaims, as he contemplates the empty dishes before him, and holds up the handle of the tea-pot without extracting a drop from the spout. "Yet I must. It's these confounded letters. I don't in the least know whether I had kidneys or bacon. There's not a vestige left on the dish to tell by. I'd smell my plate and find out in that way, only there's that confounded ass Bar-Sinister over there staring at me through his eyeglass. Deuced bore that man is! I'll just ring and ask the waiter."

When he has done so, he wonders how he shall worm it out of the man without a direct question.

"Oh, I say," as the waiter comes up; "I shall want some more—"

He stops to let the waiter fill up the hiatus. He does so by—

"Yesm'lud."

"Some—some—you know, some—"

"Yesm'lud."

"More—ahem! confound it!—bacon."

"Yesm'lud."

"Or, let me see. No. I'll have some more kidneys."

"Yesm'lud."

"Dash it—no. I'll have some—you know—what I had before."

"Yesm'lud."

His lordship grinds his teeth, with a scowl. It is useless to go on like this. The waiter seems to know but one word of the waiter-language, and that is—

"Yesm'lud."

A happy thought strikes his lordship. The scowl dissolves into a smile.

"Oh, I say. Bring me my order."

"Yesm'lud.

"Damn it man, don't you speak English?"

"Yesm'lud."

"Then, go and fetch me my order. Now, I shall know. Deuced clever dodge of mine that," and he rubs his hands together, gleefully. Two minutes pass, and the waiter returns. "Now, then, where's the order? Um? Eh?"

"Steward says he can't get it off the file, m'lud. There's so many above it."

"Confound it all! There's no help for it. I suppose I must. What—er—what did I have just now? Um? Eh?"

"D'no, m'lud."

"Don't know? What do you mean, sir?"

"'Twas Robert Dodge that served yelludship."

"Dash it, sir! Why didn't you say so before?"

"Didn't ask me, m'lud."

"Don't be impertinent, sir, or I'll report you, egad."

"Yesm'lud."

"Well, where's Robert Dodge? Send him to me."

"Yessm'lud."

"Hah! Now I'll be able to tell." More gleeful hand-rubbing, which after three minutes changed into impatient foot-stamping, until the waiter returns again, alone.

"Well, sir, where's this William Gage?"

"Robert Dodge, m'lud."

"Well, confound it! Robert Hodge, then."

"Dodge, m'lud."

"Dodge, then. Don't echo me, sir. Where is he?"

"Gone 'ome, sir."

"Home?"

"Yesm'lud. It's his turn off this afternoon."

"Afternoon? This is morning, sir. I shall certainly report your impertinence to the steward."

"Beg pardon, m'lud. It is ha' pas' twelve. There's the clock just a goin' to chime, m'lud."

Lord Bouverie looks up at the clock on the chimney-piece, just as it chimes the half-hour.

"Why, bless me, so it is. And here's a letter from Fairfield, my lawyer, asking me to be at his office in Lincoln's Inn Fields at half-past eleven. What have I been doing?"

"D'no, m'lud."

"Stupid idiot! It's pretty clear to me that this club is going to pot, employing such waiters. I'll just go into the smoking-room and send Fairfield a telegram to say I'm detained at home. Ah! clever idea that." He goes to the smoking-room, and fills up a telegraph form. "By Jove, this won't do! Dating it Binstead when the post-mark will be London. Lucky I thought of that in time." He tears up the telegram, and hastily scribbles a note to say he only reached the club at half-past twelve, and therefore, etc. He sends this off by a *commissionaire*, and then goes and sits down behind one of the window-curtains, lights up a pipe, and looks over his letters, which he still holds in his hand.

"I don't quite make out what Catherine means, I got so puzzled by that tiresome waiter. *The Delancy-Veres have asked us to go to them for a week on Monday, and as I hear that Harborough is to be there, we must get out of going to Ashwynwick. Oaktorrington is always in town, now (you know the scandal we heard from Lady Henry), so you had better keep out of his way, and I'll write and say you've been unexpectedly obliged to go to Paris, Brussels, Vienna, Berlin—anywhere—at a moment's notice. Wire me, if this will do, and say where I am to send you.* Another telegram! Egad, I shall be ruined. I don't in the least know

what she is driving at, but I dare say it's all right.
Catherine generally knows what she's about?"

He goes back to the writing-table and taking
a form, addresses it to his wife, and writes, *Yes—
Paris.* "It doesn't matter which I say, and Paris is
the easiest to get back from, if I'm not to stay away
long—ha—ha!" He then returns to the window
again. He is in the act of scratching a fusee to re-
light his pipe, when he hears a vehicle stop at the
door. He puts up his eyeglass, and looks out.

"By Jove! if it isn't—no—yes—it is Oaktorrington!" he exclaims. "A pretty hole I'm in now. He's
sure to come here, first. Blundering idiot, what the
devil brings him here? I must hide myself somewhere." He gets up quickly and goes to the door. It
is too late. Lord Oaktorrington is just entering. "Ah,
Oaktorrington, how do?" he says, forcing a smile.
"You're just the man I wanted to see. Come and
sit down here. Look here, waiter, fetch me a brandy-
and-soda."

When the waiter returns with the drink, and as
Lord Bouverie is paying him for it, Lord Oaktorrington says: "Fetch me one, also. And look here—a
cigar, as well."

Lord Bouverie drinks a long draught of his brandy-
and-soda while Lord Oaktorrington waits for his.

"Sorry we can't come to you on Tuesday," Lord
Bouverie says, as he puts down his glass on the table.
"Fact is, we've got some tiresome people coming to us
most unexpectedly, for a week. Proposed themselves.
Can't put them off, don't you know, because they've
got a lot of interest with the Duke of Cambridge.
Fitz-George is rather attentive to one of their gals,

and I want to make use of it for Jack in case the tire-some dog gets plucked again."

Before Lord Oaktorrington has time to answer, it has suddenly occurred to Lord Bouverie that this story won't tally with what he has telegraphed his wife to say. "A deuced fine mess I'm in," he mutters to himself. "Just excuse me a minute. I forgot I had to wire to Jervise not to meet me with the trap to-day. I won't be a second."

To the writing-table he toddles once more, and sends the following telegram to his wife: *Don't say Paris or anywhere. Just met O. Told him Wynd-hams were coming to us. Write that.*

While he's away, Lord Oaktorrington smiles pleas-antly to himself, as he mentally remarks:

"What luck! Couldn't have happened better."

But when Lord Bouverie seats himself again be-side him he says after a bit: "I'm awfully sorry you can't come. Harborough's coming for a week's hunt-ing. One can't—"

"What?" exclaims Lord Bouverie. "Harborough coming to you? Quite sure?"

"Positively certain. Why, you wouldn't have minded bringing your girls to meet him? I never imagined so, or I should have put him off. But as you're not coming, it doesn't matter."

"Sure there's not some mistake?" persists Lord Bouverie, with a gasping face. "I thought he was"—

"Mistake? Here's his letter proposing himself."

"A nice mess Catherine's made of it," Lord Bou-verie growls between his teeth.

"Eh?"

"Oh, nothing. I was only saying I hoped Jervise

would get my telegram before he started. By Jove"
(to himself), "I must think of some way out of
it."

They chat on in the usual commonplace fashion
for half an hour. At last Lord Oaktorrington does
the talking, and Lord Bouverie listens. He is thinking of "the way out." Presently a telegram is brought
to him. He tears it open, and reads :

Too late. Letter gone. Catherine.

He crushes it up in his hand and grinds his
teeth.

Lord Oaktorrington no more notices him than if
he were the Duke of York's statue on the monument
in Trafalgar Square. Lord Bouverie tries to steal
back to the writing-table unobserved.

"What? Going?" asks Lord Oaktorrington, before he has taken half a dozen steps.

"No. I've just had a telegram from—from "—He
can't think of who to say.

"Jervise?" suggests Lord Oaktorrington.

"No. From Macdonald, asking me to go with him
in his yacht to Cherbourg next week. I'm just going
to say I can't go."

"Macdonald?" says Oaktorrington. "Why, Macdonald's gone to America." Lord Bouverie pretends not to hear, but silently curses his unfortunate
selection.

"Oh, by-the-by, Bouverie," Lord Oaktorrington
continues. "Talking of America. We've a Yankee
coming to us to-morrow."

"A Yankee? To you? My dear fellow, you can't
mean it?"

"'Pon my soul, I do, though."

"He'll be blowing you up with dynamite if you don't look sharp."

"No fear of that, I hope. He's a friend of Freddy's—the son of a Californian millionaire."

"Eh? What? Got a lot of money, of course?"

"Rather. So Freddy says."

Lord Oaktorrington stops a waiter to order another brandy-and-soda, and when he turns around again Lord Bouverie is at the writing-table sending this telegram to his wife: *Harborough going to Ashwyn-wick. O. just told me. Rich American, also. Must go too. Write excuse to Delancy-Veres at once. Will manage the rest.*

While he is writing, the Earl of Swansdale comes in. He is a tall young man of thirty, with heavy, sensual features, who had been in the Blues, for six months, about nine years ago. He walks up to the fire with a shambling gait, and throwing himself in an arm-chair, rings the bell, and then looking over at Lord Oaktorrington says, with a side nod: "Aw! How do?"

Lord Oaktorrington nods back, and drinks his brandy-and-soda in silence.

Lord Swansdale surveys his finger-nails for three minutes, and then sings out :

"Oh, I say!"

"Hello!" answers Lord Oaktorrington.

"I forgot I've got something to say to you. I'm going for a tour of the provinces with Hyacinthe next week, and I want Val to belong to my company. She told me to ask you." The marquis winces and turns pale. Were he not so red already, he would turn that color instead. He doesn't answer.

3

"Do you hear what I say?" Lord Swansdale shouts in a loud voice that would have reached the ears of every one in the room had there been any one except Lord Bouverie. That nobleman turns sharply round, sees at a glance there is something up, and immediately busies himself with writing out a series of telegrams to imaginary people, keeping his ears wide open the mean while.

"I don't in the least know what you mean," Lord Oaktorrington replies, with the glitter of suppressed rage in his small eyes.

"Oh, I say! What's the use of your humbugging like that, and doing the goody-goody before an audience of one who knows all about it. So does everybody, for that matter. Come, give me a straight answer. Just say whether she can go, or not, that's all I want. I shan't tell the missus," and he gives a coarse laugh. "Now, then, yes or no?"

"No."

"Phoh! What's your objection?"

"I've answered your question. You said that was all you wanted."

"Hyacinth's not good enough for her, I dessay," sneers the earl.

"Well, no. I don't think she is."

"It's a damned lie!" shouts Lord Swansdale. He jumps from his chair, and swaggers up to Lord Oaktorrington.

"Thanks, awfully. It's deuced lucky there are none of the committee in the room."

"I don't care a damn for the committee. They shouldn't stop my standing up for Hyacinthe any more than you."

." It's a pity your poor wife isn't here."

" My poor wife ! Do you suppose I care a brass farthing what she thinks ? "

" No. I don't believe you do. I think you prove that every day of your life."

" And who gives you the right to preach ? An old man like you, with a wife and grown-up children."

" Suppose we end this," says Lord Oaktorrington, as the Duke of Harborough appears in the doorway. " He'll hawk it about all over town."

" Well, will you let Val come ? "

" I'll tell you what I'll do. I'll think it over, and let you know to-morrow."

" All right."

The Duke of Harborough joins them. He is a small, slight man of forty, with a bald head, pale, parchment face, a scrubby, dust-colored mustache, and black-encircled, dissipated eyes. His elegibility as a member of the " Rag " rests upon the slender basis of a year's cornetcy in the Life Guards twenty-odd years ago.

Lord Bouverie, on seeing him, immediately vacates his seat at the writing-table, and toddles hurriedly forward to meet him.

" What's the row ! " asks his Grace, looking from one to the other. " I heard a deuced lot of loud talking, and you both look devilish excited."

Lord Oaktorrington answers quickly :

" It's only Swansdale and me have been having a bit of a jaw about " (he says the first thing that comes into his head) " the new army regulations changing the names of regiments."

Lord Bouverie elevates his eyebrows, and drops his

eyeglass in the movement. He smiles grimly, nevertheless, at the chance it gives him to hold forth.

"A more iniquitous system the Duke of Cambridge
never invented," he says, pompously. "It has de-
stroyed every vestige of *esprit de corps* that the abolition
of purchase left. Look at the cads there are in the
service now! Every tradesman in London has a son
in the army or going in. Sandhurst is full of 'em.
When I think what the service was in *my* day, and see
it now, I positively hide my face with shame. Um?
Eh?"

Neither Oaktorrington nor Swansdale say a word.
Neither of them have the least idea of what Lord Bouverie is talking about; in fact, they know nothing of
the subject and its merits or demerits.

"Devilish unlucky shot of mine that," Lord Oaktorrington says in an undertone to Lord Swansdale.

"Rather. He's the greatest bore out when you
start him on the army. It's all the old duffer can talk
about. Don't answer him; that's the best way."

"Now, just look here! Fancy this. He's turned
a lot of ordinary line battalions into Highlanders.
Put kilts and trews, egad, on Cornishmen and Welsh-
men and Irishmen. Did mortal man ever hear the
like? Um? Eh?"

The duke walks over to the fire, and stands with
his back turned, warming his hands. The marquis
and earl go to different windows and look out.

Lord Bouverie pockets the snub good-naturedly.
He has grown from long experience not to mind such
trifles.

A short, weasel-faced man, with small rat-like eyes,
a long nose, receding chin, and the feet of a gorilla,

walks hurriedly into the room. He is Lord Ballyhooly (an Englishman with an Irish title), an Irish
representative, peer, and a Government "whip." He
also holds, in payment for his services, the sinecure
office of equerry to the Queen, appointed thereto by
the prime minister. He has been sent post haste to
hunt up all the derelict peers he can find and fetch
them to the House to vote in an impending division of
great importance.

"What a find!" he exclaims. "Four, and all
us ! "

All regard him with faces of disfavor, and the duke
says :

"What a confounded nuisance you are, Bobby!
This is the second time this week you've nosed *me* out.
By Jove! there's no safety anywhere. Fancy follow-
ing a man here ! "

Lord Ballyhooly is accustomed to such welcomes,
and only laughs.

" It's devilish hard lines a man can't have any peace
in a club like this," growls Lord Swansdale. " This
isn't the Carlton. If a man goes there in the afternoon and gets caught, it's his own fault. But here!
Where the devil is a man to go ? "

"Fancy having to sit squatting on those benches
in a fusty atmosphere for an hour or more, listening
to some idiot spouting about some rubbishy bill or
other. By Jove ! I must decline for one," says Lord
Oaktorrington. "Besides, I've got an engagement."

"So 've I," adds Lord Bouverie.

"I'm awfully sorry to bother you," says Lord Ballyhooly. "The chances are you won't have to stay
more than ten or fifteen minutes, and its a most im-

portant matter for the Opposition to have as large a majority as possible. It will be another black eye for the grand old man."

"By Jove! I wish I could give him a couple now," observes Lord Swansdale, holding up a brawny fist and smelling his knuckles. "Damned old scoundrel!"

"What is it about?" asks Lord Bouverie. "Deceased wife's sister?"

"Deceased wife's sister!" laughs Lord Swansdale. "That was passed last session. Even *I* know that."

"Last session? I beg to differ with you. It was two years ago," remarks Lord Oaktorrington.

"Two years! Bosh! More like four or five," calls out the duke. "Wasn't it, Bouverie? *You* know, of course."

Lord Bouverie is about to say, "I'm blessed if I know," but remembers in time his desire to please the duke, and says, "Of course it was."

"As a matter of fact," Lord Ballyhooly explains, "it was defeated the session before last."

"Defeated!" cries the duke. "Didn't Tummy vote for it? What rubbish you are talking."

"That doesn't matter. The prince only has one vote, like every other peer."

"Oh!"

"Really?"

"Fancy that!"

"You surprise me!"

"No," turning to Lord Bouverie, "this is the second reading of the Franchise Bill."

"Oh, yes," proudly, "the bill to let policemen vote. Why shouldn't they?"

"Let policemen vote!" exclaims Lord Swansdale.

' I'm not such an ass as that. There's not a greater set of blackguards in the world than policemen."

Lord Oaktorrington has in mind a recent fisticuff in Rotten Row, between the earl and Sir Charles Chatfield, and remarks :

"No doubt you have good reasons for thinking so." Lord Swansdale pretended not to hear.

"This Franchise Bill is going to let every one vote —women and everybody—isn't it?" asks the duke. "I shouldn't object to the women—but damn it, if I can go the men. Fancy your groom or footman having a vote like yourself—much they'd know about it! Gladstone's in his dotage, without a doubt."

"Of course he is, { the old blackguard!"
                   { the d—d old traitor!"
                   { the infernal old idiot!"

Lord Ballyhooly looks at his watch.

"We shall be late," he says. "You won't mind coming at once? I'll just tell the hall porter to call a couple of cabs."

"Beastly bore!"

"Confounded nuisance!"

"Rotten bother!"

"Devilish hard lines!"

"I expect we must," says the duke, looking at the others.

"Oh, yes."

"Of course."

"Must, I suppose."

"But, I say," says Lord Bouverie. "How's a chap to vote? Better know that before we go. Um? Eh?"

"*Content*, of course," answers the duke, sententiously.

"Fancy Bouverie not knowing," laughs Lord Swansdale. "A nice law-maker he is. No wonder the Radicals want to abolish us. It's fellows like him who get us sat upon. Recollect—we are all to vote with the *contents*."

"No—no—no!" cries Lord Ballyhooly, who has come back to hurry them off. "You're all to go into the *non-content* lobby. Mind, the NON-*content* lobby. You won't forget?"

There is a chorus of "Oh, no's," "Of course, nots," etc., as the four born legislators go down the steps and start in two hansoms for the House of Lords.

"Cads are good enough to envy us our lot," remarks the duke, as he steps into his cab. "They little know the hardships we have to endure."

CHAPTER III.

THE Marchioness of Oaktorrington and her two daughters, the Ladies Mary and Edith Vesey, are sitting in the drawing-room at Ashwynwick Park. They are in reality awaiting with much inward anxiety and expectancy the arrival of their son and brother Lord Frederick Vesey and his American friend; but the perfection of their drilling in aristocratic restraint and repression is such that, to even the scrutiny of a most searching observer, there is nothing betrayed, in look, movement, or act, which would give the impression that their thoughts were occupied with anything beyond the commonplace every-day occupations in which they are engaged.

The marchioness is doing some simple crewel-work with a wicker work-table full of different colored worsteds before her, Lady Mary is crocheting a crimson and yellow antimacassar, and Lady Edith is at the writing-table, writing some letters for the evening's post. The door opens, and the butler enters with a letter on a silver waiter, the brickdust envelope showing at a glance it is a telegram. Lady Oaktorrington picks it up impassively, and says in a steady voice :

"I hope it isn't from Freddy, to say his friend can't come," while her heart beats one hundred and twenty to the minute lest it bring some tidings of accident, and her daughters scarcely raise their eyes, though their breath comes and goes with trebled rapidity.

"No answer," the marchioness says, quietly. She waits until the butler withdraws and her daughters look up with the faintest shade of inquiry in their eyes :

"How tiresome of the Bouveries! or rather Lord Bouverie, for the telegram is from him," she tells them. "They're coming, after all."

"Really?" from Lady Mary.

"Oh!" from Lady Edith.

"Yes. Here is what he says : *Did not go to Paris after all, so we shall be with you on Tuesday. Jack is with us.*

Lady Edith flushes scarlet at the four last words, and stoops her head to address an envelope to some one—any one. Curiously enough she finds upon looking at it that it reads : *The Hon. John Bouverie, Binstead Hall, Talstone, Warwickshire.* Nature having

in the two minutes' lapse been got under proper con-
trol again, she tears up the envelope with an air of
thoroughbred dignity and repose, and throws it into
the waste-paper basket.

"*Jack is with us,*" repeats Lady Oaktorrington.
"I think I know what that means. One of Lord Bouverie's delicate hints. He wanted me to telegraph
back (for an answer was paid for), to invite Jack. It
will be rather a sell for him when he gets no reply.
Four Bouveries are enough at one time in all con-
science—were there no other reasons." The last five
words she adds in a whisper, her voice at its loudest
being little more. They reach Lady Edith's little pink
ears as though blared through a thousand trumpets,
nevertheless; and the blood comes back to her cheeks,
and her eyes flash resentfully. But neither she nor
her sister speaks. It is not their custom to mention
a man's name in their mother's presence or hearing.
There are not two more "properly" brought up girls
in England. Utter and complete silence reassumes her
sway. The ticking of the clock on the chimney-piece,
the dropping of a cinder now and then from the grate,
and the scratching of Lady Edith's pen, are the only
sounds to be heard. Presently Lady Edith puts down
a pen that has been idly scribbling her own name
over sheet after sheet of paper, and opens the telegram-
form case which lies on the table ; from this she stealth-
ily and slowly tears out a blank form and shuts up
the case again. She waits a minute and looks cau-
tiously over her shoulder at her mother and sister.
Both sit with eyes bent over their work. She takes
up her pen and quickly filling up the form as follows :

To Lord Bouverie, Army and Navy Club.
("I've heard father say he lived there.") *Pall Mall,*
London, S. W. We hope Mr. John will come with you.
Julia Oaktorrington.

blots it, folds it, and puts it in an envelope which she
addresses to *The Postmaster, Hertford.* Then she
places it carefully between the two letters she has
written for the post, slips out noiselessly behind a
screen and through an ante-room into the hall, drops
the three letters into the letter-box, and ere her mother
or sister have noticed her absence, is back in her seat
again with a smile of satisfaction and seemingly utterly unconscious—be the motive ever so harmless,
and the injury ever so trifling—that she is guilty of
a crime punishable with penal servitude. She is hardly
seated when her mother looks up.

"Edith, my dear, I wish you would write a line to
your father for me ; your hand is so exactly like mine
that he'll never know."

"Yes, mother."

"You've written all your own letters, dear?"

It suddenly occurs to Lady Edith that it will call
forth remark from her mother and sister (every trifle
of the sort being given undue weight) if she have no
letters to give the butler when he comes in to see if
there are any more for the post, after clearing the box
in the hall, and as she will be unable to account for
hers having been put into the box, she quickly decides
she must write another, and so answers :

"Just one more."

"Well, then, after that will do."

"Yes, mother."

She hastily scribbles a few lines to a former governess, to ask the name of a German history she used to read (the book is on her bookshelf in her room), and then says :

" Now, mother."

" Who is your letter to, dear ? "

" Fraulein.   I haven't written to the poor thing for an age."

" How good of you, dear. And the others ? "

" Only Aunt Eliza, and—and Emmy Bouverie."

Lady Oaktorrington looks round sharply, with a suspicious glance.

" Emmy Bouverie ! What on earth can you have to write to her about ? She'll be here, to-morrow. Let me see the letter."

" Oh, there, then, I'm sure I don't want to send it," and Lady Edith tears up a sheet of the paper she had been scribbling her name upon, and throws it into the fire.

" You mustn't give way to such temper, Edith, my dear. It's such very bad form."

" Yes, mother. I'm very sorry. What shall I say to father ? "

" Oh, tell him the Bouveries are coming, after all, and that he'd better come home at once to meet them."

" Yes. Anything else ? "

" Let me see. Yes. " It is against the marchioness's rule to speak to her daughters, or allow them to speak to her, about men. " Say—er—oh, I think I had best write it myself."

An idea of her own has suggested itself to Lady Edith.

."Nonsense, mother. Why should you trouble to leave your work and comfortable place by the fire. It's awfully cold out here, and too dark for you to see."

Lady Oaktorrington is very comfortable and is nothing loath to stay. After all, what harm, just this once? she thinks.

"Very well, dear. Tell him his Grace—he will know who I mean—never came yesterday, and ask him to try and see him and find out why. That is all."

Lady Edith puts all these directions into proper shape, and adds, before signing her mother's name— this time as her legal agent—*Also see Lord Bouverie, and tell him we shall expect his son Jack with them.*

When she reads the letter over to her mother she carefully omits this, and has barely time to seal and stamp it before the butler comes in with the tea-cloth over his arm, a footman following him with the lamps.

"Dear me! Five o'clock? I had no idea it was so late. Freddy must have missed his train. He ought to have been here before this."

"There he is, now," says Lady Edith, as the front-door bell rings a loud peal.

"I'm glad he's come in time for tea," says the marchioness; and after that, silence—the silence of repressed expectancy—reigns for ten minutes. Then Nature reasserts herself, and Lady Edith says:

"What a time they are coming in, to be sure! What can be the matter, I wonder?"

Her mother looks reprovingly at her.

"My dear, you shouldn't excite yourself in that way about what is very easily ascertained. Just ring, please. Oh, Dawkins, docs Lord Frederick know we are here?"

"Lord Frederick, m'lady?" asks the butler, with a bewildered look.

"Yes. That was him who rang just now?"

"No, m'lady; that was Lord Beyndour, m'lady."

"Oh? was it?"

"Yes, m'lady. He's gone to his room, m'lady."

"Very well, that will do."

"How awfully tiresome," cries Lady Edith, as soon as Dawkins shuts the door after him. "What on earth brought him, of all people? He'll spoil everything."

"Really, my dear, I don't quite understand you. Spoil everything? Spoil what?"

Lady Oaktorrington is herself quite as vexed as any one at her eldest son's unexpected arrival. But she is too well-bred to show it.

"Why, the Bouveries' visit, of course. What else could I mean? You know what Beyndour is."

"You mustn't say such things of your brother, dear. As for spoiling the Bouveries' visit, Lord Bouverie will be only too enchanted at having his girls meet him. Not that it will do them the least good. We have higher views for him than one of them."

Lady Edith knows quite well what she means, but she doesn't say so.

"Poor Beyndour," says Lady Mary. "I call it a shame of Edith."

"Do you really? Well, then, let us see how he'll get on with Freddy's American friend. I'll warrant he insults him in some way or other. There's one comfort, Ja—" She catches herself in time and completes the sentence, "Jack's a match for him," in her mind.

"Really, Edith, I must ask you to stop saying such things," Lady Oaktorrington says, while she thinks how will she ever manage to keep peace while Lord Beyndour stays, and wishes it were possible to stop Lord Frederick *in transitu.*

They drink their tea in silence for another ten minutes, when the door is thrown open with a rush and a bang, and in walks Viscount Beyndour. He is his father's counterpart, save in age, gray hairs, and the absence of beard, a thick, red mustache being his only "hirsute appendage." He says:

"How do, mother — Mary — Edith?" and kisses each in turn on the lower tip of both ears. Then he goes and stands on the hearth-rug, with his back to the fire, and, putting his glass in his eye, sticks his hands in his trousers' pockets, and looks down at his boots without another word for five minutes or more.

"Won't you have some tea, dear?" his mother asks, at last.

"Oh! Thanks, awfully."

"I thought you were above tea," says Lady Edith.

Both her mother and sister look at her and shake their heads. Her brother frowns and doesn't deign to reply.

"Beastly tepid stuff!" he exclaims, as he tastes his cup and then empties the contents into the slop-basin. "Curious thing, one always gets iced-tea out of season here."

"I'm so sorry," cries Lady Mary, in great distress; "I forgot to put on the cosy."

"Let me ring and have some more hot water," suggests his mother.

"No, thanks. I don't care for water, either cold or hot, as a beverage.

"Some more tea made, then?"

"Pfah! What rubbish you talk, mother," he answers, turning his face to the fire.

"I'm so very glad to see you, dear," the marchioness says, after a prolonged pause. No answer. "I hope you'll be able to stay with us longer than you did the last time."

"Got only a fortnight's leave," he replies. "Only stay a day or two."

Lady Edith almost bites a piece out of her cup, with repressed joy.

"Harborough's asked me to go and shoot at Beaschamp, Thursday."

"Harborough? Why his Grace wrote to say he was coming here."

"Oho!" thinks Lady Edith. "That was the 'his Grace' father's been sent after. Fancy!"

"When?" asks Lord Beyndour.

"Yesterday."

"Here, now?" He turns round from the fire with a grin (one *can't* call it a smile) beginning to develop in his face.

"No. Why, he didn't come!"

Lord Beyndour breaks into a loud laugh.

"So I thought. He's not such a fool as that. Fancy Harborough coming *here!* Haw—haw!"

"Really, my dear, I don't quite see what you mean!"

"Now, just look here. What the deuce would bring *him* here? Answer me that. *Here!*"

He looks at his mother for the first time since they began to talk, and finds her with a crimson face. He puts up his glass to regard her more closely, and then winks to himself.

"The Bouveries are coming to-morrow," says Lady Mary.

"Gals, too?"

"Yes, I believe so."

"Not that ass, Jack, I hope?"

"No, indeed," answers the marchioness, who has had time to get back her self-possession. Lady Edith smiles to herself.

"Any one else coming?"

"Yes, indeed, there is," cries Lady Edith. "Fancy our forgetting to tell him all this time."

"Well, who is it? Come—come!"

"Freddy."

"Freddy? Freddy who? There are millions of Freddies."

"Your brother, my dear," says his mother.

"What the deuce is the good of playing the fool with me like this? You know as well as I do Freddy is out in the States."

"He *was*, dear. But he's in England now, and we expect him to arrive at any moment. He ought to have been here an hour ago. Indeed, we thought it was him when you came."

"And do you mean to say father's been such an idiot as to let him come home? Why, he only went there a few weeks ago."

"My dear, the poor boy's been away six months."

"Rubbish! It seems like yesterday that he went.

4

Fancy chucking away a lot of money like that. What a beastly row father made when he had to pay up my racing bets for me last year. I'll back it wasn't half as much."

"He's bringing an American friend with him," observes Lady Edith, with a sly twinkle in her eyes.

"What?" Lord Beyndour draws himself up to his full height and knits his brows. "Fetching a Yankee here?" Then he bursts out again into a loud laugh. "Now, I know it's all a beastly lie."

Lady Oaktorrington winces. "Pray, dear, don't be so uncivil. It is all quite true."

"All I can say is, then, I'm devilish sorry to hear it. Fancy a red republican, dynamiter in this house. We shall be having Labouchere and Bradlaugh next, I dare say. What *can* father be thinking about?"

"Freddy says he's so very nice."

"As if Freddy was a judge! Have you ever had the sublime delight of meeting an American?"

"Of course, my dear."

"Who?"

"Why, Lady Ru—"

"I'm not talking of women. I mean men."

"N—no, dear, I think not."

"So I thought. If you had, you'd never allow one inside your doors. I suppose you don't know they all chew tobacco, and don't in the least mind where or when they spit. Fancy the carpets!"

"I'm sure this one doesn't. From what Freddy says, he's too much of a gentleman."

"Gentleman?" with a sneer. "Wait till you see. By Jove! Just look here! I'll back that's the reason Harborough hasn't come."

".Nonsense, dear. His Grace certainly lives in too glass a house to—"

"To throw stones. I knew you'd say that. No more he should at *us*. But, Americans are different. They're no better than shopkeepers. Fancy comparing Harborough with them! By Jove, you'll be asking Tummy down the first thing one knows, to meet Jesse Collings and Chamberlain, and wondering he doesn't come on account of *his* goings on! I dare say you and this Yankee will hit it off capitally. You should leave the Primrose League at once and join the Radicals."

" Don't be rude, dear," is all his mother says.

"Freddy says he's awfully rich," remarks Lady Edith in an undertone.

Lord Beyndour wheels round sharply, and stares at his sister.

"Eh? What? Rich, is he? Hum!" and various ideas and fancies of a monetary character flit rapidly through Lord Beyndour's brain. "Rich, eh? Of course, it's easy to say that. But who knows?"

"Freddy."

"Freddy! What rot! How does he know? All I can say is you don't get me civil to the fellow by any such rubbish as that. I'll back he's a humbug."

"We shall soon be able to tell, dear," says Lady Oaktorrington, as the front-door bell rings out another peal. Two minutes later Lord Frederick Vesey walks into the room, alone.

———

CHAPTER IV.

FREDDY'S greeting to his family is at once hearty and astounding. From his own and most other people's standpoint it is natural and sincere; from theirs, overwhelming and vulgar. He dashes up to his mother and sisters and gives each in turn a warm embrace and a kiss straight on the mouth before they know where they are.

"Well, I *am* glad to get home again!" he exclaims in a loud voice which makes his mother flinch and his brother frown. "Not that I don't like America, for I do; but its real nice to see you all again. See?"

"Yes, dear," answers his mother, faintly, slowly recovering from his onset. "I'm sure we must all be glad you've left that horrid country," and she looks meaningly at Lord Beyndour, who elevates his eyebrows and shakes his head.

"Horrid country? You mustn't call it that. It's a grand country, and I mean to go back. How handsome you are looking, mother, and I don't think I ever saw Mary look so pretty or Edith so— Well, I declare, if she isn't the prettiest girl I've seen for ever so long!"

In accordance with aristocratic canons of good form a woman's looks or personal appearance are never even alluded to—to herself; that is, before other people. Lady Oaktorrington and her daughters wince, exchange glances, and look down. Though he has been but six months away, Freddy has thrown off the shackles of family restraint, and seems to have positively forgotten the common ethics of his class. What

thoughts pass through his mother's head it is not difficult to conjecture. She looks the picture of downcast
humiliation, while his sisters, who ever take their out-
wardly appearing cue from her, wear serious, shocked
faces. Lady Edith's eyes, however, dance merrily
despite her somber countenance, and the corners of
her mouth twitch upward at times, and refuse to be
kept down. Lord Frederick is no fool. We may see
presently that he is weak from the pernicious unreality
and narrowness of his early teachings; but by nature
he is quick of perception, and in beginning to feel and
recognize the old familiar chill of repression and artificiality he recollects the rule he has broken. Six
months ago he would have felt snubbed, sat upon, disgraced, and humbled. But his little glimpse of the
world beyond the narrow confines of class, and the
strict limits of family, has opened his mind considerably, and made him independent and unyielding. He
waits a moment longer for some response, and then
turning away with a smile of pity, for the first time is
aware of his brother's presence. Before Lord Beyndour, without changing a muscle of his face, can get
further than—

" How do, Freddy ? "

Freddy grabs him by the hand with a grip of iron,
and slaps him on the back with a resounding whack :

" Why, old chap, whoever thought *you* were here,"
he shouts. "And how are you ? "

" All right, thanky," answers Lord Beyndour, civil
of word, but rude in tone and impatient in gesture,
wriggling his shoulder away and striving to withdraw
his hand. "D—don't do that, I say. You'll break
my fingers." Lord Frederick drops his brother's hand

and turns away. He feels hurt, but he won't show it. "It's only their way—their old cussed way—poor things," he says to himself. "I used to be that way myself. Well, mother, you haven't said three words to me, and as for Mary and Edith, they seem to have lost their tongues since I went away. Still no word? It's a pity I came back."

"Hear—hear," grunts Lord Beyndour, from the fire to which he has wheeled an arm-chair wherein he sits with his back to everybody. "I say, Edith," looking over his shoulder without moving. "Is that the *Hertford News* on the table near you? It is? Then just chuck it over to me. I want to see where the Tambrook meet to-morrow."

"Crown and Castle Inn, eleven fifteen," says Lady Mary. "I know. I copied it out this morning."

In common with the *passée* maidens of her sisterhood who are approaching antiquity, if there be one subject whereby to strike a responsive chord in the heart of Lady Mary Vesey it is hunting, unless horses yield their single exception to dogs. Her whole being is bound up in both, her whole existence flows in the two channels, canine and equine. Every farthing of her yearly allowance which she can shave off her other expenses goes to hunters, habits, saddles, whips, and dogs. If she is not buying or selling a hunter (of which her father allows her stable room and "keep" for two) she is going up to town to try on a habit or be measured for a saddle. When she is not consulting a vet., she is advertising or finding a place for a groom. She hunts three times a week, attends every hunt ball, and goes up to all the dog-shows at the Crystal Palace. She has four hunters (two of which she maintains out of her own pocket), six saddles, as many bridles, a dozen "crops," and a groom of her own. Her room is decorated with racks of whips, spurs, "masks," brushes, and "pads." Her inkstand is a horse's hoof —that of a favorite hunter who broke his fetlock-joint while leaping a double ditch with her and had to be shot—her paper-knife's handle a fox's pad. Of dogs she has ten—a Danish boar-hound, a collie, a black retriever, two dachshunds, two fox-terriers, a black French poodle, a white bull-dog, and a pug. The boar-hound, one dachshund, one fox-terrier, the bull-dog, the poodle, and the pug sleep in her room. "Shall you hunt to-morrow?" she asks, getting up and seating herself in a low chair by Lord Beyndour's.

"Yes. Want to go along?"

"I *am* going."

"Let you ride 'Jemima' if you like."

"You didn't fetch *her* down with you? I thought she'd just had a foal."

"No. That was ages ago."

"A colt?"

"No. Filly, just like herself, not a bit like its papa."

"How jolly!"

"Give her to you if you like."

"Thanks awfully. How good of you. Then I may ride Jemima?"

"Yes. I said so, didn't I?"

Meanwhile Freddy stands silent, an unwilling, unconscious listener. At last he sits down and picks up a magazine. He has read about four lines when Lady Oaktorrington speaks :

"Oh, won't you have some tea, dear? I'm afraid

it's cold. Mary, dear, ring for some fresh tea for Freddy."

Lady Mary doesn't hear, or pretends not to.

"Tea for me?" Freddy answers. "No, thank you kindly. I've not tasted tea since I don't know when. Men never drink tea where I've been, at all events, not at this time of day."

"Oh, don't they? Really? Fancy that!"

"Go in for something stronger, I'll back," sneers Lord Beyndour, in an undertone, for a moment interrupting his narrative to Lady Mary of how he "came a cropper" last week when out with the Garth hounds.

"Perhaps they do," Freddy says, quickly. "It can't signify much to you what they do."

"I'm not so cock sure of that; I hear we're to have one of 'em staying with us, thanks to you."

"Oh, by-the-by, Freddy," says Lady Oaktorrington, thankful for a chance to ask what she has been aching to do since Lord Frederick's arrival, the controlling proprieties of high life holding her in check.

"Isn't your American friend coming after all?"

"Coming?" says Freddy. "He's here now."

"Here now, dear? Why doesn't he come in?"

"Oh, he asked to go to his room first and make himself tidy."

"Haw—haw—haw, O—ho—ho!" laughs Lord Beyndour. "I never heard that Yankees went in for washing before."

"Surely he can't be all this time doing that," says Lady Oaktorrington.

"I dare say the poor chap is a bit shy about coming in alone and is waiting for me. I forgot all about him. I'll just go and see."

" How dreadfully disimproved dear Freddy is,"
Lady Oaktorrington says as the door closes on Lord
Frederick.

" He's simply unbearable, and wants a deuced good
snubbing. I dare say he thinks he's quite as good as
I am, with his new republican ideas." Lord Beyndour
replies, getting up to toast his back again.

" I thought I detected a slight twang ! " her ladyship
adds. " Did you ? "

" A slight twang! By jove, a *slight* twang! That's
too good. I never heard a worse one. Fancy one of
us with a Yankee twang ! And you a Primrose dame."

" Oh, my dear, don't speak of it. What are we to
do? He'll soon lose it, with us, I hope."

" Not with this Yankee pal of his to coach him on
the other tack. Of course, he's picked it up from
him."

" I'm afraid I've made a great mistake in letting
him come. Your father was so against it. But," suddenly recollecting, " he may not be so pronounced.
He's very rich."

Further discussion is stopped by the entrance of
Lord Frederick accompanied by his American friend.

" Mother," Lord Frederick says, leading his friend
forward. " Let me introduce Mr. Philip Allen."

Mr. Allen is a middle-sized young man of eight and
twenty; neither thin nor fat, but compact and wiry.
He has close-cropped brown hair, brown eyes with
long, thick, brown lashes, and a small brown mustache.
His features are small, clear-cut, and handsome, especially in profile; his complexion is pale, his teeth very
white, and he has strikingly (to an English eye) small
hands and feet. On the bridge of his nose he wears a

pair of tortoise-shell-rimmed double eye-glasses, and he is clad in a dark, small-checked, tweed traveling suit, a dark blue necktie with white spots being knotted in a sailor's loop round his neck.

Lady Oaktorrington rises (as do both of her daughters) and receives him with a gracious smile of welcome.

"I am so glad to see you, Mr. Allen," she says, kindly, "not only to welcome you to England, but to thank you for your great kindness to Freddy, who has told us how good you have been to him. Lord Oaktorrington is in London, but on his return to-morrow he will add his welcome and thanks to mine."

She has been studying up this little speech all the afternoon, and now that she has spoken it, fears she has left something out.

"Don't mention it, my lady," says Allen, with a graceful bow. "I'm sure I am only too pleased to have been of any service to him."

"Of service to me? I should rather think you were," puts in Freddy. "And look here, old chap," he whispers, as he sees Lord Beyndour smother a laugh and nudge Lady Mary. "Don't 'my lady' mother. I ought to have told you. It's not necessary."

"Let me introduce you to my daughters, Mr. Allen," and the marchioness presents him to Lady Mary and Lady Edith, both of whom shake his hand stiffly, as they look straight before them and say nothing. "And now my eldest son, Lord Beyndour. Now you know every one."

Lord Beyndour looks at him out of the corner of his eye, gives his hand an up and down pump-handle shake, says:

" How de do ? " drops it, and stands mute, gazing at the opposite wall.

The dressing-gong for dinner opportunely breaks in upon the awkwardness of the situation.   Lord Beyndour is the first to go.   He leaves the room without a word, followed by his mother and sisters in silence, Freddy and Allen bringing up the rear.   In the hall they linger a moment, lighting the hand-candles, but no word is spoken.

" What do you mean by snubbing me like that ? " Allen asks, as he and Freddy go up the stairs after the others have gone.   " I thought I was doing the thing in fine style."

" So you were, old fellow.   But equals when talking informally to each other drop the titles.   Of course, with servants and tradespeople, and others of that sort, it is different.   They never address a person of rank informally."

" Then I'm not to call your father 'my lord'? "

" No."

" Nor your sisters 'my lady,' either? "

" I should hope not.   Don't forget.   (I pity him if he does)."

" Nor your brother 'my lord'? "

" What, Beyndour?   Not for worlds ! '

CHAPTER V.

Twenty minutes later Lady Oaktorrington, in a shimmering purple satin gown, and shivering red neck and shoulders, descends to the drawing-room.   She is followed almost immediately by her two daughters, and the three sit in dignified, well-bred silence, in the semi-darkness of a recently-replenished and smoldering coal-fire, for five minutes, when Lord Beyndour rumbles in rubbing his hands with the cold. He makes straight for the hearth-rug, edging in front of his mother and sisters, and, spreading the tails of his dress-coat to the fire, adjusts the single stud of his expansive shirt-front.

"What a rotten fire!" he growls presently. "Ugh! No hunting to-morrow, Mary. It's freezing hard, Stevens says."

"How tiresome! I'm afraid I must have Snowball in my room to-night. She'll freeze in her kennel, poor dear."

"Had her puppies yet?"

"No, the darling."

"Have her in, then, by all means."

A sudden burst of flame from the igniting coals illumines the room. "Hello! Isn't every one here?"

"Only me and Mary and Edith."

"I say, what a duffer! Did you see the bowing and scraping? And 'my lady,' too! O, haw-haw!"

"Such a dreadful twang, too! No wonder Freddy has picked it up," ventures Lady Mary, personalities being her third pet topic when she can't have either of the other two.

"But just consider, dears, how few advantages he must have had," says the marchioness, in a pleading tone. "How can we expect him to be like us? He does his best, no doubt, poor fellow. One can't help being sorry for him. Considering his rough life and associations, he is quite wonderful, I think. One mustn't forget that."

"And that he is so rich," says Lady Edith, in the quietest, most unsuggestive voice imaginable.

"Quite so, dear. His money will enable him to improve himself, by putting improving influences and associations within his reach. It is really our duty to do what we can to help him on."

"What a great thing it is to have money, isn't it?" Lady Edith asks of no one in particular as she looks absently into the fire. "If this Mr. Allen hadn't it I expect it wouldn't matter what became of him."

"Really, Edith, I don't know where you get such ideas," her mother says sharply. "I must ask you not to talk so. You are too young to understand such things."

"Edith's got to talking awful rubbish lately, I'm afraid," observes Lord Beyndour. "Little girls should be seen but not heard." Lady Edith's eyes flash and the blood rushes up to her forehead, but she says nothing. "What the deuce is keeping them? I dessay it's Yankee manners to be late for dinner. I should strongly advise you, mother, to go in if they're not down when the gong goes. Who wants to bet he doesn't dress? I'll lay ten to one in ponies he comes down in 'dittoes.'"

Before the wager can be taken, were there any one in the room to say "Done," the subject of Lord Beyndour's solicitude enters the room as the gong sounds.

"By Jove, I was right! What a hatful of money I should have won!"

"I have to apologize, Lady Oaktorrington, not only for being so late," Allen says, "but for appearing at dinner in these clothes." Lord Beyndour performs an elaborate attack of coughing.   "The fact is, my port-manteau has not yet arrived from the station."

"Too large an order," Lord Beyndour whispers to Lady Mary.   "I'll back he's got no evening clothes. Curious for a rich man, isn't it ? "

Lady Oaktorrington says "Really.   It doesn't signify," and they go in to dinner, Allen arming the marchioness last.

Freddy joins them in the hall also in morning dress.   "I thought I'd keep Allen in countenance," he explains.   "My boxes haven't come either."

"I daresay you find England very different from America, Mr. Allen," Lady Oaktorrington says after the removal of the soup, during which course not a word has been spoken at the table.

Allen is nearly stunned by the originality of the question, but asks :

"In what way do you mean ?   There are so many ways."

"Oh, socially.   You have no society to speak of. How can you, where everybody is equal ?   It must be dreadfully rough—er—for a refined person like your-self (she adds as an emollient).   Freddy wrote to us all about those dreadful cowboys."

Allen smiles to himself as he thinks of New York, Boston, Philadelphia, New Orleans, Baltimore, Wash-ington, and even his own San Francisco society being called "rough," and thought to be infested with cow-boys.

"I hardly think our society is quite as bad as that," he says, unhuffily.   "We have, of course, no class dis-tinctions—"

"Your cook's as good as you are, and all that sort

of thing, I suppose, eh," says Lord Beyndour from
the bottom of the table. "You have your doctor to
dine with you, and you let your daughter marry your
dentist."

Allen looks at him straight in the eye until he
stops. He then turns away without a word of reply
and goes on speaking to Lady Oaktorrington.

"As I was saying, we have no class distinctions,
and no titles except military, naval, judicial, or clerical
ones. But that does not in the least interfere with our
society or prevent its being organized and maintained
on as solid and lasting a basis as yours in England."

"Rubbish!" grunts Lord Beyndour in an undertone, looking at the butler for an approving glance.

"I can't at all understand it," says the marchioness,
with a doubting shake of the head. "I don't see how
it is possible."

"Ask Freddy about it," growls Lord Beyndour,
rudely. "He knows, I should think."

Allen looks quickly at him as he flushes red, and
bites his lip.

"Indeed I don't," answers Freddy. "I know
nothing about it."

"What awful rot! Haven't you been in the
States?"

"Yes, I have ; but only in Kansas and Colorado—
that is, to stay. I saw nothing of society there."

"Of course not. That's just what mother says,"
and Lord Beyndour gives a sneering sniff.

"I don't at all mean that. You quite misunderstand me. I mean I saw nothing of society there
because—"

"There wasn't any to see, haw-haw!"

"Yes, there was. I simply didn't go into it. That's why I saw nothing of it."

"Oh!" incredulously.

"I was on a cattle-ranch all the time, as you know."

"My good fellow, I *know* nothing of where you were. We have only your word for it," and Lord Beyndour glances at the butler and then at one of the footmen who is handing him some vegetables. "You may have been in the moon for all we know."

Allen looks thunderstruck at such insulting language from brother to brother. Lady Oaktorrington sees the look, and fears she has let things go too far.

"I'm afraid Mr. Allen won't understand your chaffing, my dear. He is not serious, you know, Mr. Allen. You don't chaff one another in the States, I dare say.

Allen feels decidedly on edge. "I really can't say what they do in the other States. I should imagine they did say rude things to each other under the cloak of chaff, as you call it, in New York, for New York is sadly addicted to Anglomania at present. But in California—why, I've seen pistols drawn for much less than that."

"What? Between brothers?"

"No, not between brothers, for I never heard one brother talk so to another in my life before."

He looks straight at Lord Beyndour with a steady, unflinching eye as he says this. His lordship turns very white, drops his eyes, and sulks in silence for the remainder of dinner.

Allen feels uncomfortable. His irritability has given way to a sense of shame at having lost his temper at another person's table. There is an awkward pause. Lady Oaktorrington makes a face to Lady Mary to speak to him.

"Do you like dogs?" Lady Mary asks. It is the first word she has spoken since they sat down, and they are now among the "savories."

"Yes, I do—out-of-doors," he answers, without in the least knowing how he is treading on her toes.

"Oh! Then you don't like them," she says, stiffly.

"Indeed I do. I've got two dogs myself that I wouldn't part with for a good deal."

She softens a bit. "What are they? Fox-terriers, turn-spits, pugs, or what?"

"They're hunting-dogs."

"Oh, really! Then you hunt. I'm so glad!" and Lady Oaktorrington smiles and nods approval of her daughter's animation.

"It's very good of you to care, I'm sure. I do a good deal of hunting every season."

"Fancy! I had no idea you hunted in the States. Perhaps you'll come with us to-morrow. How awfully jolly!"

Allen doesn't know what to make of her sudden loquacity. It seems almost painful in its abruptness. He has no idea where they are going, but says notwithstanding:

"Thanks. I shall be very glad."

"That's capital. I shall lend you a mount."

"A mount" he asks. "Oh, how stupid of me! I see what you mean now. You are going out fox-hunting?"

"Yes, of course," she says. "Don't you hunt foxes in America?"

5

"We have no foxes to hunt in California. The nearest approach to a fox we have is the vagrant coyote. Your brother knows the animal, for they have him in Colorado, too."

"Kiotee? What an odd name! Then you hunt it?"

"Say, Vesey. Fancy hunting a coyote!"

Freddy joins him in a laugh, whereat Lady Mary gets huffy, and says something to her sister.

"I think it's rather a shame," Lady Edith answers, being *her* virgin effort at audible conversation.

Allen hasn't the faintest idea what she means or refers to, but on glancing over at her sees she is looking with a very meaning expression at him. It suddenly dawns upon him how very pretty she is. "What a fool I have been not to have noticed her before," he thinks; "where have been my eyes?" He immediately takes a deeper interest in her remark, and wonders with a dull sort of pain in his heart and a tingling of his temples if she can have meant anything derogatory to him. "Does she mean that I ought to be ashamed of myself? What for? Oh, yes, for speaking so at her brother. It was awfully rude. What must she think of me? Yet, why should I care what she thinks?" He gazes with increasing admiration at her while these thoughts rush like lightning through his head, and each second he is conscious that he does care more and more what she thinks. "I must do something to reinstate myself. But what? Speak to him civilly. That will please her, no doubt."

Lady Edith's big gray eyes have fluttered down to her plate the moment she finds his riveted upon her, and the faint little tinge of soft pink in her cheeks has

deepened into a bright red which burns itself into
neck, forehead, and ears as well. She toys with her
grapes a minute, and then steals a little upward glance
over at him. He is still looking at her, and—well, I
suppose most of us know how it makes our hearts
bump about inside when we see a pretty woman if we
be a man, or a handsome man if we be a woman, regarding us with a look of admiration which we only
can detect. Lady Edith is a natural woman, notwithstanding that she is an artificially-trained member of
the British aristocracy, and for the first time in her
life she feels her heart beat with the (to others)
well-known thump that is invariably the preface, if
not the initial chapter of "the old, old story." She
looks up again. His eyes are still upon her, and by a
sort of intuitive instinct she knows that her mother is
smiling her approval. A sense of extreme shyness
takes possession of her, and quickly becomes positive
torture. Her very helplessness, as it were, suddenly
reacts into self-possessed strength. She is angry—angry
with her mother—very angry with him. As her anger
comes, her shyness (its sole cause) departs, and with
it (for the moment) every tender sentiment vanishes
from her breast. She knows what her mother means
by smiling—she has seen her do so before—and she
will show her for the dozenth time that she is not to
be influenced in that way except in the opposite direction. As for *him*—How dare he stare at her so boldly
and impertinently, and draw her mother's notice upon
them both? No doubt Beyndour is enjoying the scene
hugely and will make it an unceasing subject of chaff
to her, and a topic to discuss when she isn't present.
She dared not look lest she should see him laughing.

Ooph! She could tear *him* all to pieces. With one blow she will shatter them both. With one stone her two birds shall fall to the ground. Allen sees all these emotions come and go in her expressive face, and reads them, alas, poor fellow! as man is prone to read a woman's eyes He unconsciously closes his a moment and the quick beating of his heart and the delicious sense of exhilaration which seems to bubble forth with every throb and suffuse his whole being, tells him that he is, to put it as mildly as possible, very happy. Dozens, ay, hundreds of girls in his own country has he flirted with and made love to in the most approved fashion, on staircases at balls, in conservatories at receptions, in secluded corners at weddings, on the veranda at Del Monte, in drives to the Cliff House, in rides in the park, and on every possible occasion, in every possible spot out of doors or in. There is not a society girl in 'Frisco who does not know "handsome Phil" to her cost, so far as the heart-ache goes. Engaged, or reported to be, a dozen times, to as many different types of femininity, he still remains free and heart-whole. Out of every skirmish he has returned scathless; out of every battle he has come without a scratch. Never before has he been conscious of the sensations which now affect him. As if impelled by some hidden, unbidden power, resistless as an avalanche and as sudden as the lightning's flash, the words rise to his lips: "She shall be my wife."

Call it the love of the eye, if you will, it is none the less deep, none the less real.

Love dawned in man's heart ere character was formed, mind cultivated, accomplishment invented, education dreamed of, rank crested, or money coined.

And so it thrives in man's heart still, for it is the true, the real, the disinterested, the unsordid love of Nature after all.

As he whispers the words to himself with a curiously fixed conviction of their certain fulfillment, he opens his eyes and looks at her again. Her anger has at that moment reached its climax. Her new-found heart has rushed back into its iron-bound case of worldliness; she is an aristocrat once more, and her mother's own daughter. Her eyes flash, her teeth are set hard, and her voice trembles beneath its thin coating of haughty defiance.

"Have you no ladies in America, Mr. Allen? I should fancy not." The words are hardly out of her mouth when she would give worlds to have them back.

Lord Beyndour bursts into a paroxysm of laughter and thumps the table with his knuckles. Freddy looks at his mother and then at Lord Beyndour, and says:

"Mother, how can you?"

But Lady Oaktorrington gives no sign of emotion. She only says in a low voice: "Scenes are such bad form, my dear."

Lady Mary might as well be in the moon from any token of interest she displays in matters mundane beyond the peeling of her forced hot-house peach.

As for Allen, he turns red to the roots of his hair, and then grows quickly pale. Indignation and resentment gleam from his eyes for a single second, and then give place to a surprised, deprecating look. He is about to reply in that spirit when a side glance shows him the marchioness's (seemingly) complacent indifference, and her son's continued hilarity.

"I—I—really—hardly know how to answer such a

question. If you mean ladies of title, I say, certainly not. If you mean by ladies, women of refinement, culture, accomplishment, mind, grace, heart, delicacy of sentiment, integrity, honor, and virtue, I say most assuredly, yes. So far as the qualifications of a lady are concerned, birth is quite a secondary consideration in America. Is it the only essential requirement in England?"

Though spoken to Lady Edith, his words are solely intended for and directed at Lady Oaktorrington and Lord Beyndour; but no sooner are they uttered, and the gratification of speaking them past, than Allen experiences with terrible retributive force the unerring punishment of ill-judged haste—unavailing regret. He is conscious that, however unwarrantable and lacking in the first principles of hospitality has been the behavior of his entertainers, his conduct as a guest accepting their food and shelter has been equally atrocious. Not only has he overstepped in one sudden stride the limits of the common proprieties of polite society, but he has—oh, spirit of chivalry within him! —measured lengths with and treated with rudeness— a woman. He feels that he has not merely disgraced himself but his country. His sense of degradation and humiliation is deep, and his eyes once more seek those of her whose displeasure, if not loss of respect, he is confident he has incurred, that he may look, if he can not speak, the contrition he feels. He has expected to find indignation and disgust written in her every feature; but great is his relief, supreme his joy, to find she is regarding him with a soft, regretful gaze, that says as plain as words can speak, "I am so sorry, oh, do forgive me."

Naturally no one replies to the question which forms the terminal point of his remarkable speech. An awkward constrained silence ensues, which is broken by Lady Oaktorrington rising with her daughters from the table.

"I think I shall go, too," Lord Beyndour says, and follows his mother and sisters to the door.

Allen holds the door open for them, and as they pass out Lady Oaktorrington smiles kindly at him, and says :

"Don't let Freddy keep you too long. We shall expect you in the drawing-room very soon."

He needs no appeasing or mollifying, yet while he is grateful for the kind, unresentful speech which smooths over much that had seemed awkward and difficult for him in the immediate future, he can not but wish that the marchioness's "soft word" had been spoken sooner.

"Look here, old chap," Freddy says, as soon as the door is shut. "Sit down and have a glass of wine. And don't you bother about this little tiff."

"I'm awfully ashamed of myself," Allen answers. "I don't know what to do about it. I ought to apologize to your mother, of course."

"Nonsense, man. You'll do nothing of the sort. You were quite right to stick up for your country, and it's a deuced shame for Edith. But mother will give her a good rowing for it, don't you fear, when she gets her alone."

"I'm sure I hope she won't. I don't in the least mind her, and it was most absurd of me to get angry about such a trifle. It's your brother who riles me. He's got such an irritating, insulting manner, and it was his fault that I said what I did."

"Oh, he's a beast. He goes on that way with everybody who is not one of his own particular pals. It's not only you. He's cordially hated about here. You see, he's the eldest son, and everything will belong to him some day, so he gives himself airs in advance. Like enough, he'll clear out to-morrow. I hope he will. Sure you won't have anything more? Well, then, let's go to the drawing-room."

CHAPTER VI.

WHEN Lord Frederick and Allen get to the drawing-room, Lady Oaktorrington and her daughters are having tea. The marchioness and Lady Mary are in arm-chairs on each side of the fire, with their cups in their hands, while Lady Edith sits far away by herself on the end of a sofa in a distant part of the room. Lord Beyndour is nowhere to be seen.

Lady Oaktorrington beckons Allen to a chair beside her:

"I have been giving Edith a good scolding for that rude, silly remark of hers to you," she says, in a confidential undertone. "I refrained from noticing it and reproving her at the time, because I didn't wish to draw the attention of the servants to it more than it was already. One can not be too careful what one says or does before servants. She is very much ashamed of herself, as you may see."

"I am so sorry you should have said anything to pain her," Allen replies, and his heart aches at the thought. "It was really too absurd of me to get so cross about it, and I am the one who should feel ashamed."

"It was really too absurd of her to say such a thing. Why, we know loads of American ladies. There is Lady Rudolph Campbell, and Lady Sanduval, and Mrs. Alfred Dodget, and Lady Haskell, and a score of others, all countrywomen of yours, and most charming ones they are. Ladies in America? The idea of such a question!"

Her ladyship's indignation would strike Allen as more sincere and consistent, did he not remember her own slurring observations about American society within a couple of hours. It is pretty evident to him that for some reason she has thought it advisable to take the opposite tack all of a sudden, and his belief in that respect is in no way lessened when she adds:

"You mustn't mind Beyndour. What he says and does seems uncivil, I dare say. But he doesn't mean them. It's only his way—only chaff."

"Indeed. Where is he?"

"He said he'd go for a pipe to the smoking-room, and then go to bed, as he was very tired."

It is a quarter to ten by the chimney-piece clock.

"He's an invalid, is he not?"

"An invalid? Dear me, no. What made you think that?"

"Oh, I don't know exactly. I seem to have got the idea somehow."

After that Allen lets the conversation flag, and finally, after a pause of three minutes, he gets up and saunters over to Lady Edith's sofa. She is leaning back with her eyes shut, but opens them as he approaches.

" Oh, you mustn't come over here," she says, quickly, in a low voice, " and talk to me by myself."

" And why not, pray."

" Mother won't like it."

" If that's the only reason, I'm willing to risk her displeasure."

" Oh, please go back. It's not our way in England, I assure you."

" But it's our way in America—my way, at all events."

" That doesn't matter. We're not in America."

" I wish to Heaven we were."

" I'm sure I don't. Will you go, please? There's mother looking."

" Is she, really, for a fact?"

" Yes, she is. She'll be awfully cross with me. She's given me one scolding already to-night on your account, and I don't want another."

" Yes, I heard about it. I'm so awfully sorry. I've come to ask forgiveness."

" I think you ought to, indeed. Aren't you going? It's most unkind of you to stay when I ask you not."

" Is it? I am unkind sometimes, people say."

" Oh, *will* you go?"

" No, I won't. There."

" Not when I ask you? Won't you do what I ask?"

" N—yes—if you ask anything else."

" I hate to have men talk to me. I never let them."

" But you will me."

" You?" with haughty disdain. " Of all people!"

Allen is an old hand in the business, and he knows as well as most men, how much value to place on what

he calls " female preliminary skittishness." But somehow this last remark rather staggers him. A man
will stand a good deal of rebuff if his self-love isn't
touched.

"Can she really mean it?" he asks himself, as the
first flush of wounded pride fades out of his face. His
self-love is not so badly hurt that it can not come to
his rescue. "No; how could she? I'll try again.
—Thanks for the compliment."

"What compliment?"

"Then you didn't intend it for one?"

"If it was for you, certainly not. Please go."

"I ought to feel very proud."

"What of, pray?"

"Your good opinion of me."

"If that's all you have to be proud of, I'm afraid
you—"

"Then you *have* a good opinion of me! Thanks,
a thousand times."

"There! I saw mother look over and frown.
She's in an awful rage."

As a matter of fact Lady Oaktorrington has been
taking in the scene through the side of her eye with a
smile of satisfaction. It is all one to her which of her
daughters it is to be, and she has already settled that
Lady Mary shall fall to the Duke of Harborough.

"Do you hear me? Mother's in an awful rage
with us."

"Is she? I hope she'll soon recover."

"How you try me! If you were an Englishman I
shouldn't have to ask you twice."

"I've no doubt of that. They are awfully behind
the times in this sort of thing, American girls say."

"What sort of thing? I don't know what you mean."

"Don't you? How queer!"

"Oh, now you're talking rubbish. I wish you'd go. I was so comfortable before you came bothering over here."

"Oh, very well, then. I'll go," and he makes the slightest step backward.

"I'm so glad," she says, with her tongue, but in pleading eyes and quivering lips, never did woman more plainly look—"stay!"

Allen's heart gives a great big throb and a bound into his throat. Without a word, he seats himself quickly on the sofa beside her.

"Oh, please don't do that. That's worse than ever. Get up, please. See, mother is complaining to Freddy about it. There'll be an awful row, you'll see. You don't seem to understand."

"No, I confess I don't. I've heard of English mothers being strict with their daughters, but I didn't think it went to the length of forbidding their being spoken to by a gentleman in their own house, with their mother close by. Is she afraid I'll carry you off, eat you up, before her face and eyes? I do not wonder," he adds, softly, while a tender look creeps into his eyes, "that she should consider my temptation to do either so great as to be almost impossible to withstand."

"If you talk like that I must go away myself. Oh, dear, I know they are talking about us, for I just saw them both look over here."

"He is really very nice," Lady Oaktorrington is saying to Freddy, "and we must not let Beyndour quiz him any more. I'm so glad you brought him, dear. He seems quite taken with Edith. She might do worse."

"Do worse? I should think so. His father's got I don't know how many millions."

"Does he depend solely on his father? Has he no money of his own?" she asks, quickly, as a shade crosses her features.

"I don't really know. I suppose so. Sons don't have regular settled allowances in America as they do here, but their fathers give them what they want, and pay up their bills, and all that. They generally start them in some business—give 'em the capital to begin, don't you see. Allen doesn't seem to be in any business that I ever heard him mention. But you see he's an only child, so it isn't likely his father will want him to work at anything. He's got no one else to leave his money to."

"How do you know these things, my dear?"

"What things? American usages?"

"No, no. About this Mr. Allen's means, and his father's money."

"How do I *know* them?" Freddy asks, not without some suddenly raised inward misgivings himself. "Why, if you come to that, I don't *know* anything, except what I've heard."

"What! Hasn't he ever said anything about them himself?" and Lady Oaktorrington's voice, held in check through fear of being overheard, attains the shrill treble of a bargaining fishwife. "What then made you suppose his father was so rich?" Her breath comes and goes with suppressed anxiety as she awaits the answer.

"Eh? A man I met in the train told me, a man from California, who knew all about the Allens."

"And is that all you had to base your—your assurance upon in bringing him here? A nice state of affairs, truly! A man under our roof by our own invitation, that we positively know nothing about, and who, for all we know, may be a penniless chimney-sweep."

"He looks like a chimney-sweep, doesn't he?" Freddy answers, quietly. "No, he's not that."

"Well, an adventurer of some sort, a nobody without a farthing in his pocket, and nothing to his name but the clothes on his back, and a glib tongue in his head. Your father was right. He was all against his coming. And so was Beyndour. What shall we do?"

"Nothing. Let things remain as they are. I'm morally certain you'll find he's all right. You see, I got into the American way of looking at things while I was there. They don't care for money as we do. If a man's clever and behaves himself, and pays his way that's enough for them. They don't run about fussing to know what money he's got before they are civil to him. Certainly Allen is all that. He's clever, he behaves himself, and he has paid his way—not only his own, but mine, since I met him. Don't forget that. He must have money to do that. Just wait. Don't act in haste and repent at leisure. I'll tell you what I'll do. There's a man who came over in the "Etruria" with us who was a great swell on board. He was from San Francisco, and he's at the Metropole. He's sure to know all about the Allens, and I'll just run up to town to-morrow, and find out from him. In the mean time—"

"I'll stop *that* at all events.—Edith dear, it is past eleven. Come, dear."

"Didn't I tell you?" Lady Edith says, as she catches a glimpse of her mother's face, and believes she is offended at her for having been conversing with Allen. "I knew how it would be."

"Good night, Mr. Allen," Lady Oaktorrington says, in such an icy tone and with such a frosty look that Allen thinks Lady Edith was right after all.

He fancies, too, that Freddy is rather awkward and preoccupied with him as they have a brandy-and-soda and a cigarette together in the smoking-room before going to bed.

"What curious people these aristocrats are!" he says to himself. "Imagine any one being offended at a trifle like that!"

Lady Oaktorrington lies awake on mental pins and needles, wondering how she shall ever be able to hold up her head again before the marquis—if he finds it out. "But why need he find it out?" she asks herself as the clocks strike three. "How can he find it out unless I tell him? Shall I? I must think about it to-morrow."

The last words that Lady Edith says before she drops asleep are those which she has been saying to herself all the evening: "What a fool I was to send that telegram!"

CHAPTER VII.

NEXT morning Lord Frederick breakfasts before any of the others are down, and goes up to town by an early train on his mission of inquiry, leaving as a rea-

son for his hasty departure that his father had telegraphed to him to meet him in London. As not only
the Bouveries, but several other guests arrive at Ashwynwick, Lady Oaktorrington has not as much time
to sit and brood over what she is pleased to regard as
the "misfortune which has befallen the family," as she
otherwise would have had. She nevertheless devotes
every moment she can spare to a mental *résumé* of the
pros and cons of the case as they suggest themselves
to her. A dozen times does she go over the same
ground and arrive at the same conclusion, only to
begin again, follow out the old course of reasoning,
and reach the identical determination once more, viz.,
to wait until she hears from Freddy and not to say a
word about it to Lord Oaktorrington when he comes
home.

"It will be no use to tell him," she argues. "It
would only make a row, and I should never be able to
hold my own with him again. It will be dreadfully hard
to wear the mask of civility to this man Allen, believing
him all the time to be an impostor. But if difficult now
when I only suspect his worthlessness, how will it be
when I know it, should Freddy return with an adverse
report, for even then it must be kept a secret from my
husband. Was ever woman tormented so !"

There is a formal, chilling, silent breakfast. The
overnight's frost having broken into a southwest wind
and drizzling rain, Lord Beyndour and Lady Mary
come to the table in "pink" and habit, eat in silence
(beyond a few interchanges of sentiment on horses,
etc.), and depart hurriedly for the meet at the Crown
and Castle Inn. Lady Oaktorrington though polite is
cold and monosyllabic in her replies to Allen, the only

one who tries to talk. He gets no more encouragement from Lady Edith, who, under her mother's eye, never oversteps the constrained decorum of the high-life breakfast-table.

Breakfast over, Lady Oaktorrington says:

"Edith, come to my room with me. There are several invitations to answer," and Allen, who learns by the merest accident that Freddy has gone to town, is left solitary and alone to his own devices. It is true that the marchioness hesitates half-way up the stairs as she thinks of the plate there is about in the dining-room. Beyond that she gives no thought to the forlorn condition in which she leaves her stranger guest. On one pretext or another she keeps Lady Edith with her all the morning, the arrival of Lady Henry Tollemache, who comes, accompanied by her maid, just before luncheon, driving over from the station in a fly covered with boxes, causing the first interruption.

Lady Henry is a "Frisky" of the most approved pattern. She is young (about seven and twenty), pretty, and bright as a new sixpence; always dressed in the latest fashion, and thoroughly self-possessed.

"I have no patience with shy women," she frequently says. "But fancy a shy *man!* Ach! *I* don't know what the word means."

And she is right. She doesn't. She is the daughter of a Yorkshire baronet, and the wife of a clerk in the Foreign Office, who is withal a younger son of the fabulously rich Duke of Westmoreland, a peer who doesn't believe in idle sons, notwithstanding his wealth, to his credit be it spoken.

Lord Henry Tollemache is a young man of fashion,

6

one year his wife's senior, good-looking, loquacious (as all Foreign Office understrappers are), and fast. One year after marriage he decided to go his own way and let his wife go hers, and he has kept his word. That she has gone *her* way almost to the jumping-off point, is no secret. How far beyond that no one knows yet. As a matter of fact the number of times she has been upon the threshold of the divorce court she can not count upon the fingers of both her little, well-shaped hands, and people say it is only a question of time when she gets dragged inside the door. In the mean time she is asked and goes about here, there, and everywhere—a welcome guest in every house worth visiting in England. They have a house in town—her husband and herself; in Hill Street, Mayfair, it is; a little *bijou* of a house. But it is let most of the year, and she and Lord Henry seldom meet except by the merest chance at a ball in town during the season, or at a country-house during the winter. Lady Henry knows every one worth knowing, many of her closest and dearest friends never having seen her husband, and is full to the brim of the slang, gossip, and scandal of the hour. Lord Henry and she have about three thousand a year between them, counting everything; and there are some ill-natured old dowagers with marriageable daughters fast approaching spinsterhood, who will tell you that her dress must cost double that, and look a large-sized? when they add: "Where does the rest come from?"

But all the same, though she is cordially hated by women she is ardently admired by men. That she is considered an addition of great value to every house party is shown by the number of invitations she receives.; and that she is altogether a charming person is the verdict of every one who meets her.

"So good of you, dear Lady Oaktorrington," she tells the marchioness after the first interchanges of greeting. "I am always so very happy here. I've just come on from the Stanvilles'—Wixstead Abbey, you know—and though they had no end of things going on all over the shop from morning till night, don't you know, and two men for every woman (*sotto voce*, the correct thing, you know), yet it was most awfully slow and dull. They're going to have 'Tummy' down next month, and have grand doings, and perhaps then it will be more lively. They asked me to meet his Royal Highness, but I don't think I shall go. One doesn't care to go, don't you know, without the princess. One can't, in fact. You see, the Stanvilles are so awfully new. The old chap only got his peerage during the summer, and they say he began life as a pawnbroker's clerk, and got on to be a great money-lender in the city. You'd be surprised to hear the swells he has yet in his books, for he keeps on the business, they say, under a different name. That's the way he got his peerage, you know. I won't mention names, of course, but two members of the Cabinet owed him such a lot of money, and they threatened to resign unless he was made a peer. You see they squared their bills in that way. I call it shameful, don't you?"

Lady Henry stops at last to breathe.

"One isn't surprised at anything in these days, my dear," says Lady Oaktorrington. "But fancy the prince staying with such people!"

"Oh, he goes wherever he's sure to get good drink and meet pretty women. I expect any day to hear ·

he's visiting Poole, the tailor, or Cross and Blackwell, or Marshall and Snellgrove. It's only a matter of proper bait for the hook they throw."

"It's too bad of him. How can he expect *us* to keep up the dignity of the higher classes when he does such things?"

"How, indeed? By-the-by, I hear you have an American staying with you."

Lady Oaktorrington gives a start at being brought thus suddenly back to a subject which she had for the moment forgotten.

"Oh, yes. A friend of Freddy's."

"How awfully jolly. I think Americans are such capital fun, don't you know. They say such odd things, and seem so pleased with everything. It's as good as going to Moore and Burgess's Minstrels to meet one, don't you think?"

"I really can't say. I never met one before. That is to say, a man."

"I was going to say I thought you knew Lady Rudolph Campbell. Of course you do. Isn't she awfully sweet, and she dresses so well."

"How on earth, dear, did you know we had an American here?" Lady Oaktorrington asks, after casting about in her mind unsuccessfully for a clew.

"Oh, let me see. Yes. Lord Bouverie told me. I met him at the Saturday Pop."

"Really?—Tiresome old fool, how did he know?" she adds to herself.

"He's awfully rich—so he said."

"Y—yes, I believe so."

"What? Don't you *know?*"

An idea fraught with much relief to her distressed mind suddenly strikes the marchioness.

"Oh, of course he is. I was only joking. He's immensely rich."

"I thought you must be. And nice, too, is he?"

"I think so. But you can find that out for yourself at luncheon."

"And that reminds me. I must go and get ready."

"That's not a bad idea," Lady Oaktorrington says to herself, as five minutes later she follows Lady Henry up the stairs and goes to her boudoir in search of Lady Edith. She is not there. The marchioness rings the bell, and orders her maid to tell Lady Edith she wishes to speak to her. In five minutes the woman comes back and says:

"Lady Edith is not to be found, m'lady. She must have gone out."

"Gone out?"

"Yes, m'lady."

"Send Lady Edith's maid, Scovill, to me."

When Scovill comes she knows no more than any one else, except that her young mistress's hat, walking-boots, and sealskin jacket are missing. The conclusion is, therefore, irresistible that Lady Edith has gone out. But where? And why? Never before has Lady Oaktorrington known her to do such a thing unattended.

"It all comes of having this—this Yankee adventurer in the house!" she exclaims, throwing herself into a chair, when Scovill is gone. "He has been undermining her principles already with his independent, rubbishy, democratic ideas. Fancy, before the servants! What must they think? I can't make a scene by sending after her. But just wait!"

CHAPTER VIII.

No sooner has Lady Oaktorrington gone down to receive Lady Henry Tollemache than Lady Edith, for the first time released from her mother's eye since breakfast, walks to the window of the boudoir and looks out. The rain has stopped, and broken clouds are flying across the sky before a fresh, warm, south wind. Every now and then the sun peeps out, throwing long shadows across the grass-lawn beneath the window, and changing the dingy rain-drops which hang upon the outer sash into sparkling diamonds. The sparrows chirp gleefully in the ivy, and a venturesome thrush or two hop hither and thither in search of the worms which come up in earthy circles to the surface of the lawn every minute. As she looks out it seems a sin to be stewing in-doors on such a day, she thinks, and she feels as though a breath of out-of-door air would do her head good, for it has been aching badly ever since breakfast. She watches Lady Henry's fly drive away down the avenue until it is lost in a distant turn, and she wishes she was the driver—anybody who has his liberty.

"If I had any one to go with me," she says. "Yet why shouldn't I go alone? What harm? I know mother will be dreadfully cross about it if she knows. But need she know?" She sees the figure of a man walking slowly up the avenue. "Who can it be?" Her heart begins to beat faster. "Yes, I really believe it is—*him*." At that moment one of the under-gardeners crosses the lawn with a lawn-mower. "I'll just run out and speak to Bridges about planting those

bulbs from Carter's.   There can surely be no harm
in *that*."

In three minutes she is dressed and out upon the
crunching gravel of the drive.   The under-gardener
has vanished.

"How tiresome of him!" she says.   "I can't go
back now.   Perhaps he has gone this way."

Taking a side-path to avoid passing the drawing-
room windows, she gains in a roundabout way the iron
gate which opens from the grounds about the house
into the avenue, and lets herself out.   Not a soul is to
be seen, nor a sound to be heard except the cawing of
the rooks as they circle about the bare tops of the
lime-trees.   She walks on and on and on, at every
step thinking she hears an approaching footfall, at
every turn expecting to see an advancing figure.   She
gets within sight of the lodge, and knows she is almost
a mile from the house.   She looks at her watch.
Quarter past twelve.   She must retrace her steps
at once or she will be late for luncheon, and her
mother know what she has been doing.   A carriage
drives up to the lodge-gates and waits to be let in.
Whoever it is will see her as they pass, and that
would never do.   Leaving the avenue she runs
quickly across the grass until she gains the friendly
shelter of a clump of deodaras, and sits down, out
of breath, to rest herself upon a bench under their
branches.

"How unlucky I am !   First to have been foolish
enough to come out, and then not to see—er—Bridges,
and last of all to be driven over here by that tiresome
carriage.   I wonder who it is?"

She becomes conscious of the smell of tobacco-smoke, and before she can realize what it means, Allen, hat in hand, is standing before her.

"This *is* a surprise. I would add what we say in America and observe that 'mother will be pleased,' but that I know the opposite sentiment to pleasure would be hers could she view this interesting scene."

He stands smiling as the bright color which her recent exercise has brought into her cheeks fades slowly away before his gaze.

"I—I—really—upon my word, one doesn't know where to go to avoid you—one is safe nowhere."

This is what she says to him after coming out to see—er—Bridges, the under-gardener.

He is really rebuffed—at last. The events of the morning have in no way sweetened his temper. Not only have they had a dampening effect upon his spirits, but they have made him peculiarly sensitive to further indignity from these people whether affected or not. He is tired of this incessant dissimulation, if such it be; and if it be unassumed it is time he accepted it at its true value. In either case he would go. He turns upon his heel without a word and walks away. He has not taken a dozen strides when he hears: "Mr. Allen! Don't go, please." In a moment he is by her side again. He stands waiting for her to say something—one, two, three minutes—they seem hours. She sits complacently looking down at the ground. At last he says,

"Well?"

She looks up with a start.

"What—*you* here? I thought you had gone."

He grinds his teeth with very vexation.

"Why, you called me back."

"Did I?   When?"

"Just this moment.   How can you go on - like this?"

"Like what?   I don't understand you."

"You know perfectly well what I mean."

"I'm sure I do not.   I really thought you had gone. Why don't you go?"

As he turns quickly from her he sees in her eyes the look of the night before.   The same pleading, unhappy, yearning look, as she bends slightly forward and puts up one hand in silent supplication.   What is he to do?   He is a man who thinks he understands women as well as most men.   He has certainly had experience enough to make him a fair judge.   He has always known just what to do with them, but this time he acknowledges himself nonplussed.   The consciousness of his superior strength and her weakness—the recollection that he is a man and she a woman—in short, his innate spirit of chivalry, comes to his aid, and molds his will.   He will obey her.

As she sees him waver and remain, the old, placid look of indifference comes back into her eyes; but he heeds it not.

"I know you wish me to remain," he says, hoarsely, "although you do not say so.   Stay!   Hear me out. For no other woman on earth would I do so—for no other woman on earth would I submit to be treated in this childish fashion."

In the frame of mind in which he is, he gives undue weight and importance to what at any other time would seem the veriest trifles.   What man does not remember how it is when the glamor is on him? Allen at last finds himself in the plight in which it has heretofore been his experience to see, and his pleasure to leave—the other party. In fine, the boot is on the other leg this time, and would that a certain score or more of American girls, who for his sake are wearing gowns of the willow pattern, were here to see.

"You do not answer—you do not speak. Have you nothing to say?"

She looks up with a face of utter unconcern, though. (did he but see it) there is a happy, restful, satisfied light in her eyes, underneath the mask she shows him.

"No. What should I say?"

"Something—anything—only speak. Let me hear the sound of your voice."

At that moment the wind wafts to them the "three-quarter" chimes from the clock in the stable-tower.

"Dear me? It is a quarter to one. We shall be dreadfully late for luncheon as it is, and won't mother make a row!"

"She is likely to do that in any event; it doesn't matter how long we are."

"Indeed it does—to me. And look! Another shower is coming up and I've no umbrella. I must really go at once. Oh, no—no—no," as Allen starts on beside her. "*You* mustn't come. Fancy what would be said! I believe my mother would turn me out of the house if I was seen walking with you."

Unaccustomed to the strict usages of the English aristocracy, and judging everything by the customs of his own country, Allen takes this speech as a fresh insult. He flushes scarlet to the roots of his hair.

"And what have I done, pray, that it would be such an overwhelming disgrace for you to be seen walking with me?" he asks in a trembling voice.

"Done? Nothing. What do you mean?"

" I mean that there must be some reason why you refuse to have me walk with you. I know there is, but what it is I no more know than the Czar of all the Russias. I can not at all understand it. I have come to your house as an invited guest, and am received with much cordiality by your mother. I have not been in the house twenty-four hours before I am treated with the most barefaced, indecent, brutal, aristocratic rudeness —rudeness so studied and high-toned in its display that it is difficult to lay hold of it, and say just what it is. But I know it. I see it. Your mother is as different to me as two women can be. She bade me good-night like an iceberg last night, and she never spoke a word to me at breakfast this morning, except to answer in 'Yeses,' and 'Nos,' and 'Ohs,' and 'Reallys,' whatever I said to her. Your brother and sister go out hunting after asking me to join them ; Freddy goes to London without saying a word to me, and you are afraid to walk with me. What does it all mean? Something. But what that something is I am as ignorant of as—"

" The Czar of all the Russias," she cries, laughing at his vehemence. Instead of being angry, her use of his former simile to fill the present hiatus seems to strike his fancy, and he joins heartily in her laugh.

" I wonder you are not too much out of breath to laugh after that tirade," she says. " I'm afraid you are dreadfully sensitive. You imagine people are rude when they are not. You wouldn't want people to be hugging and kissing you all day, would you?"

" That would depend so much on who the people were. I only expect to be treated with common.

civility. Why, I tell you a good average American Indian would be ashamed to behave to a stranger as your mother is behaving to me without the faintest cause."

"Oh, your disgraceful conduct in the drawing-room last night is sufficient cause. I told you how it would be. You forget that."

"I don't believe it—nor do you. Now, you will pardon me, I know, if I say this : I am not a fool—"

"I suppose I must forgive you for saying that," and she laughs again. "It's natural you should think so."

"Oh, no, don't turn everything I say into ridicule," and he is getting ready to mount his high horse again. "I am serious. What I mean is this : Your mother at first was all for my talking to you last night, and this morning she is just the other way."

He is afraid he has gone too far, and he watches her face narrowly to catch the first sign of indignation it may show. Instead of that, as if by the touch of some magician's wand, it turns from an expression of levity to one of stern, settled obstinacy. The word "rebellion" is written in large letters over every feature.

"Are you sure of this?" she asks, in a quiet, serious voice.

"Positive."

"Why didn't you tell me before?"

"How could I? I had no chance."

She thinks to herself a minute or two, and bites her lips nervously. Then she says :

"You may walk home with me. Come."

CHAPTER IX.

LADY EDITH and Allen, both occupied with their own thoughts, walk on side by side across the grass and among the park trees for some minutes in silence. Each is following out a train of thought, and Allen is the first to arrive at a conclusion. As they leave the grass and step into the broad roadway of the avenue, he stops short.

"I don't think I shall go any farther with you," he says, decisively. "It is better not."

"What! After begging me to let you, and my giving in to please you? So like a man! You're afraid of the consequences," and Lady Edith gives a slight sneer.

"Yes, I am—for you."

"Oh, pray don't think of me."

"Yes, I must. I didn't quite realize the situation in all its bearings at first; but I see now what it would bring upon you. No; for the sake of ten minutes more alone with you I can not subject you to the consequences of what it would entail. I am not so utterly selfish."

"Nonsense. I don't mind. At all events, you can walk on as far as the iron gate. We shan't be seen from the house until we get there, if we keep close under the trees on this side."

There is more silence as they walk on, and then Allen says:

"Yes, I've made up my mind. I shall go at once."

"Oh, we're not half-way to the gate yet."

"I mean leave here—leave the house."

As he says this, and before Lady Edith can answer, the rumble of wheels comes from the direction of the house, and before they have time to escape to the grass again and get out of sight behind a tree, a one-horse fly rounds a bend and comes toward them. As it turns out it is the carriage which Lady Edith saw at the gate, returning empty after leaving some one at the house.

"This is most opportune," Allen continues. "I shall keep it to take me to the station."

"You are not in earnest?" she asks, quickly.

"Indeed I am."

"Going to run away and leave me to face it all alone! That is your idea of manliness, is it?"

"No, it is not. But my going will so gratify your mother, that she will quite overlook your being late for luncheon and unable to account for it."

"Oh, I shall be able to account for it, no fear."

"How?"

"I'll tell her I turned on my ankle getting over a stile. It will be rather a bore, though, having to keep up a limp for the rest of the day, but there is no way else."

Allen is regarding her with eyes full of wonder and regret. He is no "prig"; there is no man less one, as his rousing Saturday-night stag-parties in Frisco can amply testify. He doesn't mind or question what a woman is if she be but truthful. That is his one hobby, his single requirement in woman—given, of course, that she be fairly, reasonably well-looking to start with.

"Pray don't say that," he says, earnestly.

"Why not?"

"Because it is not true."

"Rubbish! Who is to find out? Who will know?"

"Yourself."

It is neither Allen's custom nor inclination to preach. He is one of the last men in the world to lay down rules for anybody except himself, and he has never cultivated the habit of inveighing against vice or extolling virtue. But it is doubtful if a sermon, couched in the most elaborate diction, and embellished with the most ornate verbiage of some acknowledged ecclesiastical light of the Established Church, could have appealed more eloquently and directly to Lady Edith's sense of right than this single, earnestly-spoken word. She reddens and bites her lip, and looks confused, as the monition goes straight home to her heart. But the taint of worldliness, the baneful influence of a life of daily association with high-bred artifice and dissimulation, where self-interest is the paramount, if not only sentiment, taught and fostered and encouraged by frequent example, is too deeply rooted in her nature to be shattered by one blow. She is not to be won over by a word.

"Dear me, how particular we are to be sure! I am sure I can not see the faintest harm in shielding— protecting one's self against injustice."

"By just means—yes. But is deception just?"

"Yes. Under some circumstances."

"You are a sophist, and I do not wonder. The life of the average English aristocrat is one of sophistry, pure and simple. In everything he does his conclusion is drawn from false premises; he finds a justifiable reason and excuse for the most mean and petty, the most dishonorable and unprincipled actions. His sole aim and object in life is the conservation of him-self—as an individual member of a certain class—and through him of that class in the aggregate. To this end it matters not what he does, so long as he can jus-tify it on the ground of class custom, usage, mainte-nance, or protection. He is always doing (or willing to do) evil that good may come—in the cause of his class."

"I'm afraid you'll think me very stupid, but I can't quite follow or understand all you say. You see, I have never heard anything *we* do questioned or criti-cised by any one."

"No. I dare say not. Not even in the pulpit. The clergy know too well on which side their bread is buttered, to have them admonish the nobility of their faults."

"I expect you are quite right. I really never thought about it much. One sees every one do just the same. But, of course, when one looks at it prop-erly, it must be all wrong."

"It *is* all wrong, and it is the easiest thing in the world to fall into such ways one's self without being aware of it. Now, I myself, with all my talk, was going to do a mean, dishonest thing, a minute ago, cal-culated to deceive and mislead. I have changed my mind; I will walk on with you to the house. And then —but I declare if the fly hasn't driven past and gone without my knowing it."

"I don't wonder," Lady Edith says, with a smile. "I saw it while you were talking."

"How unkind of you not to tell me or stop it for me."

"I am not such a f—fussy person as to interrupt people when they are talking."

Allen smiles to himself. "Of course, I can have one sent for. They'll be too glad to get rid of me, I should think. There's a train at 3.27 I can just catch. I know, for I've looked it out in Bradshaw."

"You are very silly," Lady Edith says, after a long pause, as they walk on.

"Because I am doing what is straightforward and honest in walking home with you?"

"No. Because you are going away. Would—would you stay if I asked you—begged of you to?"

They have all but reached the gate of the iron fence that incloses the grounds about the house from the park-land, and she stops, and turning, places her hand upon his arm. In her eyes is the old pleading look, while tears tremble upon their lids. A flush of excitement suffuses her cheeks, and her lips, half open, disclose the tips of the whitest teeth. To Allen (with all the circumstances combining to make it so) it is the loveliest face his eyes have ever rested upon. The climax of a passion, which has been growing steadily in his heart, is reached sooner than even he expected. His heart beats, and his temples throb with the sudden ecstacy of love, which seizes and takes possession of him. He is about to answer in words of intensest love and devotion when—prosaic destroyer of his short-spanned bliss!—a voice sounds behind them, and a striding, lumbering step comes quickly on.

CHAPTER X.

"HELLO, Sissy! Fancy *you* being out like this!"

The new-comer is a tall, raw-boned youth with short, sandy-brown hair, and a smooth, sunburned,

7

shiny face. He wears a check tweed jacket and knickerbockers, long, coarse brown-yarn stockings, and thick-soled shooting-boots. In his hand is a stout ash walking-stick, on his head a small tweed cap, and in his mouth a short briarwood pipe. He strides up to Lady Edith, grasps her by the hand, and stoops down and kisses her on the cheek before she can collect her wits to speak. Allen's first impulse is to knock the fellow down for his astounding behavior, and he has sprung toward him with that intent, when Lady Edith stays his uplifted arm:

"Bertie, of all people! What on earth brings you home? I thought your vacation didn't begin till just before Christmas."

Her surprise is not unmixed with vexation as she says this—vexation for the future as well as for the present.

"No more it does," the youth answers, a grin slowly taking the place of the frown with which he has been regarding Allen. "The fact is, a pair of confounded bull-dogs hauled me up for smoking in the street yesterday, and this morning the blackguard old proctor sent me a polite note saying I was to pay him six or seven bob. 'No fear,' says I, and I hooked it home the first train. Beastly jolly sell for the proctor."

"Father will be very angry, I'm sure."

"Can't be helped. Don't catch me chucking money away like that, to keep the jolly dons in old port. But I say," lowering his voice, "Who's this duffer? Never saw him before."

"Oh, I beg your pardon. How stupid of me! Mr. Allen, my brother Bertie."

Allen looks at the youth a moment and mutters to himself:

"Another brother!" and then puts out his hand, which the other "pump-handles" in sulky silence.

"I say, what are you doing out here like this?" Bertie asks his sister, as he drops Allen's hand and turns away. "It's uncommonly strange, isn't it? Who's this chap? It isn't possible that he's staying here?" and he gives Allen an impertinent look over from head to foot. "Looks like a foreigner."

"How rude you are, Bertie! I'm positively ashamed of you," Lady Edith whispers, as she sees Allen flush with anger and knows he must have overheard. "Yes, he is staying here. Why shouldn't he?"

"I'll back the gov'ner's away," Bertie says, with a meaning wink.

"You may consider yourself lucky that he is. I don't think you'll stay long after he returns."

"Two to one in half-crowns on it. Come, do you take me?"

Lady Edith does not answer, but turns to Allen and says:

"We shall never get home like this," and walks on with him beside her.

"By jove, no. You don't shake me off like that. I'm not quite so green," and Bertie, with another wink and a knowing nod, strides on by her other side.

"After all, perhaps it's just as well, if not better," Lady Edith muses. "His coming will distract mother's attention from us, and she will think I have really been with him. Happy thought! I will be civil to him and get him to say so." She is about to broach the subject to Bertie, when Allen's recent warning comes back to her. No she won't. She will begin being honest, straightforward, and truthful from that moment. Allen's words have borne their first fruit already.

As they come in sight of the house a telegraph messenger passes them going away.

"I hope it isn't anything bad," Lady Edith says, very pale; "I never can see a telegraph messenger without being anxious and nervous until I know what he is fetching. Do hurry on. Perhaps father is ill."

With a heart beating from a now double source she runs up the steps followed closely by Allen.

"Now for it," he says, as the first person they encounter is Lady Oaktorrington, telegram in hand, standing just inside the open drawing-room door. He braces himself, and is about to shut his eyes to receive the first outburst, when, before he can do so, Lady Oaktorrington comes forward with a beaming smile and outstretched hands:

"Mr. Allen—Edith. I am so glad to see you—together. Had I known that you were with her, Mr. Allen, I should have been spared much anxiety. You naughty girl to go out without telling me," and she shakes her finger good-naturedly at her daughter. Allen and Lady Edith exchange puzzled glances. In their state of mingled bewilderment and satisfaction of mind at the unexpected and unaccountable turn affairs have taken, they have time to do that.

"I must apologize for being so late," Allen begins.

"Oh, yes, mother, I'm afraid we're awfully late for luncheon."

"It doesn't signify in the least. We have come out, but everything is being kept hot for you. Will you please ring the dining-room bell, Mr. Allen, when you go in? I hope you'll find something to eat," and the marchioness smiles again graciously.

In the revulsion of feeling from anxious anticipation to relieved realization, which Lady Edith has just experienced, she has quite forgotten her fears about the telegram. She sees it in her mother's hand. "Anything unpleasant, mother?" she asks. "I was afraid father might be ill, or that there had been some accident on the railway or in the hunting-field."

"No, my dear," her mother says, soothingly. "It's only a telegram from Redfern to say the jackets have been sent off. Hadn't you better go and have some food. You must be very hungry."

"What on earth can it all mean?" Lady Edith says to Allen as they wait in the dining-room for the dishes to be brought in again. "It is past my comprehension."

"And mine," Allen replies. "She is not like the same person."

They have grown upon a very familiar footing, these two, in their short acquaintance, without seeming to be aware of it.

"I can't help thinking," Lady Edith says, presently, "that it might be that—" she stops short.

"That what?"

"Oh, never mind, now. Perhaps I'll tell you some other time. By-the-by, what's become of Bertie? I had quite forgotten him."

"Not a very direful disaster if you had," Allen says, with a trifle of impatience in his voice. "I fancy he is old enough to look out for himself. In my opinion the less a girl sees and thinks of her brothers the better—after they're grown up."

" Do you ?   Why ? "

" Oh, they are always in the way, loafing and idling about—I am talking only of England, mind, for in America all your three brothers would be in some business, or have some occupation that would keep them busy away from home."

" My three brothers !   I've got four."

" Great Scott ! another ! "

" I'm sure you ought not to find so much fault with them.   If it hadn't been for Freddy we should never have met."

" True.   And for that one reason I forgive them everything else.   You want to know what became of Bertie ?   I will tell you.   When we came to a path near the iron gate he left us abruptly and turned into it.   I saw him."

" Do you mean just inside the iron gate on the left ? "

" I do."

" Oh, that is the short cut to the stables.   He's gone to have a chat with the stable-boys."

" Humph ! " and Allen, with a facial contortion evincing much inward irritation, drops his eyeglasses off his nose.   Luckily they are attached to a slender silk cord and do not come to grief.   " Do you know the more I see of the English aristocracy the more inexplicably inconsistent, the more extraordinarily self-contradicting do they appear to me to be.   We Americans are blamed and abused for our ' universal equality notions '—as you call them—and are twitted with calling our servants ' help,' and with being on equal terms with them.   You do this—"

" I'm sure I never said anything of the sort."

"I mean you collectively. I say you do this with one breath, and with the other you go to your stables and have a familiar chat with your grooms and stable-boys, and see no harm in it. Stay—I make no point of its being intrinsically wrong. It's harm depends on the sort of people these grooms and stable-boys are. They may or may not be advantageous companions for young gentlemen. The chances are they are not. It is not because they are grooms or stable-boys, but because—especially in England—association with such people, as you commonly find them, is not likely to improve a youth's mind. Otherwise, there can be no actual harm. But it is not that I am thinking about. It is the glaring inconsistency of the thing on the part of people who despise *us* for not having our servants say 'sir' and 'ma'am' to us every two minutes, and who at the same time associate with their own servants on a far more familiar footing than we do with our 'help.' All I can say is, if you do these things you have the right neither to criticise us, nor to exclude from your intimate acquaintance anybody on the mere ground of class."

Allen stops and rearranges his eyeglasses to look at her.

"Why do you wear those things?" she asks.

Allen is rather put out by her seeming indifference to his remarks:

"Why does a miller wear a white hat?"

"Then you wear them to keep your eyes warm? What an extraordinary reason?"

"Oh, you always turn everything I say into ridicule."

The entrance of the butler and a couple of footmen

with their luncheon puts a stop to further conversation—save of the most conventional character—between them.

CHAPTER XI.

THE Bouveries arrived before afternoon tea in a formidable family party of five—father, mother, two daughters, and, much to Lady Oaktorrington's surprise and ill-concealed vexation—Jack.

Lord Oaktorrington still remains in town. He is *detained by important political events*, he writes to his wife by the evening's post. *An important division on the Ground-Game Bill is expected to-night*, he goes on to say, *and Salisbury has made it a personal favor, my remaining. I have an especial reason for wishing to please him, as you know he has eight livings in his gift, and one must think of Bertie. Besides, should the Government be defeated, her Majesty will send for Salisbury at once, and he has hinted his intention to offer me a seat in the Cabinet as Lord Privy Seal, or the Lord-Lieutenancy of Ireland, whichever I like. I expect to get home to-morrow, but in any event I shall not be kept much longer, as Parliament must be up in a day or two, now.*"

"I don't believe a word of it," is Lady Oaktorrington's comment, as she throws her husband's letter down on the table. "It is only another excuse."

As a matter of fact, Lady Oaktorrington is wrong. Though the marquis has cried wolf so often without just cause that when at last he means it his cry is discredited, this time (with one exception) his statement is quite true. The single exception is, however, but a mistake, and a minor one to him. The measure under

discussion in the House of Lords is the Local Government for Scotland Bill, the Ground-Game Bill having
been passed three years before !   It is really all one to
Lord Oaktorrington.   To him it doesn't matter in the
least what the measure is, so long as he knows which
way he is to vote.   As for the marchioness, her knowledge of politics and political history dates but from her
enrollment as a Primrose League dame by the Hertford Habitation a year ago, and consists chiefly of a
hazy, indistinct, but nevertheless bitter hatred of
Gladstone, and of Mr. Joseph Chamberlain the accred-
ited leader of the Radical party.

She takes up the marquis's letter once more, and
reads it through again.

"No.   Just as I thought.   Not a word about Harborough.   The man I wanted hasn't come, and the
man I didn't want has.   I can't understand it."   She
is in a complaining humor, with no one to complain to.
It is dull work growling to herself, and she misses her
husband, who is her usual safety-valve in that regard.
She has no confidences with her daughters, and her
sons, with the exception of Freddy, are too unsympa-
thetic to listen to her five minutes without yawning in
her face.   In her extremity she turns for comfort to
Lady Henry Tollemache.   They are all in the drawing-room at five o'clock tea—that is to say, tea is over,
and everybody is sitting about the room talking in
couples.   Lady Bouverie, a tall, thin, vinegar-faced
woman, whose distinguishing characteristics are huffi-
ness (called sensitiveness by herself) and family pride,
is conversing in whispers with Lady Mary, on what
subject it is difficult to conceive, for they have not one
thought in common.   However, as their lips move oc-

casionally, it is presumable they are saying "something or other about something." Lord Bouverie is talking to Allen, Lord Beyndour to Emily Bouverie, and Lady Edith to Jack, while Augusta Bouverie sits alone and crochets.

"I don't know what you'd think of it," Lady Oaktorrington begins, as soon as she sees everybody settled, and makes sure there are no listeners, "but to me it is a most unheard-of thing."

"What is, dear Lady Oaktorrington?" asks Lady Henry, all ears in a moment, thinking she is on the threshold of some startling scandal. "Pray tell me. It shall go no further, I assure you."

"Why, having a man come uninvited to your house."

"Who has done that?" Lady Henry asks, looking round questioningly at the male guests, so as to shape her answer accordingly. "The American gentleman?"

"Oh, dear, no!"

"It's rather like them, you know. They do that sort of thing among themselves, don't you know, and think they can introduce their customs among *us*. I was told a curious thing about a Yankee the other day, by-the-bye, which is rather à propos. You know the Delancey Veres, of course. Well, Lady Charles and her maid were coming home from Cannes, and were crossing from Boulogne to Folkestone. On board, as usual, were a lot of Americans. One of them, a lady, noticed Lady Charles was looking rather ill, don't you know, and, seeing her sitting on deck, where she went for the air, supposed she had no cabin. So she went up to Lady Charles, introduced herself as Mrs. General, or Judge, John T. Spaulding, of New York, or

Cincinnati, I forget which, and insisted upon Lady Charles going down to her cabin, where she and her husband, a fearful snob, had a couple of bottles of iced champagne, and made her drink some. Poor Lady Charles was all alone, don't you know, except her maid, and was afraid to refuse for fear of a scene, these people were so pressing. Indeed, they wouldn't take any refusal, and the general, or judge, actually came up and assisted Lady Charles down the companionway with his arm round her waist. Just fancy!"

"How dreadful! Why didn't she send for the captain?"

"Poor thing, I expect she never thought of that, she was so bewildered. She goes about very little, don't you know, and it was her first journey abroad."

"What a mistake—traveling alone like that! It shows how dangerous it is."

"It does indeed. But that is not the worst part of my story."

"I suppose the champagne was drugged, and they robbed her," suggests Lady Oaktorrington.

"Oh, not quite so bad as that," smiles Lady Henry. "They kept with her all the way to Charing Cross, forcing themselves into the same compartment in the train, and were actually almost carrying her off in the cab with them to the Langham Hotel, when luckily her footman appeared and rescued her. She says they never rested till she gave them her name and address —she was shrewd enough to give them false ones—and gave her a pressing invitation to visit them in New York or Chicago—I wish I could remember which it was—as if she would ever go to the States, and actually invited her maid, too!"

" How disgraceful ! "

" Lady Charles tells me poor Gilman acted so well about it. She never answered or took any notice of them."

" How clever of her ! "

" Yes, wasn't it? And such a sell for them, not finding out who Lady Charles was. I dare say they've been passing their time trying to find the " Duchess of Yorkshire " at " 45 Regent Square (that's the name and address she gave them—there's no such title, as you know, and no such square, ha, ha !), and will go back to America and say all sorts of uncivil things of the English nobility in consequence. But you haven't told me who came without being asked. It can't be Lord Bouverie ? "

The marchioness shakes her head.

" Oh, no, of course not. Then it must be Jack Bouverie. Don't you think I ought to have been a man and gone to the bar? You don't mean to say Jack did such a thing as that? Shan't I give him a jolly good rowing."

" I certainly beg you won't. I've told you in confidence."

" Oh, yes, of course ; I forgot.—Poor Jack," Lady Henry says to herself, " I wonder why you weren't asked? Ah, yes, of course," and she shuts her left eye slowly after regarding Allen for a second or two. " One eye is enough to see *that*.—Of course, this American gentleman—I forget his name—ah, yes, Allen. I suppose, of course, he's awfully rich. They all are, don't you know—in England."

Lady Oaktorrington doesn't quite catch the last two words, but there is something in Lady Henry's face which makes her heart drop down—bump!—into the soles of her shoes.

"Why, what do you mean?"

"Oh, nothing. He's very rich, isn't he? Oh, yes, I remember, you told me he was to-day."

· "Yes, he is," Lady Oaktorrington answers, buoying up her drooping spirits, and fortifying her doubting heart (as one often does) by the self-deceiving assumption of firmness.

"Oh, you know, of course." There is ever so slight an emphasis on "know," and the marchioness is now enough on the alert to detect it. Her heart can not drop any further, but she gets a choke in her voice as she answers:

"Y—yes—we know."

She thinks of Freddy's telegram in her pocket, and wishes she might have another look at it to make assurance doubly sure. She has not had time to read it once all the afternoon, since she got it, and then she only glanced hurriedly over it.

"Because," Lady Henry goes on, "one hears such odd things, sometimes, of the way they impose upon us in England by their pretended wealth. Now, only the other day— But it can not interest you or be à propos of your friend, so I—"

"Oh, do tell me, I beg of you, dear Lady Henry," Lady Oaktorrington says, with anxious eyes. "I should so like to hear."

Lady Henry smiles cruelly behind her handkerchief, and reels off as she spins:

"It's not very much. Only this: Sir Charles Heathcote, who has lately been over to the States, fell in with an American on board the steamer coming home. A·

most agreeable, pleasant, well-mannered fellow he was,
Sir Charles says. They occupied the same stateroom,
and became very great friends. I forget the name of
the young man, but at all events he seemed to have
plenty of money to chuck about, and was a great favorite with every one on board. They traveled up together from Liverpool to London, and had a compartment together It was at night, and Sir Charles fell
asleep, and didn't wake up till they got to St. Pancras.
Sir Charles there bid his new friend good-by, the young
man saying he was going to stay at the Grand Hotel.
Well, to make a long story short, next morning Sir
Charles found his pocket-book was missing, with a
couple of hundred pounds in it in circular notes. Poor
chap, even then his suspicions weren't aroused, and he
posted off to the Grand Hotel to tell his American
friend his loss, and, would you believe it—"

"The young man wasn't there, had never gone
there," the marchioness suggests between quick gasps.

"Half right and half wrong. He *had* been there,
but had left by the early morning Tidal for Paris. He
left a note for Sir Charles, to say he had been telegraphed for by his brother, but would return in a few
days. And fancy, Sir Charles swallowed the threadbare excuse, and is anxiously awaiting his return ! *I*
should have communicated with the Paris police without a moment's delay, shouldn't you ?"

"Y—yes, dear, I should," the marchioness answers,
absently, staring straight before her.

"So one can't be too careful, don't you know, can
one ?"

"N—no, dear, I suppose not," and Lady Oaktorrington's eyes rest thankfully on Jack. "How glad I

am *now* that he is here," she thinks. "How silly I was to speak of it.

"I can't get over Jack's behavior," Lady Henry says, after a short pause. "I think I really must give him a good rowing," and she rises from her seat.

"Not for worlds, dear. I beg of you not," the marchioness implores. "Do, pray, sit down again. I want your help about something. I'm in a tangle about how I'm to send them all in to dinner. You see, I of course must take Lord Bouverie, and Beyndour Lady Emily, and that will leave only Jack Bouverie or—or —this American gentleman for you, dear Lady Henry. I'm so very sorry."

"Oh, I don't mind in the least," Lady Henry says, airily. "Pray don't trouble about me."

"We expected that Lord Alfred Pictou and Montie Vereker, whom we've asked to stay, would be here to-day; and the Duke of Harborough actually wrote and proposed himself for yesterday, and he—"

"Harborough coming here?" and Lady Henry's voice shows much agitation. "You—you never told me," and she gives a mental stamp with her foot.

"I didn't think of it. Why, my dear, *you* don't mind meeting him, do you? I thought, of all people—"

"Oh, it's not that. But never mind. Which, then, am I to have, Jack or the Yankee?"

"Whichever you like."

"Oh, give me the Yankee, by all means."

Lady Henry watches the marchioness's face narrowly as she says this, and sees, by the look of relief which comes into it, that both her stories have taken root already.

"Thanks so much, dear," Lady Oaktorrington an-.

swers. "That will leave Jack for Mary, and the Bouverie girls will have to go in by themselves with Edith. It's all settled so nicely, although I wish I had some other men."

The words are hardly out of her mouth when the door is thrown open, and the butler announces—

"The Duke of Harborough!"

As the name rings out through the room Lady Oaktorrington, every thought of her now unsettled plan merged in but one of supreme satisfaction, and beaming with smiles, rises quickly and goes to meet his Grace; Lord Bouverie stops in the middle of a long dissertation on the Queen's regulations for the army in his day, with which he has been regaling Allen, and toddles forward with a fawning grin; Lady Bouverie gives a slight start, but instantly lapses back in bolt-upright placidity; Emily Bouverie screws up her mouth and winks at Lord Beyndour, who takes not the faintest notice; the other three girls sit demurely oblivious as all properly brought up young ladies should under all circumstances; Lady Henry turns as red as she can under her powder, and looks a curious mixture of annoyance and pleasure; and Allen, with a face of utter and silent amazement, glances quickly over at Lady Edith.

CHAPTER XII.

LADY OAKTORRINGTON's plan of sending in her guests to dinner receives a further disruption by the arrival, just before the dressing-gong goes, of the Honorable Montague Vereker. Montie Vereker, by which name he is best known, is a younger son of Viscount Hampstead. He is a "young man about town," as the phrase goes, who, on an allowance of four hundred a year from his father, manages to live well, dress well, have chambers in Bennet Street, St. James, to belong to three or four swell West End clubs, and to do the London season every summer, and a round of country-house visits every winter. Besides amusing himself he does nothing. It is not that he has not brains enough and natural ability enough with which, if set going in the right direction and through the proper channels, he might accomplish by work something to do him credit and honor; but simply that his education and bringing up have fitted him for nothing but aristocratic (though economical) idleness. He goes to two or three balls a night from May to August, seldom misses Epsom, Ascot, or Goodwood—the Derby and Cup days never—and is generally to be found at Sandown and Newmarket. He is a swimmer "in the swim" if any man is, and is, in short, a fashionable idler. He is young—about six and twenty—and though, except on account of his rank, not considered an "eligible," and then only by the title-seeking parents of some trade-made heiress; he is one of a large army of useful and ornamental, though comparatively impecunious, young gentlemen in aristocratic London society, who can dance, flirt, talk fluently the gossip and small talk of the hour, and who make the "men" at every entertainment during the season, from state balls at Buckingham Palace to "small and early" dances in Belgravia and Mayfair. He is eminently safe on the marriage question. He was never known to commit so vulgar, ill-bred, and altogether unaristo-

8

cratic an error as to fall in love; and such a thing as
entertaining a serious idea of any of the dozens of girls
with whom he dances, flirts, and gossips from one year's
end to the other, has never entered his head. He
knows better. It is his utter neutrality which obtains
and retains for him the *entrée* to the best houses, and
gives him unlimited and free access to the society of
young girls, who from other men of less circumspect
habits and equally light purses, are guarded by lynx-
eyed papas and mammas as from the approach of raven-
ing wolves. He is an authority on everything fashionable, from the last figure introduced in the *cotillion* to
the latest cut of trousers or style of shirt-collar; and
has at his fingers' ends all the scandal and tittle-tattle
of the hour, from the whispered name of the co-
respondent in the next divorce case before Sir James
Hannen or Sir Charles Butt, to all the minor legacies
in the will of every rich maiden aunt or bachelor uncle
in the kingdom. He is a fund of information on everything considered useful in society but nowhere else.
So long as he cultivates the qualities which at present
distinguish him, and observes a strict adherence to the
rules and regulations which they entail, so long will
he never want a dinner to eat or a bed to lie upon
from the fathers and mothers of girls needing partners
at balls, and a helping hand generally to make not only
their coming out a success, but their going through a
second season a possibility. He has assisted a dozen
or more girls to good marriages, and one of these days,
when he finds his social power and prestige on the
wane, and his grip upon society loosening, he will think
of marriage himself, and will select the heiress of some
title-hunting city magnate of obscure origin but pletho-

ric bank account, or retired millionaire brewer who began life on sixpence ; and in the dowry he gets with his wife will find ample amends for red hair, freckles, vulgarity, and *h*-dropping.

The proper adjustment of the niceties of the scale of precedence which controls the British aristocracy as by a rod of iron, and which is never more strictly observed than in the sending of guests in to dinner, is a science in itself ; and if a thorough knowledge of all the intricacies and ramifications of rank can entitle her to the honor, Lady Oaktorrington may justly be called a scientist. But she has nothing on the present occasion to test her skill in this respect. The rank of each guest is too clearly defined to admit of any question. There are no conflicts arising out of similar titles, no claims of superiority that can not be seen at a glance without consulting the peerage for creation dates. She herself will, of course, go in last with the Duke of Harborough, Lord Beyndour will take in Lady Bouverie first, then Lord Bouverie will follow with Lady Henry Tollemache, and after them will come Montie Vereker and Lady Mary. Up to this point it is all plain sailing with her. After this her troubles begin. And her troubles consist of but one difficulty, and that lies in the answer to the question of not *where,* but *with whom* she shall send in Allen. As an American gentleman he is legitimately and logically the peer of any man. If the status of a man in his own country be the criterion, no one should outrank an American in any other. Unfortunately, this is not admitted in England (at all events among the aristocracy), where all Americans must take rank with English " misters " who have no title, if indeed Americans are allowed to have any rank at all. But it is not Allen's rank or right of position which troubles Lady Oaktorrington's mind. *Where* he ought to be placed never enters her head. If that were all she would soon come to a decision. As a matter of fact she believes (in common with her class) that as an American, and because he is an American, he should yield precedence to every Englishman present, and be content to be sent in the last of her guests. To do this she would not hesitate if it becomes necessary upon her settling the real difficulty in her mind—*with whom* she shall send him. The duke's coming has dislodged Lord Bouverie from his place of honor with her, and makes it imperative, much to that lady's disgust, that he should be allotted to Lady Henry Tollemache, the next lady in order of rank. That leaves Allen free, and who his partner shall be partakes very much of the character of a dilemma. In fact, two dilemmas stare the marchioness in the face. She doesn't want Lady Edith to have him, and she does. The new doubts which Lady Henry's tales have raised in her mind support the negative of the proposition, while Freddy's telegram takes the affirmative side. In the one case she should shield her daughter from his attentions ; in the other, she should not throw any obstacle in his way. If he doesn't take in Lady Edith he must Emily Bouverie, and Emily Bouverie is about the last girl on earth in whose way she would throw any young man on whom she had an eye for either of her daughters. This is dilemma No. 1. Then, if she doesn't let Allen take in Lady Edith, there is but one man left for her to go with, and that is Jack, and Jack is almost, if not quite (in her mind), as bad as Allen may be. There is the difference of the present and the future between them.

"I can't send Jack in with his sister," she reflects. "That would be simply outrageously bad form. And yet I must if I don't let him go with Edith. What shall I do?" This is dilemma No. 2.

She is still in doubt when she goes up to dress for dinner. While her maid is dressing her hair, she gets her first fair chance to read Freddy's telegram again. It reassures her immediately, and she decides at once in Allen's favor on all points. She reads the telegram once more :

" *Treat him civilly. He is all right, of course.*"

This is all it says.

She reads it again, and the warm sense of security and satisfaction about her heart quickly falls in temperature. As no doubt most of us have experienced, the more she studies and reads and thinks, the more uncertain does she feel. By the time she has read and weighed the words half a dozen times they bear a totally different construction from that which she put upon them at first. Freddy has seen no one, it is evident, and has really found out nothing, and his telegram is no more than a mere opinion based upon no further information concerning Allen than that with which he went away in the morning.

"Oh, dear me, yes," she cries to herself. "*Of course*, shows that. I know Freddy's "of courses." They're always meant to bolster up some real doubt in his own mind which he finds easier to dispose of by two self-assuring words, than by the trouble of an investigation. Fancy my forgetting this! And yet, perhaps I am wrong and he does know. It's all the fault of these tiresome telegrams; they never make anything clear. But I dare say I shall hear from Freddy to-morrow. In the mean time I shall follow his advice, so far as I can. I'll be civil to him, but I'll be on the safe side about Edith. She shall go in with Jack. Jack's a gentleman at all events, and though he may not have the money we want, would not do anything dishonorable. That's all settled. But I wish I could see my way to avoid sending the other in with Emily Bouverie. Augusta I shouldn't mind. She's so dull."

The first person she meets on entering the draw-ing-room is Bertie. Her delight is unbounded. "So good of you, Bertie, dear, to come so cleverly to my rescue," she smiles, as he walks sheepishly up to her, expecting from her the displeasure at his unwarranted absence from his college which his father would have shown; "I don't in the least know what I should have done with poor Augusta Bouverie, but for this. Thanks, dear, so much," and she accepts a dutiful kiss from the truant on each cheek. "You must take in Emily Bouverie—mind. *He* shall go with Augusta. I hope he'll enjoy her society."

And so, when dinner is announced, Allen has the satisfaction of seeing himself placed below every one else, and given as his companion the lady whose rank is the lowest of the entire company. And this, while the highest position and greatest honor is graciously bestowed upon a man whose name and fame as the most immoral profligate of the British peerage are—thanks to the American press—as well known publicly in the United States as they are privately in England.

CHAPTER XIII.

ALLEN's naturally quick temper is sorely tried by this exhibition of (to him) aristocratic flunkeyism. He can forgive the slight insult to himself, if it be not intentional; but he can find no excuse for the homage done to a man so degraded as the Duke of Harborough. He does not know that the strict rules of precedence, which to the English nobility are as the laws of the Medes and Persians, demand this social elevation of a duke, libertine though he be, above the heads of his fellow-men who rank below him; and that to none save a prince would he yield precedence. Accustomed as he is to see only men of merit and brains, ability and valor, given place in his own country, he contemplates the spectacle with a sense of humiliation that he should be obliged to be even an unwilling assistant at so degrading a ceremony. With brows knit and teeth set hard he takes his seat, a latent fire in his eye telling that he but waits his opportunity to give vent to his feelings in some wholesome expression of opinion on the shallowness of monarchical institutions, and all the empty follies which they entail upon the people who are so weak as to be ruled by them. A sweet and sympathetic smile from Lady Edith, who sits opposite, does much to mollify him; and after a somewhat prolonged silence, during which he eats his soup in mechanical abstraction, he turns to Augusta Bouverie.

To begin a conversation with a person with whom one has no interests in common, of whose tastes, predilections, opinions, and views one is totally ignorant, is not an easy task for any man—at a dinner-table espe-

cially. The first remark must partake of the forced
abruptness of a question, as to the answer to which
you are utterly indifferent; or else of the lugged-in-
by-the-head-and-shoulders character of a comment on
some passing event, which comes into your head *à propos*
of nothing at all. You only speak because you must
speak, because you are expected to talk about something, or be put down for a dolt and a fool; and while
the sound of your voice seems to you harsh, discord-
ant, choky, and unnatural, you are conscious that several pairs of ears besides those possessed by the person
you are addressing, are wide open to listen and criticise and quiz your every utterance. To a shy man
the position is one of untold misery. Fortunately for
himself, as well as those with whom he is thrown in
contact, Allen is not shy. Never was a man less so.
But were he afflicted with this painful, and, in his own
opinion, unmanly malady of sensitive diffidence, the
resentful humor he is in would temporarily overcome
and cure it. There are plenty of things that he would
like to say, and would say, but that his inward sense
of delicacy and refinement holds him in check. He is
not usually at fault for something to say at any and all
times, but now he seems unable to think of anything.
His companion in no way suggests a topic. She sits
bolt upright in her chair, with her hands folded in her
lap, and her eyes demurely bent down, contemplating
the table-cloth immediately in front of her. Through
the corner of his eye Allen sees Lord Beyndour making signs to Emily Bouverie to look at him; he is dimly
conscious, for he dares not trust himself to look, that
they are both laughing over some mutual joke of which
he is the subject; his ears grow hot and his forehead

flushes red. He dashes at the first thing that comes into his head :

" Do you admire Irving ? "

" I—I—don't know who you mean," with a slight blush.

" Why, Henry Irving—" still a look of oblivion— " the actor."

" Oh !" with a start. " I don't know anything about actors—that is, real ones. We have private theatricals at home, sometimes."

" Do you take part in them ? "

" Me ? Oh, dear, no. But Emmy and Jack do."

" But you go to the theatre, don't you ? "

" No."

" If I lived in London I should go almost every night."

" We don't live in London. We live in Warwick-shire."

" Why, your father spoke to me before dinner about his house in London."

" Yes, that's our town-house. We don't live there. We only stay there in the season."

This seems to Allen much like a distinction without a difference.

" And you never go to the theatre. I thought English people were so fond of the theatre."

" I expect you are thinking of the middle classes. *We* don't care for the play."

" Then you have never seen any of Shakespeare's plays ? "

" Dear, no. Mamma wouldn't let us see them ; they're too dreadful."

Allen adjusts his eyeglasses to look at her.

"Are you serious?" he asks, after a minute of silent inspection.

"Yes. Quite."

"Don't you know that Shakespeare's plays are the grandest, most superb writings in the English language; and that he is acknowledged to be the greatest of English poets?"

"No, I'm sure I don't. I know nothing at all about him, and mamma would be awfully shocked if she thought I did."

Allen is thunderstruck, and regards his companion with eyes of honest pity.

Lord Bouverie has been watching the pair with calm satisfaction, while carrying on a determined struggle with Lady Henry for the exclusive use and possession of the personal pronoun I. At the same time he contrives to catch enough of their conversation to tell its drift. Both eyes and ears warn him that everything is not going on as swimmingly as he would wish. He leans forward in front of Lady Henry, who separates him from Allen.

"I'm afraid, sir, that Augusta's ideas do not agree with your own about something," he says, with a smile to Allen which merges into a frown as he catches his daughter's eye. "You are talking of Shakespeare? Pray don't mind anything she says. She knows positively nothing about him."

"So she tells me. And I confess I am surprised. In America we have the greatest veneration for him. I thought it was the same here in England."

"I'm sorry to say I'm rather ignorant myself about him. I believe there's an actor in London who, under the patronage of Lady Burdett-Coutts, has been doing some of his plays lately. I'm sorry to say I've not seen them."

"Sorry?" exclaims Lady Henry. "I'm sure if you'd been with me you *would* be sorry. You know Berkeley Villiers? I thought you did. He's gone on the stage, you know, and Henry Irving, whose real name, by-the-by, is John Brodribb, it seems was originally a clerk in the city in an insurance company's office of which Berkeley's father was a director. So Irving engaged him for very small parts at his theatre, and one night last summer he sent me an order for a box with a note begging me to go and see him act. Just to please the poor fellow, don't you know, I went. It was one of Shakespeare's plays—'Romeo and Juliet'—I think there is such a play, isn't there?" and she looks at Allen for enlightenment.

"I believe I have heard of a play of that name attributed to Shakespeare," Allen answers, dryly. The sarcasm is, however, quite thrown away.

"Thanks. I thought you'd know—you Ya—Americans know everything. I never saw such people. Well, as I was saying, I went to see this play, and of all the dull, trashy, tedious, vulgar productions as it was. I don't think I ever saw anything more utterly absurd. Men were fighting with their swords out every two minutes, somebody was taking poison every three, and such rubbishy stuff as the people talked! Love-making it was, nauseous and vulgar from beginning to end. Now, fancy a man being such an utter idiot as to talk to a woman like this, and fancy her putting up with it! I remember it especially because its silliness made a great impression upon me. Romeo talks to Juliet under her window late at night—imagine any *lady* going in for such things—and says, 'Would I were a glove upon that hand, that I might touch that cheek!' Just fancy that! It's positive drivel, and about on a par with the rubbishy stuff in the railway-stall novels which my maid pores over all day long. It's just the sort of thing she would like to have said to her by her young man in Fortnum and Mason's shop."

"I quite agree with you, Lady Henry," shouts Lord Beyndour, from the bottom of the table. "Shakespeare writes most awful rot. The other night I went —for something better to do—to see Irving as Shylock in—I forget the name of the play. Shylock is a Jew, and he lends a merchant a lot of money, and takes as security a pound of the poor chap's flesh. If Gilbert or anybody else put such stuff as that into their plays in these days they'd be hissed off the stage in no time. Shakespeare, indeed! The Jews in the City want better security than that nowadays. Try 'em and see."

Allen elevates his eyebrows to Lady Edith, and turns to Lady Henry.

"Do you hunt?" he asks.

"Rather, when my friends are good enough to mount me. I'm too poor to have horses of my own. And you? But of course not. You Americans sneer at our hunting, don't you?"

"Do we?"

"Oh, yes, you know you do. You see, you are not fond of sport as we are."

"Possibly not, if you limit it in that way. We certainly don't care much for such mechanical sport as fox-hunting."

"I won't listen to you, you shocking heretic. Fancy calling our dear hunting a mechanical sport!"

"What else is it? You preserve the animal you hunt from all harm until you want to use him, and in the mean time he's devastating farmyards and doing no end of damage. Then the sport is so dreadfully uneven. There's one poor solitary half-tame fox with no means of defense but his heels, pitted against say, a hundred horsemen, and as many dogs. What danger is there in it except to the fox, and what skill is required? It is danger and skill that make sport."

"What! No danger in riding straight across country? I never heard such a man!"

"Yes, perhaps in riding straight. But who ever rides straight? Did you ever see any one? I'm sure I never did. People make for every gap and open gate they can find, and ride along the roads."

"Oh, that's to save their horses. I'm sure that's right enough."

"Perhaps it is. But it isn't riding straight, all the same."

"Oh, you only talk like that because you're an American. If you were an Englishman, you'd hunt, never fear."

"Perhaps I couldn't afford to have any horses of my own."

Lady Oaktorrington and Lord Beyndour catch all but the first word of this speech, and exchange glances. Lady Henry sees an opportunity to find out something she has been anxious to know before wasting any ammunition upon Allen, for she has mentally selected him for a victim, should events recommend and justify it in her estimation.

"What bosh!" she exclaims. "All you Americans are so awfully rich. Aren't you?"

Lady Oaktorrington pays no heed to something the duke is saying to her, but sits breathless awaiting Allen's reply :

"I—I—really—I can't answer for all my countrymen. Some of them are very wealthy, I dare say. Vanderbilt, for instance, and Jay Gould and Gordon Bennett and Mackay. But they are only four."

"Oh, come, you know you yourself are said to be enormously rich ?"

"Am I ? People talk without book sometimes."

Lady Henry grows desperate.

"Well, aren't you ?"

"What ? said to be enormously rich ? I don't know. You say so."

"Oh, no; you know quite well what I mean. Aren't you awfully rich ?"

Allen winces and reddens, at the point-blank question, and his disgust at the grossness of its personal character is doubled as he becomes vaguely conscious that everybody is silently listening for his answer.

"You must pardon my declining to answer," he says, stiffly. "There is nothing I detest more than discussing myself at any time, and especially for the edification of a whole dinner-table."

"By Jove! if he hasn't shuffled out of it. I thought he would," mutters Lord Beyndour to himself but loud enough for his neighbors to hear. "He's afraid to lie before so many people, of course. I say mother ! Freddy ought to feel proud of himself, don't you think ?"

The marchioness who hasn't this time caught Allen's answer owing to an inopportune remark from the duke, replies by a puzzled, questioning look, whereat

Lord Beyndour shuffles his feet under the table in a
temper, and says :

"By Jove, she can't think of anything but Harborough."

"I'm not going to have such an answer as that,"
Lady Henry says, with a little laugh, fearful of having
gone too far in her rudeness to a man whose evasive
reply to her questions she is woman enough of the
world to know is better proof of his riches than if he
openly declared the fact to her. She must try and
make up for it, she thinks, and for the first time it
dawns upon her that Allen is "awfully good-looking."
Not that that fact would have had much weight with her
had she not now felt morally convinced of his wealth.
She throws into her eyes all the suggestive power that
can come from half-closed lids veiling upward turned
pupils, and says in a soft, cooing voice, that dozens of
men have known to their cost :

"You must tell me some other time soon, all to
myself. Promise me, won't you? I shan't tell any one.
I never tell any one anything—not even my husband," and she opens her eyes for one second and
shoots a glance full of meaning at Allen. He is not the
man to misunderstand her. No man knows woman
and her ways better than he. He is conscious of a
slight quickening of his heart-beats, and sense of sudden heat in his temples as she speaks, for she is really,
by candle-light, a very pretty woman.

"You will tell me?" she persists.

"Certainly I will," he answers in a low voice. "But
it must be under the condition you mention, you must
be alone. And—" He looks up and catches Lady
Edith's eye. She is looking at him with her great big

soft gray eyes full of wonder and reproach.   He colors
and stops short.

"And—what? what else?   Oh, I'm afraid you're
wasting your time if *that* is your game.   She's engaged to be married."

"Yes?   And to whom?"   ·

"To the man she's sitting next and with whom she
came into dinner—Jack Bouverie"—this in a whisper,
for Lord Bouverie's ears are wide open.

"I should hardly have fancied he filled her ideal."

"Girls in these days are not allowed such incon-
venient impediments to matrimony as ideals, my dear.
We find our ideals *after* marriage, not before.   Some
of us find them and some don't.   I'm still looking for
mine," and the old look comes into her eyes.   "Perhaps I shall find it sooner than I thought."

"And do you mean to say, she is really engaged to
that young man?   Are you sure?   It has not been
formally announced?"

"No, not yet.   But they have been engaged for
more than a year, I know.   Lady Oaktorrington, told
me.   There! will that satisfy you?   But you mustn't
breathe a word of it to any one for it is a secret yet.
But there.   How tiresome!   Lady Oaktorrington is
putting on her gloves.   You won't stay long, promise
me—and," in a low whisper, "come to me directly you
can.   I've got something I particularly want to say to
· you."

CHAPTER XIV.

WHEN the ladies retire, Allen is left to the tender
mercies of Lord Bouverie, in whose demeanor to him
he notices a marked change.   The old warmth of

manner, and glaringly apparent desire to ingratiate himself with the rich stranger by overdone attentions and forced interest takings have vanished, and in their place he finds cold and distant civility. After a few interchanges of words of the most commonplace character, during which Lord Bouverie gives indisputable evidence of a wish to listen to, if not join in, the talk of the others, Allen lets the conversation drop, and sits silent and alone among his own conflicting thoughts. No one utters a word to him, no one takes heed of his presence, and the only part he takes in the assembly is to mechanically pass on the decanters as they come his way in their periodical circuits of the table.

"I say Monty ; heard anything of Bazzy, lately?" asks Lord Beyndour.

"Who? Bazzy Paget?"

"Um."

"No, only that he's gone to the dogs, neck and crop."

"The devil! you don't mean it?"

"I do it mean it, though. He's been tumbling downhill fast enough the last two years for anybody to expect it, I should think."

"Tumbling downhill isn't going to the dogs, though, is it?" remarks the Duke of Harborough, dictatorially. "Not quite, at all events," and Allen thinks he ought to be an expert on such matters. "I knew he'd got awfully in debt, and heard whispers of his having to leave the army on account of a little affair with his colonel's wife. But that was before he came into the title more than six months ago. I thought the title cured all that."

"I dare say the title may have hushed up the little

9

scandal you mention, but it didn't pay his debts. He'd anticipated every farthing of ready money there was in bank, and the estates wouldn't stand another ha'penny on mortgage, so there he was. Even the succession tax was paid by his uncle. I met him coming out of the Rag one afternoon last month, and he told how up a tree he was, and that he thought of sending in his papers to sell—"

"Pardon me one moment, Vereker," says Lord Bouverie, who has been waiting his chance. "Not to *sell*, my dear fellow. Purchase was abolished in—let me see—seventy-two, no, seventy-one. You can't sell what you've not bought. Um. Eh? I remember once—"

"It doesn't signify in the least," Vereker replies, curtly, knowing what they will be treated to if prompt measures are not adopted. "My belief is that Bazzy Paget went into the Blues in seventy, before purchase was abolished—"

"Well, then, of course—"

"Er—er—it doesn't signify in the very least, my dear Lord Bouverie. I believe I said so. Where was I? Oh, yes. He said he was thinking seriously of going out to America—"

"Fancy Bazzy Paget on a cattle-ranch!" laughs Lord Beyndour, whose sole ideas of America are associated with his brother Freddy.

"Cattle-ranch? No fear, my dear boy. Cattle-ranching wasn't his little game. He thought he'd go over and pick up a Yankee heiress, with a million's worth of plating over her twang."

Allen turns crimson, and the veins in his temples stand out like knotted whipcord with suppressed anger

as he sees Lord Beyndour look over at him and laugh
to himself. Jack Bouverie and Bertie exchange winks,
and cough pointedly at each other.

"Oh, for one—just one—of the boys, Al Freeman,
Joe Spaulding, Ed Billings, or any one of them, to
back me and see fair play, and I'd tackle the whole
lot of them, duke and all!" groans Allen, helping
himself to some grapes to appear indifferent. "Why,
oh, why, did I ever come among them? Why, indeed?" and his thoughts flow into a different
channel.

"Poor chap," says the duke. "Fancy being
driven to that extremity."

"By-the-by, talking of Yankee heiresses, have
you seen Haskell's wife?"

"No, I haven't. Have you?"

"Yes, I have. I met her—"

"Stop a bit," interrupts the duke. "Is that the
girl from 'Frisco? If so, I can tell you something
about her. But go on, Vereker, I'll wait."

"I met her and Sir George staying at the Charter-
ises up in Yorkshire last winter. I believe she's got
two millions and a small foot, but there it stops."

"Oh, I say now," shouts the duke, "draw it mild,
Vereker. I happen to have seen her myself and she's
deuced pretty."

"Tastes differ. She said 'yes *sur*' to me when I
spoke to her first, but when we got 'bettur 'quainted'
as she called it, her favorite form of acquiescence in
any of my observations were 'that's so,' 'you bet
you,' and 'I should remark.' I stopped counting the
'guesses' after the first ten minutes."

"Oh, come now," exclaims the duke. "That's too

large an order. I've met loads of Americans myself,
and though I should be deuced sorry to be so hard
put as to have to take one to wife, they don't talk like
that. Give the devils their due."

"That's just what I am doing. I'm telling you exactly the sort of woman Haskell's Yankee wife is.
They call her 'the mustang' up in Yorkshire."

"And more shame for them, is all I can say!" exclaims Allen, quickly, unable longer to restrain his
tongue. "I don't know what you may think about
it yourselves, but to a foreigner like myself, such a
remark applied to a lady is simply atrocious. English
chivalry must, indeed, have gone to the dogs—if it
ever existed, which I begin to doubt—when it can
permit any *man*, I won't say gentleman—to call a lady
'a mustang.'"

The men look from one to the other thoroughly
taken aback, for a minute. Then Lord Beyndour
sneers and tries to laugh, while Lord Bouverie wakes
up from a doze, and asks :

"What's the row? Um. Eh?"

The duke is about to say something disagreeable,
from the look in his eye, when Vereker, with a very
pale face, thinks discretion the better part of valor,
and says, with a pacificatory smile to Allen :

"What harm? I don't in the least know what a
mustang is. I had a sort of idea it meant a fairy,
or—"

"Oh, ho—ho—ho! Ha—ha—ha!" shouts Lord
Beyndour in an explosion of laughter. "That's too
good. A fairy! oh, ho—ho—ho!"

"Or a foreign princess, or something of that sort,"
procceds Vereker, as soon as he can make himself

heard. "I thought it was something complimentary, at all events."

"Fancy sucking up to him like that!" says Lord Beyndour to the duke. "He needs a devilish good snubbing for his impertinence."

"I'll give him one presently," the duke answers. "Just wait."

"I'll tell you what a mustang is," Allen says, "and you'll see how complimentary it is. It's a half-bred Mexican horse, half-broken, half-wild."

"It may not be complimentary," says the duke, "but I call it damned appropriate."

Allen rises quickly from his seat.

"I have assumed that I was addressing myself to gentlemen," he says, hoarsely. "Am I to understand that I have been wrong? I happen to have the honor of knowing the lady, and were it not so, she is a country-woman of my own. As she is a friend, a country-woman, and a woman, may I ask you to refrain from further comment upon her in my presence?"

"Certainly—of course—we didn't know," explains Vereker, who is a man of some knowledge of the world outside the radius of English aristocratic society. "Pray sit down."

"Perhaps you'll allow me to speak, Vereker," scowls the duke, "our answer to you, is this: Mr.— what's his name?" aside to Lord Beyndour.

"I'm blessed if I know," Lord Beyndour answers with a grin.

"Well, then, our answer to you, sir, is this: We propose to talk upon any subject we see fit, without any dictation from you. If you do not like it you can—"

"Retire. Which I most assuredly shall do." And Allen leaves the table and walks out of the room, without a voice or hand to stay him.

"Beastly cad!" exclaims Lord Reyndour, as soon as the door is shut. "It serves mother right for asking him here."

"Who is he?" asks the duke.

"A Yankee friend of Freddy's he picked up on his journey home."

"It's deuced lucky the servants had left the room," remarks Lord Bouverie. "Um? Eh?"

CHAPTER XV.

ALLEN goes directly to his room. He finds a fire burning brightly in the grate and candles lighted on his dressing-table. He draws an arm-chair up to the fire, lights a cigarette, sits down, and tries to think. There is a feeling of warmth and comfort about the room, an atmosphere of noiselessness and dried lavender that fills his brain with a sense of repose, and seems to chide him for his ill-temper. After all, these people do not treat him so badly. Perhaps he has been too exacting? No, he has not. It has been one insult after another heaped upon him. Who wants their candles and their fire? He will blow out the one and extinguish the other with the water-jug in two minutes. Yet stay. They don't know that his room is so comfortable. It isn't them he has to thank for it. It is only the work of the servants in anticipation of a good tip when he goes away. Money, again! But can one blame them with their betters setting them the example?

"Now, then, what am I to do?" he asks himself, as he breaks his reverie to light a fresh cigarette. "I can't stay here after this, and I won't, unless some apology is made to me, and that isn't a likely thing to happen. There isn't anything for me to do. None of them will fight. It's against the law they tell you. A nice law that enables a man to insult another with impunity! They simply shield themselves behind a law of their own making for their own protection. No wonder England is become a bear-garden! Yes, I must go. The fact of the matter is I ought never to have come here. I wish I hadn't for many reasons. I should never have seen *her*. Not that it can matter now. Who would have thought her such an arrant little coquette? And such a man to oust one! Is it true? Can it be true? Yes, it must be. Everything confirms it. What a fool I have been! I, who have gone through fire a score of times unsinged. How lucky I didn't commit myself this morning. And how I cursed her brother for interrupting me. Poor chap, I ought to feel deeply grateful to him for it. It was a narrow escape. What would Fanny and Carrie and Kittie and Jennie and Lou and Syb and Hattie and Nellie and Minnie say if they were to hear of it. I could never live in 'Frisco again."

He smiles to himself at the thought, but his smile fades away as he studies out some problem imbedded in the red coals, and his cigarette burns away into a long, crisp ash between his finger-tips.

"Is it not all a yarn of this Lady Henry Tollemache? It is clear what her game is, and she may only have invented it all to serve her own ends. I ought to feel immensely complimented, of course, but all the same,

I should like to know for sure. How can I find out? Ask her. Tax her with it. But when? My only chance is to-night, for I must go as early as I can to-morrow morning. How I hate going down among them again! Yet, I suppose I must. Shall I get a chance to speak to her, with this fellow Jack hanging about her? More than likely not. I'll tell you what I'll do. Yes, that's the way."

He seats himself before the writing-table and writes *Accept my congratulations. I hope you will be happy. I go to-morrow morning. Oh, how* COULD *you?*"

" Now, the next thing is, how to get it to her? It would require the sleight of hand of a skilled conjuror to pass it to her before all those eyes. I must find some way." He folds the sheet and puts it into an envelope, and has just done so when there is a knock at the door.

" Please, sir," says one of the footmen, " his lord-ship sent me up to say as how if you wanted to smoke, sir, there was a smoking-room. Every one's been wondering where the smoke came from, sir, and her ladyship's in a great way about it, sir."

" I'm so awfully sorry. It was very stupid of me. I quite forgot. Just open the window. And here's a trifle for your trouble," putting half a sovereign into the man's palm.

" Yes, sir. Hope no offense, sir. Young master's orders, sir," says the servant, touching his forehead at every second word.

" No, no. That's all right. See here. I want a note delivered unknown to any one in the house. Can you do it for me?"

" Yes, sir."

"Mind, it's not so easy as you think. It's for a lady."

"Lady Henry, sir? Not the first time, sir," and the footman grins.

"Oh, isn't it? Well, it's not for Lady Henry this time. It's for Lady Edith. Think you can manage it?"

"Certain sure I can, sir. If you please, sir—he—he—beg your pardon, sir. I be keeping company along with Lady Edith's own maid, sir. I'll get her to slip it to her young missus, no fear, sir."

"To-night?"

"Yes, sir, when her ladyship goes to her room."

"All right," and Allen puts another half-sovereign with the letter into the man's hand.

"Thanky, sir."

"And now, I suppose, I must go down. This confounded smoking will be another thing to face. However, it can't be much worse," and Allen goes down to the drawing-room. Self-possessed as he is, it takes a good deal of nerve to open the door and go in. As it is he stands for a minute or so with his hand on the door-handle before he can get courage to turn it. He is received in silence. Lady Oaktorrington is talking to Lady Bouverie, Lady Mary is telling Augusta Bouverie all about her dogs, and Lord Beyndour and Emily Bouverie are whispering and laughing together on a distant sofa. Lord Bouverie is fast asleep in an arm-chair. The others are nowhere to be seen. He walks over to a table, picks up a photograph-album, and sits down. As he turns over the pages of princes, dukes, marquises, and all the grades in the peerage down to honorables, he catches a scrap now and then of what his neighbors are saying :

"Yes, I can smell it quite strong," Lady Bouverie says. "Fancy a young gentleman in *our* day smoking in the house!"

"Ah, yes, but then one so seldom met foreigners, my dear Lady Bouverie."

This has clearly been said in a loud tone purposely, for the voices become almost inaudible again.

Presently he hears Lady Mary say:

"Oh, they've gone to the billiard-room," and in two minutes he is out in the hall on his way there himself.

Lady Edith and Jack are playing against Vereker and Bertie.

He makes straight for Lady Edith, who at the moment is standing alone just having made a stroke. She turns very pale as she sees him coming, and, he thinks, looks annoyed.

"I had no idea you added this to your other accomplishments," he says, trying his best to smile and look at ease.

"No, it's Jack's turn," she says, in answer to Bertie, and then looks at Allen.

"What did you say?" she asks, with her brows a trifle puckered.

"It doesn't matter in the least. I came to say—"

"What? what? Don't look like that at me here before the others."

"I think I shall say good-night, now, as I'm going—"

Bertie looms up along side. "My turn?" and Lady Edith goes to the table. She has some wonderful luck considering that her cue shakes as much as it does, and makes a good break. When at last she misses and comes back to her former place, Allen is gone.

As Allen turns to go, a different door from that at which he entered opens, and the Duke of Harborough comes in fastening a spray of stephanotis in his button-hole. The doorway is nearer to him than the other, and in his anxiety to get out of the room as quickly as possible, Allen makes his exit by it. Instead of in the hall, as he expected, he finds himself in a narrow ante-room, the far door of which stands ajar. He walks on and enters a small, cosy apartment. In the grate a fire of glowing coals casts a rosy hue over the room, the effect being enhanced by a lamp on the table, with a rose-colored shade. Standing by the fire is Lady Henry Tollemache. Allen's humor at the moment of leaving the billiard-room is one which pretty nigh verges on desperation. Not alone is he now convinced that Lady Edith's engagement to Jack Bouverie is true, but he feels like some hunted animal, only too glad to obtain succor and comfort at the hands of any one. In his present frame of mind the "any one" in his case is a very pretty woman, a trifle rouged, perhaps, and made up as to the eyes; but in that light, and under those circumstances, with all the fascinating adjuncts of the female toilet as it can be expressed in full evening dress, she seems a veritable houri. She looks up and greets him with a smile.

"What a time you have been?" she says. "I waited for you in the drawing-room, for ever so long, and at last thought you were not coming, and had gone to bed."

Her kind words when every one else is cold and cruel, is the finishing touch. For the moment, he is

(or feels as though he were, which amounts to pretty
much the same thing) madly in love with her. Without a word, he steps forward and grasps her gloved
hand.

"Not now," she says, quickly disengaging it, with
a slight reproving frown. "You've not told me what
you promised."

"What?" Allen asks, hazily. "I haven't told you
what?"

Lady Henry puts her foot impatiently on the floor.

"Oh, you remember what I asked you at dinner."

His face clouds.

"Never mind that now. Don't let us mix such
sordid thoughts—"

"But you must tell me at once," she answers, seriously. "I dare not stay here a minute longer. Any
one is likely to come upon us at any moment, and
just fancy what people would say!"

"Who cares for people?" says Allen, grandly.

"*I* do. Oh, no, no, no! You mustn't lock the
door. We should be in a pretty trap then. Fancy
such a thing! I ought to be awfully angry with you."
She looks really annoyed for a moment, and then says,
with a smile. "I'll forgive you if you tell me." Allen
does not reply. "Will you tell me, or will you not?"
she asks, impatiently.

"Why do you want to know?"

"Why do you object to tell me?"

In the midst of the fascination which spurs him on,
Allen is conscious that he is making a fool of himself.
His better sense tells him this. Yet, manlike, the
glamor is on him, and he does not hesitate.

"Do you wonder that I should want you to like

me only for myself?" he asks, with a hoarse tremu-
lousness in his voice that is such old and well-known
music to Lady Henry's ears that she smiles inwardly
as she looks at him with her most winning pout.

"No.   But suppose I should be very mercenary—
most women are, you know, though they pretend
they're not—you'd have to tell me then, wouldn't
you?"

"Um! Yes; I suppose I should."

Lady Henry's mental powers of perception are
sufficiently keen to let her see in this answer all the
information she wants.   Her heart gives a great bound
of joy.   She puts the hand she had drawn away on to
his, and says in a soft, cooing voice.

"I do like you so much.   How happy I could be
if—"   She pauses and looks down.

"If what?" Allen asks, quickly.   "You had another husband? I've—"

"No," she answers deliberately, shrugging her
rounded white shoulders.   "Marriage makes no difference, I think, except that it changes one's name.
It's not that."   She gives a little sigh and bites her
lips.   "I'm in a good deal of trouble about something.   You won't mind if I tell you? You have
such kind, sympathetic eyes."

"Pray tell me what it is," he says, earnestly.
"Perhaps I may be able to help you out of it."

Her eyes brighten at his words and the smile
comes back to her lips.

"Yes, you could," she says, slowly.

"You *could*," and she puts a sweetly smiling emphasis on the word.   "But how can I expect a
stranger—"

"Pray don't call me that," he cries, eagerly. "In more ways than one the word grates upon me."

"I won't then, dear—oh, what on earth am I saying! What must you think of me?"

"Shall I tell you?" Allen exclaims, hotly. "I will. That you are the most charm—"

"Stop! stop! I can't hear another word. It's most awfully unfair. Wait till you hear what I am going to tell you. Know, then, that I've—you are sure, you won't mind my telling you?"

"No, no. Quite sure. Do go on."

"Well, then, you must know that" (a long pause beginning with a serious face and tearful downcast eyes, but ending with a beamingly hopeful upward glance) "I've—I've overdrawn at my banker's. There! I'm so awfully ashamed," and she covers her face with her hands.

"Nonsense. Is that all?" Allen says, gently taking down her yielding fingers from her eyes. "That's easily remedied. I shall be only to hap—"

"Oh, thank you so very much," she cries, breaking away from him. "I knew you'd understand about it. You Americans are so quick to see one's meaning. Englishmen are so awfully dense, don't you know, when there's a question of money."

"Are they? I should hardly have thought so. But you must tell me how much you—"

"Not to night. I'll tell you to-morrow. What's that? Voices? Hush!"

They listen in silence awhile, but no sound reaches them save the chimes of the hall clock. "Eleven! I must go back to the drawing-room at once. No, no; you mustn't come with me. That would never do. I shall go by this door alone and you can return to the billiard-room by that. Or else you must wait here till you are sure every one is gone to bed, and then come out through the drawing-room. Goodnight."

"Just wait one minute," Allen says, in an eager voice, then stops short, and fumbles with his watch-chain.

"Well, what do you want?"

"I—I—can't—can't you give me a bit of this?" and he touches the bunch of stephanotis in her corsage.

"Not for worlds!" she exclaims, covering the flowers with both hands. "Another time I will—perhaps—but not to-night. Don't ask me."

"I saw the duke with one as he came into the billiard-room from here a few minutes ago. You gave him one."

Her eyes flash for a moment as she mutters some words of vexation to herself; and Allen has sense enough left to see he has made an unwary speech.

"Did I?" she asks, in as careless a tone as she can command. "I don't remember in the least. But even if I did—which I don't admit, mind—that would be a good reason why you should not want one, also, wouldn't it?"

Allen thinks a minute to get her point well into his head, and then says, rather sulkily and disappointedly:

"Yes, I suppose so."

She turns to go. "One minute more," he says, recovering some of his usual courage as if by an effort "I dare say you'll think me foolish, silly."

She shakes her head.

"I'm sure I shan't do that," she whispers, sweetly. "Why should I? You are far too kind."

"Well, exacting, any how. I won't ask for the flower; but I do want something you have worn—something that has touched you."

Half an hour ago he would have quarreled with his best friend had he predicted such a scene for him as this with any woman—but one. In less than half an hour hence he will realize the degradation of his treason and awake from his fleeting and self-enmeshed enthrallment. He is but a mortal at best, and *Nemo mortalium omnibus horis sapit.*

Lady Henry is about to smile contentedly to herself behind her fan at his words. They speak such unconditional surrender to her charms; such unqualified success in her "plan of campaign." But there is a look in his eyes which, experienced as she is in such scenes, fairly frightens her. She takes a step backward and hurriedly holds her pocket-handkerchief up to him. "Will this do? You can give it to me to-morrow. Now, really, good-night, or I shall lose my character." She glides quickly away through the doorway and is gone.

Allen stands waiting a few minutes, the handkerchief held tightly in his hand. He puts it up to his lips. It breathes the same delicate perfume which seems to pervade the atmosphere when she is present, and in obedience to the influence of the instant he is about to kiss it, but something tells him not. He rolls it up quickly, and puts it in his pocket. He feels triumphant, and yet a trifle ashamed when he lets himself think. But reflection is a mental operation fraught with too much pain to him just then not to have him seek relief in physical activity. He can wait no longer standing idly there, so he retraces his steps through the anteroom to the billiard-room door. He hears the click of balls within and hesitates. What if she be there still? How can he play the spaniel in her eyes by coming back? And how can he have the heart to enter her presence -fresh from such a scene as that in which he has just played so recreant a part. His treason is beginning to dawn upon him already, and he feels as though he could not meet her eye without a flush of honest shame. Yet, there is no other way. He must face the ordeal. He opens the door and to his intense relief finds it is only the duke and Bertie having a game together. All the others are gone. He walks quickly through and out by the other door into the hall, utterly unheeded by the players. The drawing-room door is standing open. All is dark and silent within. He lights his candle and goes up-stairs ; and as he passes through the main corridor on his way to the bachelors' wing where his room is, he sees lying on the mat just outside one of the bedroom-doors a spray of stephanotis. " Hello ! That's a nice way the duke treats her flower, and she refused me one. I'll have this any how even though it does come second hand," and he picks it up. "She'll wonder how I got it when I show it to her— What? Eh? Is this the duke's room? And—why, I left him down in the billiard-room. Faugh ! " With a face of loathing he flings the flower to the other end of the corridor.

––––––

10

CHAPTER XVI.

" MUST you really go ? " Lady Oaktorrington asks, freezingly, as Allen comes into the breakfast-room next morning before prayers, ere any other guest is down. The marchioness always reads prayers for the servants when her husband is away, and consequently has to be on hand earlier than other people. " And you won't stay and have breakfast ? "

" I shall lose my train, if I do, thanks, very much. I can get a bite in the refreshment-room at the station that will last me until I get to London. Good-by. I must thank you for your generous hospitality and kindness."

" Oh," is all Lady Oaktorrington can say. To do her justice she is inwardly ashamed, but discipline will not let her say so. " Good-by." And she gives Allen two fingers to shake. He is out in the hall where the butler and footman are helping him on with his ulster, when the marchioness follows him.

" Oh—will you be so good as to send your—your bill, don't you know, for what we owe you for Freddy to our lawyers, the Messrs. Fairfield and Jenkinson, Lincoln's Inn Fields, and they will settle it. Allen does not answer. He dare not trust himself to speak ; but turns without a word and leaves the house. As he is stepping into the fly which his friend the footman has procured for him from Hertford, the latter says to him. " In the inside breast-pocket of your ulster, sir, you will find a letter. Thanky sir."

And the fly goes lumbering down the avenue.

Ere the wheels have performed a dozen revolutions Allen has the letter open in his fingers.

I don't know what you mean, it says. *If any one has told you that I am engaged to be married to any one, it is false. I think I can guess who told you. It is so like her. If you get this in time, which I hope and pray you may, I beg and implore you not to go, until I see you at all events. If not, write to me at Lord Hartworth's where I am going on Saturday to stay for a week. The address is Willesden Manor, North Allerton, Bucks. On no account write to me here.*

Allen's first impulse is to stop the fly and go back. But before he can get the window down, the sober second thought comes to him and says—No. " I would face the whole lot of them again, and put up with any fresh indignity they could concoct, for her sake," he thinks. " I don't care a button for that. But in the first place, I can think of no possible excuse to make that would not eventually involve her ; and in the second, I can not meet that woman again. Oh, how could I have been such a fool ! When I think of last night I feel positive degradation."

So he drives on to the station, and in two hours is walking up the steps of the Hotel Metropole.

At precisely the same moment another fly drives up to the door at Ashwynwick, and Lord Frederick Vesey gets out. He goes at once to his mother's boudoir where he knows he will find her.

" You got my telegram ? " he asks, after the usual double-cheek kissing.

" Yes."

" And acted upon it, I hope."

" To tell you the truth, dear it was so vague, that

I didn't know what to do. Here it is. Look at it yourself."

"Vague? Can anything be clearer than *treat him civilly?*"

"I dare say. But *he is all right, of course,* was so indefinite and unsatisfactory. I knew you had heard nothing new. And besides other circumstances have occurred to shake me—first, some things Lady Henry told me, and then something Beyndour and I overheard him say himself at dinner about not being able to afford something or other. After that Lady Henry asked him outright if he wasn't awfully rich—"

"How disgraceful!"

"—and he refused to tell her."

"Poor chap! I can imagine the sort of life you've led him."

"Then again I expected a letter from you this morning and you never wrote."

"Where was the good when I was coming myself? I must go and smooth it over with him as best I can. Of course, you've been abominably rude to him. I can see that."

"Why, why, dear, you haven't ascertained that he is all we thought?"

"All we thought? Just wait till you hear. When I got up to town I went to see the man from the steamer, and found he had left the night before for the Continent. I didn't know what to do, when I suddenly thought I couldn't do better than go and ask Fairfield's advice. He said the best thing to do was to write to the English consul at San Francisco. I told him we couldn't wait all that time—five weeks

it would take—for an answer.   So he said then he'd
cable."

"Cable, dear?   What's that?"

"Telegraph.   Don't you know there is a tele-
graph-cable to the States."

"I'm sorry to say, dear, I—"

"Well, never mind.   He said he'd cable at once,
and might get the answer by night.   It was tedious
work waiting in town, for London's as empty as it
can be.   By-the-by, I met father.   At least, I saw him
in a hansom out in St. John's Wood.   He didn't see
me.   Well, I waited and waited, and thought it safer
to send you the telegram I did, for Fairfield said he
had, he thought, heard the name of Allen in connection with some enormous American railway transac-
tions on the Stock Exchange.   I went to their office
a dozen times at least, but there was no answer.

"How tiresome for you, dear!"

"At last, about nine o'clock at night, it came.
Fairfield, who'd stayed at his office on purpose, sent it
to me at once.   Here it is."   Freddy unfolds a long
sheet of paper.   "I'll read it:

"'*Philip Allen's father is one of the richest men in
California.   Philip is an only child.*'

"It was an expensive job—cost three pounds for
both telegrams."

"Oh, dear!"

"It was well worth it, though."

"I'm not thinking of that.   What on earth are we
to do?"

"Do?   Why?   Come, don't worry over it, mother,"
Freddy adds, kindly, struck by her face of abject misery.   "I'll soon square it off with him, never fear.

He's an awfully good chap." And he starts for the door.

"Stay, dear. I'm sorry to say you can't do that. He's gone."

"Gone?"

"Yes, dear. He left this morning."

"The devil! Oh, a nice mess you've made of it! It serves you right."

"Oh, dear, don't say that. I acted for the best. I must think of Mary and Edith."

"And a nice way you've thought of them! Hunted away the best match Edith will ever get. If this doesn't cure you of your money-worshiping, I don't know what will. Yes, money-worshiping, for it's nothing else. Unless you know a man has plenty of money you are not decently civil to him. It doesn't matter what he *is*; it is only what he's *got*. You needn't look so cross. You know it is perfectly true. For my part, I'm utterly sick and tired of this incessant money, money, money, and I'm ashamed of having had anything to do with this telegraphing to America about Allen; I wouldn't have had if you hadn't forced me into it."

"You really mustn't say such dreadful things, dear. You know I only want the girls to be comfortable when they marry."

"Comfortable? It certainly takes a lot of money, in your eyes, to make 'em comfortable."

"I know, dear, you don't at all really mean what you are saying. So I sha'n't be angry with you."

"Don't I mean it, though! I tell you I'm ashamed to belong to the English aristocracy. You profess to think only of rank and family. But let the son and heir of a Jew pawnbroker come among you and you'll welcome him with open arms, and lead up your daughters to him to choose one of them, whereas, the son of what society chooses to consider a poor nobleman, is watched and snubbed and insulted in every conceivable fashion."

.. Lady Oaktorrington sits silently and passively submissive to this long harangue. It is not that she sees one word of truth in what her son says—she is too dyed-in-the-wool an aristocrat to admit the possibility of the aristocracy's fallibility in any of its rules, customs, or actions. But, unable to answer his assertions were she inclined to do so, she knows it will shorten the discussion if she says nothing.

"Well, dear," she asks, when Freddy has finished. "Can't you suggest something? Can't we get him to come back? Won't you go after him?"

"Me? By Jove, I should be ashamed to look him in the face. Besides, he wouldn't come."

"Nonsense, dear. He'll be only too glad. He was immensely taken with Edith, I could see."

"I know he was. What an awful pity it is! She'll never get such another chance."

"Yes, she will, if you'll go after him. You'll do it for her sake, I'm sure."

"It will do no good. You don't know the spirit of these Americans. I do. They are a deuced sight more like noblemen than we are."

At any other time Lady Oaktorrington would have flounced out of the room in high dudgeon at such a speech. But now she is willing to submit to anything in order to gain her point. Freddy is the only one who can persuade Allen to return, she feels confident.

"I'm sure you can get him back if you try. Follow him at once, without any delay. I'll get Edith to write him a nice little letter for you to give him. She shall put off her visit to Willesden, and I'll give you a check for a hundred pounds if you succeed."

O fallible and inconstant man! O unerring, unvarying potency of gold!

Like mist beneath the rays of the noonday sun, Freddy's objections vanish; his eloquent condemnation of the power and influence of money among the aristocracy (with which the air is scarce done reverberating) is forgotten. He is an aristocrat once more, and his mother's true son.

"All right," he says. "Give us the check, and I'll do my best. No one has seen me arrive except Dawkins and Wilson," he adds, entering into the scheme with a will. "At least, I saw no one as I came in. I can square it with them right enough not to tell. No one need see me go. I can slip out through the conservatory, and get to the stables without meeting a soul."

"There's no one about except Lady Henry and Edith. All the others are gone to the meet at Upton Grange."

"All right, then. Let them think Allen ran up to town to meet me—in fact, you can tell people so if they ask—and when we come back together it will look all proper."

"Capital!" says the marchioness. "How clever you are, dear. Then you feel confident you will bring him back with you?"

"Double the check and I'll swear to it."

One hour later Lord Frederick Vesey is speeding up to London again as fast as the Great Eastern Express can carry him to Liverpool-Street Station.

CHAPTER XVII.

"By Jove! Where's the Yankee?" asks Lord Beyndour, as the house party meet for the first time at tea. "Keeping up his sulk, is he?"

"I never saw a fellow with such cheek," says the Duke of Harborough. "Fancy ordering us to shut up about some Yankee friend of his, because, forsooth, she was a woman—a 'laydee,' I beg his pardon."

"They should have heard you shut *him* up," adds Lord Bouverie. "It was the neatest thing I've seen in an age, Harborough. Um? Eh? I remember once when my battalion was in—"

"Ahem—er—let me see," interposes Montie Vereker. "Who was it? Oh, yes, to be sure. Haskell's wife. He flew into a rage because I said she was called 'the mustang' up in Yorkshire, and a mustang is only a sort of horse they have in the States."

"Fancy being angry at being called like a horse!" exclaims Lady Mary. "I should consider it a compliment."

"I should call it deuced hard lines on the horse," says Lord Beyndour.

"When did all this occur?" asks Lady Oaktorrington, anxiously. "In the smoking-room?"

"Oh, dear, no. He never shows his face in the smoking-room. He's a cut above that," Vereker answers, holding out his cup for some more tea.

"Prefers his own room," says Jack.

"Do you know I once knew a chap like that in the Ninth Lancers," begins Lord Bouverie, helping himself to some bread and butter. "It was in '53, and we—"

"Ah—er—no, it wasn't in the smoking-room," Vereker goes on. "It was in the dining-room after you had gone, Lady Oaktorrington."

"And you were all rude to him?"

"By Jove, the boot was on the other leg," exclaims the duke. "He was confoundedly rude to us. It was just like a novel or a play. When I told him we should talk about whoever we liked, he got up, put his hand in his breast, and said, 'Then, I shall retire'—"

"No, no. '*Re*-ty-urr,'" shouts Lord Beyndour. "Give it the proper pronunciation."

"All right," says the duke, holding his nose between his finger and thumb. 'Then, gentlemen, I shall *re*-ty-urr,' and out he stalked."

"Ha—ha! Capital!" cries Lord Bouverie. "You're as good as Corney Grain, Harborough. It's a pity you're not obliged to go on the stage. Um? Eh? By-the-by, do you know Tindal of the Seventh Hussar's? He's an out-and-out good mimic. He commanded the regiment in —"

"Oh?"

"Did he, really?'

"Fancy!"   ·

"Never!"

"Yes, and—"

"Oh, look here!" shouts Lord Beyndour. "Did you see that duffer Kerr-Jones, come a cropper?" and the sporting people fall to talking of the run they have had with the Chill-will hounds.

"Tell me, dear Lady Oaktorrington," Lady Henry Tollemache asks, in a low voice; "where *is* Mr. Allen? I haven't seen him all day. I'm afraid he's gone away. Yes, I see it in your face. He *has.* How low of him!" she adds to herself, as she thinks of last night.

"Yes, dear. He went up to town this morning to keep an engagement he had with Freddy."

Lady Henry's face falls, but revives with a dawn of new hope in her eyes, as she whispers:

"He's coming back again?"

"Oh, of course. He and Freddy are coming together to morrow."

"I'm so glad. We must do our best to make it up to him as much as we can for the shameful way he's been treated, poor fellow."

"Ye—es," Lady Oaktorrington says, dubiously, scenting danger in the encouragement of any extra attention on Lady Henry's part. "N—no. I wouldn't just yet, if I were you. It might look too marked. Better leave it to me."

"Shall I, indeed, you old she fox," is Lady Henry's mental reply, as she answers aloud:

"Oh, certainly, if you wish it." As soon as she can, Lady Oaktorrington takes Lord Beyndour into a corner, and shows him the San Francisco telegram. His lordship emits a low whistle.

"The deuce! We *have* made a jolly mess of it, haven't we?"

"I should think you had. If it were not for Harborough being mixed up in it I should be excessively angry."

"Oh, come, now. I don't think you have been so

overpoweringly civil to him yourself. You needn't put it all on us."

" I think you might have prevented it."

" You see, I didn't know about this," and Lord Beyndour gives the telegram another look over. " Of course, there can be no mistake?"

"Impossible."

" I'm awfully sorry. But I'll square it with him, never you fear. I'll go and begin sucking up to him at once. Where is he, I wonder?"

" In London. Hush! He's coming back. And you must get Harborough to be civil to him."

" May I show him this?"

" Good heavens! No. That would show *us* up, don't you see."

" So it would. But divil a bit will he believe me without."

" Try him and see. Tell Montie also. But you needn't mention it to Lord Bouverie. He'll only bore him all day long with attentions for the sake of his girls, if you do."

" Rather hard on the old chap, though, don't you think? He's only followed our lead in being cold to the American. You can't blame him."

" Nasty, mercenary old thing! It will be such a sell for him when he finds later on the mistake."

" Oh, don't you fear. He's not such an old ass as that. He'll pretty soon twig our change of manner, and trim his sails to suit."

" At all events, let him stay in the dark as long as possible. And now," Lady Oaktorrington says, coming forward : " Won't some one help me about this Primrose meeting. I have to preside at the first meet-

ing of our habitation to-morrow, and I don't know
in the least anything about it all. I depended on Lord
Oaktorrington telling me."

"Haven't you got a book?" asks Montie Vereker.

"Yes, I have. But it doesn't tell one anything. It
assumes one knows everything, when one knows nothing. I want to know such lots of things I hardly know
where to begin. For instance, what are the principles
of the Conservative party? It's the Conservative party
that the Primrose League belongs to, isn't it?"

"Most decidedly," Lord Bouverie answers, pompously. "It was founded by Lord Beaconsfield, and
he was a Conservative."

"Oh, yes, I forgot that. It's kept up in his honor,
of course. How silly of me! But, the principles of
the Conservative party, what are they?"

"I'm blessed if *I* could tell you *one*, let alone the
lot of 'em—if there are any—" says Lord Beyndour.
"Except that it's against old Gladstone."

"And supports Lord Salisbury," adds Lord Bouverie, grandly. "That's quite sufficient. Um? Eh?"

"But what do they mean by calling it the Constitutional party?"

"Because it upholds the Constitution," says the
Duke of Harborough. I should think any fool could
tell that."

"Upholds the Constitution? What Constitution?"

"The Constitution of the Primrose League," replies Lord Bouverie, with a sweep of his hand. "Um?
Eh?"

"I fancy it means the Constitution of England,"
suggests the duke, humbly dismounting from his high

horse as the road becomes more difficult. "England's got a Constitution, hasn't it?"

"Upon my word, I couldn't tell you. I d'say it has," answers Lord Beyndour.

"Yes, I think it must have," adds Montie Vereker, with one eye shut and the other gazing into space. "Else what do they mean by talking of the Constitutional party?"

"Why don't you ask mamma," says Emily Bouverie. She's a dame. So are Augusta and I, for that matter; but we know nothing about it at all."

Lady Oaktorrington looks inquiringly at Lady Bouverie, who has been sustaining a well-bred, aristocratic, self-conscious silence while the talk has gone on. Indeed, her words could be almost counted on one's fingers since she has been at Ashwynwick.

"Can *you* tell me anything?" the marchioness asks.

Lady Bouverie looks startled either from overweening shyness at having attention drawn to her, or from the novelty of being addressed.

"I—I—am sorry to say that I can't," she whispers. "I've been to one or two meetings, but there was never anything explained to us."

"It doesn't really matter, I should think," says Lady Henry, "so long as you get people to vote for the Conservative candidates at elections. That's really all you've got to do if you're a dame. You haven't had an election here? No. Well, we had one the other day at Lord Grafton's where I was staying. No one said anything about such boring stuff as principles and constitutions. We just bought a lot of things at the shops, and gave the village people a grand treat with buns and tea for the women, and bread and cheese

and beer for the men. Everything was decorated with
primroses, don't you know, and there was a large
portrait of Lord Beaconsfield framed in laurel-leaves
out on the lawn. Of course, there were a lot of leaflets
sent down from London to be distributed, showing up
the villainy of Gladstone and Chamberlain."

"Oh, pray don't mention that dreadful man's name
again," cries Lady Oaktorrington. "He wants to de-
stroy the Church and plant atheism in England in its
place, I hear."

"So does John Bright, the old square-toed, psalm-
singing scoundrel," says the duke. "He and Chamberlain want to abolish *us*, too. A nice pair, truly!"

"I wonder they are not put in the Tower," says
Lady Oaktorrington, " or beheaded—or something.
The Queen is far too lenient and forgiving."

"I quite agree with you," says Lord Bouverie, sol-
emnly. "I wish *I* were on the throne. You'd see a
different state of things in England then, I can assure
you."

"I haven't a doubt of it," assents Lady Oaktorrington, unconsciously. "You were telling us, Lady
Henry, about Lord Grafton's, when I'm afraid I interrupted you."

"Oh, there isn't much more to tell. We got no
end of people to vote our way. I know that was the
chief thing—in fact, the only thing—thought of. The
Radical man was defeated by an immense majority.
I assure you, there's not the least necessity in knowing
anything about politics or things of that sort. You
must know how to get men to vote for your candidate."

"Hear—hear!" shouts the duke and Lord Beyndour in a breath. "And you needn't be overscrup-ulous as to the use of—palm-oil," adds his Grace. So long as you're not found out, of course."

"Or intimidation," says Montie Vereker. "Threat-en to withdraw your custom from a Radical trades-man, and he becomes a Tory on the spot. They're awful blackguards, Radical tradesmen. How they hate saying 'sir' to one or touching their hats. Yet they do it to get your custom."

"It's that dreadful worship of money among the lower classes," bemoans Lady Oaktorrington. "I oft-en wonder some of them are not afraid."

"Shocking, isn't it?" assents Lady Henry. "Why can't they be like us, for instance? I believe they'd most of them sell their souls for a check, or the hope of one."

"It's fortunate they are that way," bursts out Lady Edith, no longer able to contain herself, "or the Primrose League wouldn't be of much service, would it?"

"Edith, my dear, I beg of you not to express your-self in that way. You are too young to comprehend such things," her mother says with a soft voice but a face full of daggers.

"I'm afraid she's getting rather ahem — er — re-publicanized," Lord Bouverie remarks, *sotto voce*, to Lady Henry. "I wonder at her mother having such a person as that—er—Yankee man here. Um? Eh?"

"Oh, yes, a great pity, it is. I wonder, too."

"You see Lady O. is so confoundedly fond—of—of money, she'd have any one here who had it."

"Yes, I'm afraid you're right."

"But the best of the joke is, the fellow's an impostor—a starving beggar."

"Is he? You don't mean it?"

"Why, didn't you hear what he said at dinner last night?"

"Hardly. It was after we had left the room."

"Ach! I don't mean then. Don't you remember what he said about his working every day in America?"

"Oh, yes, of course. I forgot."

"That's enough, I should think. Um? Eh?"

"Oh, quite. Dear Lady Oaktorrington," she whispers as the marchioness passes her, "do rescue me from this dreadful old bore. Ask me to sing, or anything."

At that moment Dawkins comes in with a telegram on a silver waiter, and hands it to Lady Oaktorrington.

There is utter silence in the room while she reads it, and mental notes are taken of every expression that flits across her features.

"Nothing unpleasant, I hope?" asks Lady Henry, to the delight of every less audacious person in the room.

"Oh, no. It's only from Freddy, to say he's going to keep Mr. Allen in town with him for a few days."

What the telegram says is:

Allen won't come. Is going on the Continent, and has asked me to go, too. I'll stick to him.

Freddy.

11

CHAPTER XVIII.

*I can not tell you how sorry I was not to come back
with Freddy* (Allen writes from Paris to Lady Edith at
Willesden Manor), *especially after your sweet little note
which he brought me. It was a sore trial for me to refuse, but I thought it best for more than one reason to do
so. What those reasons are, I will tell you some day.
In the mean time I am very wretched. Everything
seemed to go wrong when I was with you. I wanted to
tell you something, but I never was able to get a chance to
speak to you alone, and what I wished to say had to be
spoken to you alone. There was only that one day—that
happy, happy day, how I cherish its memory in my heart
of hearts !—only that one day, and even then just as I was
about to tell you, your brother interrupted me. I feel that
I must tell you now, for I can not bear this suspense any
longer. You won't think me presumptuous if I tell you
now. It is so much easier to write it than speak it. I
love—*

Lady Edith reads as far as this, and then with a
heart that seems to leap within her, crushes up the letter in her hand and thrusts it into her pocket. She
feels as though she must run away and hide herself
somewhere. A vague idea that the eyes of every mortal she knows have been peering over her shoulder
while she read and are now staring at her takes possession of her. She covers her face with her hands
and leans her elbows on the table in front of her. Yet
she is sitting alone in her room at Willesden Manor,
even her maid having been dismissed by her half an
hour ago, on the plea of being too sleepy to have her

hair brushed so that she might read Allen's letter, which had come by the evening post, and which she had found on her dressing-table when she came up to bed. A thousand conflicting thoughts rush through her mind, while her temples throb in unison with her heart-beats. A sense of shame takes possession of her, and quickly grows into resentful anger. How dare he write to her so? What right has he to take this advantage of her permission to him to write to her? Yet was it not rather a request on her part? She had really forced him to write, and he had fairly paid her out by—by—insulting her. Is it not a low way of retaliating upon her for the treatment he had received from her mother and brothers? If so, is it manly of him? He can not be serious. It is impossible that he can be sincere. He has not known her long enough to justify the sentiment he professed. It is preposterous.

"And yet—," (ah! the comfort of an "And yet "—who has not felt it's temper-soothing, anger-softening, disappointment-curing, hope-inspiring power?) "And yet, why may it not be as he says?" her heart whispers to her as she thinks, and her resentment cools. "It is not impossible," she cries, clinging to the glimmer of happiness that suddenly illumines her soul. "Why should he not l—like me? I am not hideous." Slowly her hands come down from her face, and she looks in the glass before her and—blushes. "And why should it be presumptuous in him to—to love me—there, I've said it!" Her heart goes thump, thump, thump, up to the top of her head, and the blood tingles in her very finger-tips, as the born and tutored aristocrat oozes out through them and Nature takes its place

in her being. She takes the letter from her pocket
and goes on reading it.

"*I love you, Edith darling.*"

A sense of sudden overpowering ecstasy seizes her.
She seems to be lifted from her chair and to be float-
ing in the air. She clasps her hands together in a
paroxysm of delight and murmurs:

"He loves me—he loves me! *I love you, Edith
darling. Let me read it a thousand, thousand times.
You are not angry with me, for telling you? Would
that I could feel that you did not hate—despise me for it.
Oh, that you could know the happiness it gives me to tell
you! Will you write me ever so short a letter to tell me
you are not angry with me, and if after this you care to
see me again, tell me so, and I will come at once. I feel
that I must see you again—once more before I go home.*"
Her soul sinks within her as she reads these last
words. All her new found happiness fades and vanishes away. A lump rises in her throat and a sharp
pain, as though from a dagger, pierces her heart.

"Before I go home—before I go home," she repeats. "Oh, that, must not be, if word of mine can
hinder it."

She seats herself quickly at her writing-table, and
takes up her pen. Though her heart would tell him
in burning language, could it speak, the words that lie
hidden within it, she can not with her hand impart
them to paper. It is doubtful, if, were he here, she
could get her lips to express the thoughts which fill
her mind. A dozen times she puts the point of her
pen on the paper, but further than that it will not
move. Altered as she is in thought and feeling, when
called upon to *act*, the old teachings of high-born re-

straint and aristocratic repression still hold dominion over her. She can not write as she thinks. She must then only write as her but yet partially conquered tyrant will let her :

My dear Mr. Allen (the " *My* " is a great concession from the enemy) :

" *Thanks very much for your letter, which I need not answer now. I am sure my father and mother will be delighted to see you if you will come to England again. I shall not be at home for at least a fortnight, as I have one other place to stay at after leaving here. So, pray, do not come while I am not at home. You must not think of going home without seeing us again. I hope Freddy is well and enjoying himself. I fancy he is sure to do the latter.* Believe me,"

Yours sincerely,

Edith M. A. E. Vesey.

" It is hardly the sort of letter to satisfy a man who feels as I do," Allen says, on reading it the next evening in Paris. " It is cold, distant, and formal. But it is only so on the surface, for underneath I can read in everything she says all that I need to know. She is not angry with me or she wouldn't have written, and she bids me come by telling me to postpone my return while she is away from home. Though the chill of aristocratic ' form ' pervades every pen-stroke, beneath the thin coating of artificial ice the limpid waters of reality reveal themselves. I am not thankful enough. What if she hadn't written at all ? "

CHAPTER XIX.

THE snow lies deep upon the ground at Ashwynwick this December morning, and a leaden sky droops
low over the cheerless landscape without. The leafless trees stand out grim and bare like dim skeletons
against a vast expanse of white ; icicles hang from the
window-sashes ; and but for the fire which blazes brightly upon the hearth of Lady Oaktorrington's boudoir,
and exhales a genial warmth throughout the room, the
window-panes would be crusted with frost. It is the
first real snowfall of the season, and hunting is stopped
for the nonce. Parliament after an autumn session
protracted beyond a point almost unheard of in the history of that august body has at last been prorogued,
and Lord Oaktorrington, unable to find further "just
cause or impediment" to his return home, has been
compelled to come back from town. There being
nothing for him to do out-of-doors, he is passing the
morning in his wife's society.

"I see by the 'Morning Post' that Lord Argenton has bought Tillotson Towers, the Delancy-Veres'
place in Devonshire," says Lady Oaktorrington. "Who
on earth is Lord Argenton ? I certainly never heard
of him before."

"You certainly never did," answers Lord Oaktorrington, curtly, without raising his eyes from the letter
he is reading.

"Pray, be good enough to explain what you mean,"
says Lady Oaktorrington. "I thought I knew every
man in the peerage."

"You'd have to live at Salisbury's elbow to do

that. He's full as bad as Gladstone when it comes to increasing *us*."

"Don't go on talking in riddles. I asked you who Lord Argenton is, and I shall be glad to have you answer my question."

"If you want to know who he *is*, I shall be obliged to tell you—Lord Argenton. If you desire to know who he *was*—that is a horse of quite another color!"

Lady Oaktorrington frowns and tosses her head.

"I'm in no humor for joking," she says, impatiently.

"I assure you, it's no joke—far from it," says his lordship, making a face. "It's too nauseous a subject for joking."

"How long do you intend to keep up this ridiculous harlaquinade?" Lady Oaktorrington asks with a pitying sneer. "You do it so very badly."

"Do I, really? Then you'd best not encourage me."

Lady Oaktorrington regards him with mute surprise. Every time he stays any length of time in town by himself, he comes home more independent of speech and less afraid of her. But other times have been bagatelles—mere patches on this one. Some counter-influence to her own is, of course, at the bottom of it. She is not slow to guess the source, and guessing with a woman's brain, jumps to the inevitable female conclusion, and puts the saddle on a woman's shoulders.

"Have you been outbid for a horse at Tattersall's this time, too, that you are in such a vile humor?" she asks, pointedly, fixing her eyes to meet his point-blank when he raises them.

"Eh—what the deuce do you mean?" he says,

quickly, looking up, but dropping his glance again like a shot bird before hers. "Who—who's talking in riddles now, I should like to know? You want to know who Lord Argenton was, eh!" he adds in such a tone of incipient surrender that Lady Oaktorrington smiles to herself at the bull's-eye her chance shot has made. "He *was* John Grubs, the Birmingham brass-founder. Salisbury's just made him a peer, to spite Chamberlain, people say. It is hardly the use you'd expect him to make of the House of Lords, is it? The fact is the peerage is going to the dogs neck and crop, and I say with Chamberlain, the sooner we're abolished the better."

Lady Oaktorrington, happily for the tranquillity of her aristocratic temper does not hear the concluding words of her husband's speech, so immersed is she in her own thoughts.

"He's rich, of course?"

"Rich? Rather. A couple of millions at least."

"Any sons?"

"Yes; two I believe. One's in the Blues with Beyndour. Haven't you ever heard him laugh at Jacob Grubs, and call him a howling cad? Fancy, the Honorable Jacob Grubs! Salisbury has a lot to answer for."

"Salisbury?" says the marchioness, with a look of sudden awakening. "Then he's got back into office again?"

"Yes, he has," grumpily.

"I thought he was going to make you something in the Cabinet, or Lord-Lieutenant of Ireland, or something."

"So did I," says Lord Oaktorrington, feelingly.

"And so he promised—ahem—before the division that turned out Gladstone. But, bless you, he's like every one else. Now, he says he'll give me one of the vacant Garters."

"That will be something, at any rate," says Lady Oaktorrington, in a "half a loaf is better than no bread" voice. "I should rather have liked to go over to Ireland, though. It would have given poor Mary a chance, don't you think? By-the-by, has this Lord—Lord (looking in the paper) Argenton—has he any daughters, do you know?"

"Yes, one that I know of. She was presented at the last drawing-room. I remember your laughing at the name, and wondering how Lady Bouverie could present such a person."

"Did Lady Bouverie present her? How tiresome! It was for Jack, of course; one can see that now. Fancy one's degrading one's self like that!" and Lady Oaktorrington holds up her hands. "Tillotson joins Tewtorlock, doesn't it?"

"Yes, it does. More's the pity," says the marquis. "If it wasn't entailed I'd sell it like a shot."

"Sell it? Indeed, you should do nothing of the sort. We must stay there next winter," Lady Oaktorrington says, decisively.

"What on earth has got into you now?" Lord Oaktorrington asks, in amazement. "Stay at Tewtorlock? We haven't stayed there for twenty years. Fancy the damp! You can't be serious."

"Fancy *not* staying there with these rich people next door to us! You forget—"

"Oh, yes, I know—the girls. But I thought you had Harborough selected for Mary."

"Oh, I've given that up. He wouldn't so much as look at Mary while he was here. You couldn't drag him away from Lady Henry—"

"Lady Henry? And do you mean to say you were such a fool as to ask her here with Harborough?"

"I'm afraid I was," Lady Oaktorrington says, humbly. "It was a great mistake."

"In more ways than one," his lordship says, *sotto voce*, knitting his brows; "as I'm afraid you'll find out. What fools women are! And what about the Yankee? I thought he was allotted to Edith. Another failure there?"

"Not exactly," and then Lady Oaktorrington gives her husband a fairly correct account of Allen's visit, ending up with the information received from San Francisco.

"You *have* made a charming mess of it!" Lord Oaktorrington exclaims.

"That's what Beyndour says. But he's coming back. I've had a letter from Freddy this morning from Florence saying—"

"Freddy in Florence? I thought he was out in the States."

"How can you be so silly?" You knew quite well he was coming home before you went up to town. I read you his letter—"

"Oh, yes, yes. To be sure. And the Yankee is a friend of his. Of course. How stupid of me."

"You needn't be angry at his coming home. I assure you he has been most useful."

"I'm not angry," Lord Oaktorrington says. "On the contrary I'm confoundedly glad. I'll tell you why. I've got a letter here from Harborough in which he says he'll support any candidate I may put up for the Bridgeleigh vacancy made by—curiously enough—this same man Grubs's elevation to the House of Lords. It's awfully good of him, for Bridgeleigh belongs to him, and it will be a walk-over. I'll let him have Freddy."

"Freddy, dear? Isn't he too young and inexperienced to be a member of Parliament?"

"He'll know enough to follow Smith into the right lobby when there is a vote on anything, and that's all we want. It's all the most of us do in the Lords. It will strengthen me with Salisbury wonderfully," he adds, reflectively.

"I'm so glad, dear. And it will be another advantage for Freddy with this Lord Grubs's daughter, don't you see," and Lady Oaktorrington smiles benignly at the happy thought. "It will be so nice to be succeeded by one's son-in-law at Bridgeleigh. How charmingly it all happens! One could almost fancy one was reading a novel, dear, couldn't one?"

The sunshine of his wife's smiles is a temperature in which Lord Oaktorrington is not wont to bask. It is not that he cares for the warmth of marital congeniality. The effect is more of comfort than bliss, and while he enjoys the novelty of it, his pleasure is rather negative than positive in the absence of the jar and contradiction to which he is commonly accustomed in her company, rather than in the presence of anything likely to especially gratify him.

"Yes," he answers, restfully; "so one could if everything else went so swimmingly. This *contretemps* with the Yankee rather spoils the harmony of the scene."

"We shall soon put that right," Lady Oaktorrington says, hopefully. "He and Freddy will be here
to-morrow."

"But Edith is not at home."

"She is coming home to-morrow, oddly enough."

CHAPTER XX.

PHILIP ALLEN's second arrival at Ashwynwick Park
is a gratifying contrast to the first.

Lady Oaktorrington meets him in the hall with both
hands extended, and a smile of sweetest affection illu-
mining her aristocratic countenance.

"So charmed we are to see you back again, Mr.
Allen," she says, in her softest voice. "This time I am
delighted to say my husband is here to add his welcome to mine," and she leads Allen to the drawing-
room, where he is met at the door by Lord Oaktorrington.

"I am most pleased to see you here, Mr. Allen,"
his lordship says, with as warm and tight a grasp of
the hand as he is able to give any man. "I was so
awfully sorry to miss your last visit to us, and to have
to defer for so long my thanks to you for all your kindness to my son Freddy. Pray accept them now." Having said this neat little speech without miss or blunder,
Lord Oaktorrington thrusts quickly into his pocket the
small piece of paper on which it had been written out
for him by the marchioness the night before, and being
left to his own mental resources without coach, sticks
his glass in his eye and surveys his guest with a silent
though friendly smile.

Even Lady Mary, at a prearranged signal from her mother, emulates the weather in a "universal thaw," and comes forward to greet him.

"You must really come out hunting with us this time," she says, after as warm a shake of the hand as she can muster up. "We shan't let you off again. You shall ride polo; and—and—I've got a new dog to show you."

Allen is about to say that he does not remember having seen the old ones, but tact stops him in time.

"It is all very absurd," he tells himself, "this marvelous alteration. I can't at all make it out. It is another phase of aristocracy, I suppose, whose ways are quite beyond me. If it makes them happy I don't care. Let by-gones be by-gones." So he says to Lady Mary, politely:

"You're very kind. I should like to see him of all things."

"He is such a dear," Lady Mary goes on. "A darling skye, with not an eye to be seen for love or money."

"Pray, Mr. Allen, come and sit down here. You must be dreadfully cold after your long drive," Lady Oaktorrington says, placing an arm-chair for him at the fire. "Edith, don't you see Mr. Allen?"

Lady Edith has been standing pale and motionless near the chimney-piece, a silent witness of what to her appears to be nothing less than her family's degradation.

"Oh, how can they? How can they?" she says to herself again and again, as some fresh piece of flagrant toadying exhibits itself. "Can they not see that he must notice it? I am most awfully ashamed. What must he think of us all?"

In the midst of these painful reflections her mother's words jar upon her. Is she, too, to be dragged forward to pay him court upon compulsion? Must she, also, humiliate herself in his eyes with the others? No, she will not be a party to such barefaced money-worshiping. Rather will she go to the other extreme. As Allen comes up to her she puts out her hand and says, stifly :

"How do you do?" without so much as looking at him.

To Allen, who has come all the way from Florence, full of happiness and hope, her greeting is a glass of cold water in his face. After the first impulse of anger as it comes upon a sudden and unexpected blow, he is conscious of a sense of great weariness. He is heartily sick and tired of her meaningless caprice ; he is worn out with the artificiality of manner which, without the slightest warning, and without apparently the faintest reason, she is wont to assume to him ; he is jaded past endurance with the never-ending obstacles to an understanding between them, or which she is forever throwing in his path with seemingly no object whatever but the gratification of a spirit of natural and heartless coquetry.

"After all, is the game worth the candle?" he asks himself. "Is such a girl worth a minute's anxiety on the part of any man? No."

For the moment he is sensible of that delicious feeling of relief which comes to all men upon their deliverance from the despotic thralldom of love for one woman. It matters not whether their fetters are broken by their own will or against it; or whether their freedom is gained by their rude awakening from a delusion, or by the discovery of unworthiness in the object of their affections, the effect is always the same; the return of a light heart, buoyant spirits, and a good appetite.

As Allen turns from Lady Edith without another word, he is in full and joyous possession of these three concomitants of happiness for just twenty seconds. Then he looks up at her. In her eyes is the old yearning, pleading look, the dumb show of self-reproach, repentance, and love. Down flops the flag of independence with a run, and snap-snap go the shackles of slavery on wrist and ankle again. He is about to speak when Lord Oaktorrington walks up:

"Glad to say it's thawing. We're going to shoot the Wampstone coverts to-morrow. Fetched a gun?"

"No," Allen tells him. "I'm sorry to say I haven't."

"Oh! Don't shoot, perhaps. You Ya—a—hem—Americans don't care much for sport, I dare say."

"I'm sure I don't know why you people in England should think so, but I constantly hear that said. It is altogether wrong. If there is anything in it, it is that our ideas of sport differ from yours. We don't hunt foxes, stags, and hares on horseback, and we don't have covert shooting. With us the preservation of game (except as protected by law) is the exception. With you it is the rule. But we have plenty of wild game to shoot, and plenty of what *we* call sport in hunting and shooting it in its wild, uncultivated state."

"Oh! Really?" But d'ye mean to say you have no gamekeepers, or people like that, on your estates to feed the pheasants, and shoot cats and stoats and things like that, don't you know?"

"I don't know what they may have in the Eastern States, now," Allen says, with a smile. "I dare say that Anglomania has imported gamekeepers as well as foxes. But out West a gamekeeper would be mobbed."

"How do you keep poachers off your property?"

"We have no poachers. At least, we don't consider men who shoot on our land such. Everybody shoots over everybody else's land indiscriminately, by a sort of common consent. The privilege is never abused. Besides, every one doesn't shoot as in England. Men, as a rule, are too busy, too much engrossed with business and their occupations and professions to pass their time with shot-guns in their hands. They only shoot when they have the time to spare."

"Oh! Do—do you shoot, by chance?"

"I? Well, I should say I did. Somewhat," and Allen smiles to himself when he thinks of his regular September and October campings-out in Marin and Humboldt Counties, and among the Mount Diablo foot-hills, and Gabilan Mountains of the Coast Range; and his December and January "duck hunts" among the Carquinez terles, and the head-waters of the bay.

"Oh? Not a great deal! I'm sorry, because you'll find it rather dull work here by yourself, when we're out to-morrow."

"I shall be very glad to go out with you. I dare say Freddy can fit me out with a gun."

"Oh, I can lend you a gun if that's all; I've half a dozen. But—but—don't you think if you're not accustomed, don't you know—to—ahem—you know what I mean—why, you may find it awkward, don't you see. All the fellows I've asked are devilish good shots, you know."

"I dare say I shan't be able to hit anything," Allen answers, dryly. "But I shan't mind that. One must learn, mustn't one?"

"How confoundedly tiresome of him," Lord Oaktorrington says to his wife, who at that moment calls him away. "He insists on coming out shooting to-morrow. Of course, he can't shoot, and will make an infernal guy of himself."

"Never mind that, dear," Lady Oaktorrington replies. "You must humor him, for Edith's sake. And now, dear, let us come away and leave them together."

CHAPTER XXI.

"HAVEN'T you one kind word to say to me?" Allen asks, after waiting several minutes for Lady Edith to look up. She has seated herself near a window, and is trying to unravel a skein of floss-silk.

"One kind word?" she replies. "About what, pray?"

He walks over and sits down beside her.

"Let me hold that for you," he says. "You'll never manage it alone."

"Why not? I've done hundreds."

"But you'll fail this time. See if you don't. I'm sure you will."

"I'm sure I shan't."

A long pause, during which she winds off about a yard of silk.

"Why don't you go out-of-doors for a walk, or anything," she asks.

"Because I prefer being here—with you."

12

"Englishmen don't sit in-doors with women on a fine day like this."

"I'm not an Englishman, as I've told you before."

"Then Americans do, I suppose."

"Like ladies' society? Yes. I don't think Englishmen, so far as I have seen, care much for—ladies at any time."

"Don't they? Why?"

"Oh, you must ask them that. I can only guess why?"

"There! That is the first time I've heard you use that word. I thought you—"

"Oh, I know. You thought I'd say 'I guess' every minute or two before you met me. Come, confess."

"I really don't remember. I don't think I thought at all about it."

Allen bites his lips.

"Pardon my presumption, please," he says, stiffly.

"Don't be huffy. You Americans are so awfully touchy. You are always taking offense at something."

"Are we? I don't think you have any right to say that of me. I'm sure I've stood a good deal of roughing lately."

"Of what?"

"Roughing."

"What's that?"

"I guess that's another Americanism."

"Is it? I never heard the word except applied to what is done to horse's shoes in frosty weather. You don't mean that, do you?"

"Well, harsh treatment—insult, if you will."

"Where?"

"Here."

" Here ?   By whom, pray ? "

" Oh, everybody—yourself among the number."

" Me ? "

" Yes, you.   And I've stood it all for—for your sake."

" For *my* sake ?   I don't quite understand."

" Yes, you do.   You know quite well what I mean. I—I told you in my letter—"

" Please don't speak of that letter.   I was very angry with you for writing so to me."

"Were you ? "

"Yes, I was."

" Are you still ? "

"What ?   Ye—oh, dear me, what a tiresome knot. I shall have to break it."

" Let me try."

Allen takes the silk from her, and in doing so gives her hand a little squeeze.

" You mustn't do that.   I don't like it."

" What?   Undo the knot for you ? "

" No.   What—what you did just then."

" What did I do ? "

" You know very well.   You hurt me very much."

" Did I?   Then let me kiss it and make it well. There ! "

" How dare you," pulling her hand away and jumping up.   " I never had such a thing done to me in my life."

" I'm awfully glad to hear it.   Please sit down again.   I promise I won't do it—"

" No Englishman—no English gentleman would do so."

" English gentlemen are awful muffs, then."

"They know how to behave to ladies, if that's what you mean."

"They don't know how to behave to ladies. That's what I mean. Pardon me if I say so, but I never saw such rude, uncivil, *gauche*, ill-mannered men with women in my life as are what you call English gentlemen. Why, they treat women like cattle. Such a thing as sentiment for a woman never enters their heads. They only marry for money; love is not only unprofitable in their eyes, but vulgar. I don't suppose an English gentleman ever in his life told a woman whom he wished to marry that he loved her."

"I don't know, I'm sure."

"I'll bet none ever did to you."

"I should hope not," drawing herself up. "Certainly not, until he had asked my father's consent."

"Oh, that's the formula, is it? The artificial, mechanical, stony-hearted, aristocratic formula. And must I go through the empty, meaningless form?"

"You really must excuse me, Mr. Allen. I forgot I have some letters to write for the post."

She rises and walks rapidly toward the door. Allen stops her half-way.

"You shan't go until you answer me one question. I shall never get such another chance as this, and I've frittered away too much time already. It is something I must know before I go back to America, and I sail from Liverpool on Saturday."

Lady Edith starts visibly, and changes color.

"You are not going—really?" she says. "You only say that to make me stay."

"Indeed, it's too true. I've told you already that I loved you."

She catches her under-lip with her teeth and looks down at the floor, while her breath comes and goes quickly.

"I now ask you to be my wife. You do not answer. Is it yes, or no? You refuse me."

She stands silent and still, her eyes still bent upon the carpet at her feet, and her fingers twitching nervously as they clasp each other.

"At least, say good-by to me, for I must leave this house at once," he says, in a voice hoarse with emotion.

She looks up at him, and the old pleading look is in her half-closed eyes, the old supplicating gesture in her quickly raised hand.

"Don't go," she murmurs, softly. "You must not do that."

In an instant his arms are about her, holding her firmly to his breast.

"My darling, I will take that as your answer, and seal it thus."

She puts her hands up to her face, but before she can get them there he kisses her lips.

She gives a little sigh as the blood comes rushing back into her cheeks, and says:

"I feel so ashamed. What must you think of me!"

His only answer is to kiss her again.

"Oh, let me go, please. I hear some one coming."

Allen releases her, and they stand listening a moment or two, but no one comes.

"I'm so awfully happy," Allen says. "I could dance and sing for very joy. All my troubles are over now."

A shade crosses Lady Edith's features.

"I'm afraid they have only just begun," she says, shaking her head. "Marriage with us is a more difficult matter than you think."

"Difficult? Why, every difficulty is past. Unless you mean to take back your consent. Do you mean that?"

"No. I wish it all lay with me. It would be easy then."

"I don't understand you. It does all lie with you."

"There's father."

"Oh, nonsense. I'll make it all right with him."

"And mother."

"I shan't have any difficulty with her."

"Don't be too sure. Are you quite certain you won't mind if they ask you a lot of questions?"

"Of course. But what can they want to know? I can tell them I love you very dearly, and will take good care of you, and do my best to make you happy. What more can they want than that? That should satisfy any father and mother."

She shrugs her shoulders.

"Not fathers and mothers of our class."

"Oh, I see," Allen says, quickly, with a sudden cloud on his brow. "I'm not good enough, I suppose. Yes, I forgot that."

"No, no, no. It's not that. It's something else. I'm afraid you have made a great mistake in liking me. It will never answer."

"Never answer? What on earth can you mean?"

"I know it will annoy you—the things they will ask you."

"No it won't. I shan't mind anything, when I think it is for your sake, dear."

"I wish I felt sure. You will promise me, then, that you won't mind?"

"Yes, I promise."

"Well, then, see them at once. The sooner you get it over the better. I hear them coming now. I'll run away by this door like a great coward, and leave you to do battle alone." She stops a second in the doorway, says, "You won't mind?" and shuts the door after her, as Lord and Lady Oaktorrington enter the room.

CHAPTER XXII.

"WHAT, alone, Mr. Allen?" the marchioness asks, with a disappointed face, while her eyes visit quickly every nook and corner of the room. "I—I—thought Edith was here. How tiresome of her," she whispers to her husband.

"By Jove, yes, the little minx," he grunts back.

"She *was* here," Allen says.

"For long?"

"It seemed to me but a few seconds," he answers, with a meaning smile, hoping thus to crack the ice at least. Neither the marquis nor marchioness see it. They only mutter:

"So like her" and "Isn't it?" to each other.

"I'm afraid you must find it very dull," Lady Oaktorrington says, after a moment or two's whispered conference with her husband. "I can't make out where Freddy has gone."

Lord Oaktorrington smiles behind his hand.

Freddy has received strict orders to keep out of the way, and is at the present moment engaged in forwarding his two-hundred-pound check to Coutts & Co., to be placed to his credit.

"Lord Oaktorrington will take you a drive in his phaeton after luncheon.   Won't you, my dear?"

His lordship says :

"Oh, yes.   Delighted," aloud, and "Blow it all!" to himself.

"Like to have a look about the place?" he says to Allen.   "Seen the stables?"

"No, I haven't."

"Come along, then."

"I should like to have a few words with you both, first," Allen says.   "It won't take long."

Lord and Lady Oaktorrington exchange glances. It can't be possible, they think, that he can mean anything about Edith, so soon as this.

"Oh, certainly," Lady Oaktorrington says, with a hopeful smile, notwithstanding.   "I wonder what it can be about.   Sit down, my dear," to her husband.

"I am not surprised at your feeling wonder," Allen goes on, "for I have known her—"

At the sound of the personal pronoun, Lady Oaktorrington gives a slight cough, and elevates her eyebrows at the marquis.   He replies by a wink.

"Such a short time."

Allen pauses.

"Yes?" says Lady Oaktorrington, bowing graciously.   "Pray go on."

"I don't generally find it awkward or difficult to say what I mean," he continues.   "But I confess to considerable hesitancy in speaking to you on this matter."

"How infernally long-winded these Yankees are!" mutters the marquis to himself. "Why can't the fellow speak plain English?"

"Yes, yes. Pray tell us. It is some trouble Freddy has got into I'm afraid," Lady Oaktorrington says.

"I'm blowed if I pay another farthing for the beggar, if that's it," growls the marquis.

"It hasn't anything whatever to do with your son," Allen answers. "I will not waste words further. Know, then, that I love your daughter—"

Lady Oaktorrington straightens up with dignified astonishment. "Really. This is indeed a surprise, Mr. Allen. And may I ask which one?"

"Edith, if I may call her so."

"Edith? Why, you have scarcely exchanged two words with the child. You can not be serious."

"Indeed I am."

"Pray go on."

"Of course, you must know what next I would say. I ask your consent—yours and Lord Oaktorrington's to—to—"

"To your speaking to her?" kindly helps out the marchioness. "I hardly know what to say. I really know so little about Edith. She is so secretive and silent, and never confides in me, poor dear. Her affections may be engaged elsewhere, and—"

"I can answer for that," Allen says, proudly. "I know they are not."

"Oh, you do? And pray how do you know? Who has told you?"

"Herself."

" The deuce ! " exclaims the marquis.

" Herself ? " echoes Lady Oaktorrington, drawing back and knitting her brows. " And do you mean to say you have spoken to her already ? "

" Why, of course."

"And engaged her affections without first asking our permission ? "

" I'm very sorry, but—"

" Really, Mr. Allen, this is most unheard of. Such a thing never happened with *us* before. What would all our relatives say, were they to hear of it ! "

" I'm sure I can not see that you should be so offended," Allen says, in a hurt tone. " Perhaps you consider it a presumption on my part to aspire to the hand of—"

" Oh, no, no, not that, not that. Pray don't think that, Mr. Allen," Lady Oaktorrington cries, seeing that she may be carrying family dignity a trifle too far. "Of course, it is a great compliment." Allen bows, while she elevates her eyebrows at her husband, who replies by a grimace.

" I assure you I consider the honor all on my side."

"It's very good of you to say so, I'm sure," Lady Oaktorrington says, graciously. "Of course, you don't understand our ways. You can't be expected to. But in England a gentleman of our class never dreams of approaching the subject of love with a girl without first declaring his intentions to her parents."

" Does he not, indeed ? " says Allen. " It's a pity the rule is not followed out as strictly after marriage— and the husbands of pretty wives accorded the same right," he adds, to himself. " There would be fewer divorces, then."

There is another pause.

"Well," says Lady Oaktorrington, "I suppose, then, you mean that you want our consent to—"

"Our marriage. I'm sure you will have no objection. I dare say I may have no rank, but I love her truly and dearly, and I'll be very good and kind to her and take such care of her."

"Then you've actually proposed to her and been accepted without our knowing anything about it."

"Yes."

Although mutual glances of satisfaction are immediately exchanged between Lord and Lady Oaktorrington, her ladyship thinks it incumbent upon her as an upholder of aristocratic propriety and decorum to display her high-bred indignation. She is now quite safe, she thinks, in doing so.

"Really, Mr. Allen, you must pardon me when I tell you that you have been guilty of a gross breach of etiquette. *We*, don't allow our daughters to be treated as our footmen treat their sweethearts."

Allen's eyes flash.

"It's a pity you don't," he says, before he can stop himself. "There would be less artifice about them, and more nature, if you did. But let us forget all about that," he says, good-humoredly, fearing he has jeopardized his happiness by what he has said. "I'm very sorry, and I won't do it again," he adds, with a smile. "I can't say more than that. I may feel, then, that I have your consent?"

Lady Oaktorrington looks at her husband and nods. He nods back.

"Yes, I suppose so," she says. "I suppose so."

"Oh, thank you so very much. It is very good of

you.   You have made me very happy.   I'll go at
once and tell her."

"Come," he thinks to himself.   "They are not such
dreadful ogres after all."

"Wait a moment," says Lady Oaktorrington, as
Allen is making for the door.   "Not quite so fast,
please.   There are one or two conditions, you know."

"Rather," acquiesces the marquis.

"Yes?   What?" Allen asks, with a surprised face.

"We must know about your affairs, don't you
know."

"Oh, of course," says Allen, lightly.   "That's all
right.   You needn't have any fear about them.   I
don't think I shall experience much difficulty in keeping a wife handsomely.   I suppose that's all you want
to know."

Lord Oaktorrington laughs outright.

"Is it, indeed?" he says.   "I think we shall want
to know a little more than that."

"Recollect," says Lady Oaktorrington, "that we
know positively nothing about your means—your—
ahem—your money, don't you know."

"Quite true," says Allen.   "No more you do.
Nor about my family at home and my relations.   I
haven't got much of either.   Only a father, a couple
of uncles, one aunt, and—"

"Oh, we don't care about them," says Lady Oaktorrington, impatiently.   "We want to know about
your money."

"Don't you think he'd better go up and see Fairfield?" suggests the marquis.   "It's an awful bore
for us."

"Who's Fairfield?" asks Allen.

"Our lawyer—our family solicitor," answers Lady Oaktorrington.

"What have I to do with him? Must .I get his consent, too?"

"Yes, in a measure. If he's not satisfied with your money-matters, we can not give ours."

"But you have given it."

"Oh, come," says the marquis. "We're only wasting time bandying words about it. You may evade telling us, but he'll get it out of you, never fear."

"Get it out of me?" says Allen, quickly, "I don't comprehend."

"You don't comprehend anything, it seems, unless you want to," replies the marquis, standing up.

"Hush, my dear," says Lady Oaktorrington, and the marquis sits down again. "There's no good in quarreling over it; and perhaps we can do without Mr. Fairfield's assistance for the present, if you will tell us, Mr. Allen, what your income is, and what your means and prospects are."

"I have no fixed income," says Allen.

"What?" cry the marquis and marchioness in a breath.

"Father gives me all the money I want. He's never refused me a cent—a penny—yet."

"Then you have no means of your own?"

"Yes, I've got ten thousand dollars invested in a quartz-mine."

"How much is that in our money?" asks Lady Oaktorrington with returning confidence.

"About two thousand pounds."

"Good heavens! That's only about—How much dear?"

"Sixty pounds a year at three per cent," says the marquis. "Our butler has more than that. Just fancy!"

"Really, I am surprised at you, Mr. Allen, expecting us to give you one of our daughters, with no more than that."

"Yes, but I know father will give me something regular. He's the director of two or three railroads, and will get me put in as secretary on one of them. That will give me a fine salary. Besides, he'll build us a fine residence to live in, and I know, if I manage him right, he'll give us all the money we shall want to live upon."

"Then you are really and actually dependent upon your father for everything, and have nothing but indefinite prospects?" says Lady Oaktorrington. "Of course, you can't settle anything on Edith?"

"Settle? No, of course not. But what need to settle anything. Father will leave me everything. In fact, General Hodge, his attorney, told me in confidence the old man made his will that way. Won't that be enough?"

"It's very uncertain and indefinite. He might change his mind and revoke his will at any moment. Wouldn't he settle something on your wife?"

Allen shakes his head.

"I should dislike to ask him. He's very crotchety about such things, and his great fear is that some one should marry me for money. It would spoil all to ask him to settle any money. He wouldn't understand it."

"Don't you have marriage settlements in America?"

" I never heard of one, there."

" Does he know of your wish to marry our daughter? "

" Yes. I've written to tell him."

" Then he must know the necessity of some settlement being made."

" It is about the last thing to enter his head. He is not a very great believer in marriage, at best, and of all things he detests most is a marriage for money. My mother married him when he was a poor man, struggling for his living."

Lord and Lady Oaktorrington again exchange glances.

" Fancy not getting money with such a low connection! " thinks one.

" Talk of the degradation of the peerage after this! " thinks the other.

" You haven't said anything to him about money, then? " asks Lady Oaktorrington.

" Not a word. I know better than that. He'd be against my marrying at all. I know if we leave it as it is it will be all right. I know I can manage everything."

" Oh, we could never agree to that," says the marchioness. decisively, with a haughty stare.

" No fear," mutters the marquis. " We're not quite so green as that."

" You see," Lady Oaktorrington continues, "it is not as though we could give Edith much ourselves."

" I don't want anything," replies Allen, quickly. " I want nothing with her, and nothing but her."

" Oh, of course we should settle something upon

her. It can't be a great deal, for we haven't it to give."

Allen opens his eyes in amazement.

"No doubt you think it strange," Lady Oaktorrington goes on. "But all the estates are strictly entailed, and go to our eldest son. Then from what remains we must first provide for our other three sons."

"Three?" says Allen. "I only know of two."

"You've never seen Cecil. He's at Eton, you know, and only comes home for the holidays. Then, after them, come our three daughters."

"Three?" repeats Allen. "Is there a third?"

"Yes, Maude. You've not seen her either. She's in the school-room still."

"Oh, at school. I didn't know."

"No, not *at* school," replies Lady Oaktorrington, contemptuously. "Fancy our sending one of our girls to school! She has a governess, of course."

"Where is she?"

"Where? Why, here, of course, where should she be?"

"And I've never seen her?" asks Allen. "Is she an invalid?"

"Indeed, no. Girls in the school-room are not likely to be seen by any one. You wouldn't be likely to see her until she comes out."

"Poor thing," says Allen. Has she much longer to stay in—in—" he is all but saying "her prison," but tactically substitutes, "the school-room."

"Only seven or eight years."

"And does she never go out of the house?"

"Of course she does—with her governess."

"And do you mean to say you never see her either?"

"Really, Mr. Allen, you show a marvelous interest in the child. Certainly, I see her at least twice every day. I go to the nursery when she has her dinner, and look in to say good-night when she goes to bed."

"Have all your daughters been treated like that? Edith, too?"

"Exactly like that," Lady Oaktorrington answers, stiffly. "You seem to disapprove of our way of bringing up our girls."

"I must say it's awfully artificial and unnatural," Allen replies, candidly.

"You are quite satisfied with Edith, however?"

"Yes, I am, I admire her more than ever now. What a lot of character she must have!"

"Suppose we go on with what we were talking about. I say we can only give Edith a few thousand pounds."

"And I say I don't want a farthing with her."

"Then, all the more reason is there that you should make some settlement upon her. Now, to be plain, as you can't do so yourself, your father must. Otherwise, we must decline your offer."

"But don't you see, can't you see, dear Lady Oaktorrington," Allen urges. "that I can't ask him."

"Skittles!" says the marquis, "you must, if you want Edith. You must communicate with him at once, and on his answer depends our consent."

Lady Oaktorrington rises, and Lord Oaktorrington, like an unchained dog, makes a break for the door.

"Stay a moment, please," Allen says. "I will do as you wish, but I honestly tell you I fear the consequences. I shall cable to father at once. A letter would take too long. Have you a telegraphic blank— a form, you call it here? Now, then."

He seats himself at the writing-table, and takes up a pen. As he is about to begin, he pauses and thinks for a minute or two: "You are quite determined not to allow her to marry me unless I do this?" he asks.

"Quite," says the marchioness.

"Rather," observes the marquis.

"And you wont allow her to marry me in the way I suggest?"

"Decidedly not."

"No fear."

"Would she marry me herself without their consent," he asks himself. "She is of age. No, this would never do. It would cause a scandal that she could never face. It will be time enough to think of that if this fails." He takes up the pen again and writes rapidly:

"*Will you settle   dollars on my wife?*"

He hands the form to Lady Oaktorrington, and says:

"I have left the sum blank. Be kind enough to fill in what you think right."

Lord and Lady Oaktorrington read it over together, and confer in an undertone.

"We don't know anything about dollars," Lady Oaktorrington says, handing the paper back to Allen. "Can't you put it in pounds."

"If you will say how much in pounds you want, it will be sufficient," Allen says, "I can turn it into dollars.—Talk of the heathen Chinese buying their wives!" he thinks to himself. "And these people are the cream of civilized Europe! I feel as if I were bargaining for a horse."

Lord and Lady Oaktorrington have a whispered conference, while Allen is left to his own thoughts.

"We think," says Lady Oaktorrington, at last, "that thirty thousand pounds would be right."

Allen takes the paper with a sarcastic smile.

"Is that all? Why that is only a hundred and fifty thousand dollars. You ought to have said a million while you were about it. Father would give it quite as willingly."

He can not keep back a sneer as he says this. These English aristocrats will, he finds, stand anything for money.

"Eh? What?" says the marquis, all alive in a minute. Then in an audible whisper to the marchioness: "I told you you didn't make it high enough. You were a fool not to double it."

Allen looks at him with a face full of repugnance and disgust, but the glitter of gold is too strong in the marquis's eyes for him to see it.

"Never mind. This will do," he says, folding up the paper. "And now, how can I get this sent? It ought to go at once."

"I'll drive you in to Hertford myself," Lord Oaktorrington says, ringing the bill.

As Allen goes to his room to make some preparations for the drive, he meets Lady Edith on the stairs.

"I'm afraid you've had a dreadful time of it," she says, with a white face and wide open eyes as she studies his features for a clew to the result. " It has all gone wrong. I feared it would."

" No, indeed, it hasn't," he answers, with a smile. "It has gone right enough. Not, perhaps, exactly in accord with my views, but—"

"Oh, I know. There's been a lot of trouble about money."

"What of it? You are worth every bit of it."

"Every bit of what? The money?" with a deprecating look.

"No; the trouble."

CHAPTER XXIII.

LORD OAKTORRINGTON's shooting-party assembles next morning at eleven. It consists of six guns : himself, Freddy, three neighbors—viz., the Earl of Wentworth, his son the Honorable Percy Knollys (pronounced *Knowles*), and Sir Herbert Wemyss (pronounced *Weames*)—and Allen.

" I don't know if you understand breechloaders," Lord Oaktorrington says to Allen, pointing to the gun he has lent him. "I dare say not. But I've given directions to one of my keepers to stay by you, and he'll show you how it works."

"Thanks," Allen replies, with a smile. "I think I shall be able to manage."

"Much cover shooting in the States?" the marquis asks, as they walk along.

"None at all that I ever heard of," Allen tells him.

"What?" exclaims Lord Oaktorrington. "Then, of course, you know nothing about it. Perhaps you'd better not come, you know. It's awfully difficult and sharp work, and unless you understand it, you'll find it very stupid and dull. I should strongly advise you to go back."

"No, thanks," says Allen, carelessly. "I expect to make a fool of myself, but I shan't mind."

"I shall, though," groans Lord Oaktorrington to himself. "What an ass I was to lend him the gun. It will be the joke of the county for a month. Look here, then, if you will persist in coming, let me give you a few hints. When we get to those trees over there we shall stand round them about twenty yards apart. The beaters will go in and drive out the pheasants. As the birds fly out we pot 'em, don't you know. You must be careful not to shoot at another fellow's bird, and always fire low. Of course, you know, you must only shoot at birds on the wing."

"Really!" says Allen, "you don't mean it?"

"Deuced lucky I told him," thinks the marquis.

"Then I mustn't shoot at a bird sitting?" Allen asks. "I shall never hit one flying, I'm afraid."

"I shouldn't try. Suppose you just look on at us to-day, and next time you'll know how to do it yourself."

"I can't think how you can have time to aim at a flying bird," Allen goes on. "I should think it would be impossible to hit one."

"Wait until you see," says Lord Oaktorrington, proudly. "We'll show you."

They reach the cover, a clump of leafless trees some two hundred yards in circumference with a thickish undergrowth of bushes, and the party ranges itself around it without loss of time. Allen, who insists on "having a try," is placed in a wide vacancy, the distances between the other men being lessened to give him the extra room.

"Devilish clever dodge of mine, that," thinks Lord Oaktorrington. "And mind, Smith," he says to one of the keepers, "that you stick close by him, and see that he gets on all right. He's rather inexperienced. You understand?"

"Yes m' lud," the man replies, touching his hat. "He do look different, that's true. I'll lay a tanner he knows more than he lets on," he adds to himself.

On Allen's right is Lord Wentworth, a pompous old gentleman with a red face and gray whiskers; on his left, Sir Herbert Wemyss, a downy-faced boy with long legs, a narrow chest, a thin neck, and an eyeglass. Lord Oaktorrington has put himself as much out of harm's way as possible on the other side.

The beaters set to work vigorously with voice and stick, and presently a babel of tongues bursts forth.

"Mark cock to the right!"

"Mark cock to the left!"

"Mark cock forward!"

"Mark right!"

"Mark left!"

"Mark forward!"

Allen who is nearly stunned by the noise, and bewildered by the conflicting announcements, then hears six double shots follow each other in quick succession. A cock pheasant flies straight up from the left, giving a sort of aërial start as Lord Wentworth discharges both barrels into space after him, and keeps on past Allen. As the bird's head and neck cross Allen's front, he raises his gun lightly, and fires. The bird seems to explode a bunch of feathers in the air, turns head over heels, and drops with a thump at Allen's feet.

"By cricky!" says the keeper behind him. "I knowed he was the right sort."

Lord Wentworth and Sir Herbert Wemyss immediately approach each other:

"My bird," says Lord Wentworth, motioning to the keeper to pick it up.

"Aw. Beg pardon," says Sir Herbert, adjusting his eyeglass. "I was on the point of making a similar remark myself, don't you know. Eh?"

"What? Do you mean to say you claim it? Nonsense. It was my last shot that fetched him down."

"Awfully sorry, don't you know, but I was the first to fire. I saw him stagger, and timed him to fall about here."

"If you will excuse me, my lud, and you too, Sir Herbert," says the keeper. "But this be this here gentleman's shot. I see's him shoot the bird with my hown heyes."

"Don't be impertinent, sir," answers Lord Wentworth, "or I shall at once complain to your master."

"I never heard the like," says Sir Herbert Weymss. "I shall certainly speak to Lord Oaktorrington about you, sir."

"I hopes no offense, my lud," the keeper begs. "This gentleman hisself will say the—"

"Oh, never mind," says Allen, with a laugh. "It doesn't matter in the least. I have no doubt the bird belongs to—both of you."

By this time the entire party have come together,

and discuss the claims of both parties, ending by allot-
ting it to Sir Herbert."

"We all know a pheasant will carry a charge of
shot five minutes before he falls," decides Lord Oaktorrington.

"Of course, if Sir Herbert fired the first shot, and
saw the bird, as he says, stagger, why, of course, the
bird must be his."

"I never heard such awful rubbish," shouts Lord
Wentworth, with flashing eyes. "Fancy any one abid-
ing by it! I shall go home at once. It's useless to
waste cartridges here."

"Oh, pray accept the bird," Allen says to Lord
Wentworth.

"Accept the bird?" exclaims Lord Wentworth.
"What do you mean, sir? The bird is mine, not yours
to give."

"Well, have it so. Don't let us waste any more
time haggling over it. It isn't worth it."

"And pray, sir, who are you?" Lord Wentworth
demands, in an angry tone. "Your face is unknown
to me."

"I dare say it is," says Allen, impatiently. "So is
yours to me."

"Come, come," shouts Lord Oaktorrington. "Let
us end this squabble. I quite agree with Mr. Allen
that it is not worth it. We are losing the best part of
the day."

Lord Wentworth turns away, muttering, and the
party return to their stations. But not another pheasant can the beaters scare up.

"I thought as much," Lord Oaktorrington says.
"The birds have all taken themselves off while we have

been jawing. We'll just have time before luncheon for a try at the covers on the home farm. Come along."

"Bosh!" says Lord Wentworth, to Sir Herbert Weymss. "The fact is the Ashwynwick preserves are not what they used to be. They're gone to pot. Small wonder, too, when 'pot hunters' are let loose over them," and he looks vindictively at Allen.

"I quite agree with you," says Sir Herbert. "I expect he'll be giving us a load of shot to carry home before the day is out. Did you ever see such an ass? Fancy trusting him with a gun! Who is he?"

"No idea. Oaktorrington's tailor, no doubt."

The home farm covers are productive of but two more pheasants, one of which falls to Freddy's gun, the other to Allen's.

"It's rather late in the season," Lord Oaktorrington says, apologetically, to Allen, "and the birds are wild."

"Hear that?" asks Lord Wentworth of Sir Herbert, elevating his eyebrows. "If it was me, I'd discharge my gamekeeper on the spot, or shut up shop at once. Late in the season! Ha, ha!"

"Don't catch me here again," replies Sir Herbert.

"I should hope not," says Lord Wentworth.

The party then wends its way across an open meadow to the agent's lodge, where luncheon is prepared. Allen is rather disappointed at not meeting the ladies, whom he has heard make it a custom in England to come out and join the shooting party at luncheon. He says as much to Freddy.

"Oh, that's only in September and October, when the partridges and pheasants are fresh, and the weather warm," Freddy tells him. "It's too far on for that sort of thing now, don't you know." Everybody's temper is better after a plentiful meal of Irish stew and copious draughts of home-brewed beer, with bread and cheese and a mouthful of Scotch whisky to end up with. But there isn't much better luck in store for anybody. An hour and a half's more shooting results in but four more pheasants and one hare. So, at three o'clock, the party breaks up, and Lord Oaktorrington, Freddy, and Allen walk slowly and silently home.

CHAPTER XXIV.

THE first person Allen sees as he enters the hall and is about to go up to his room to change his clothes, is Lady Edith. She is standing just within the doorway of the library, the door of which she holds a few inches open. Her face is pale and her eyes wide open and anxious. She beckons silently to Allen, and he follows her into the room.

"It's come," she whispers, hoarsely. "I've had such a time of it keeping it from mother and Mary. They don't know it's arrived, for I waylaid the messenger in the park. I thought this the safest place to keep it, for no one ever comes near this room."

Allen looks puzzled a minute, and is upon the point of saying "What?" when she goes quickly to one of the bookshelves, takes down a large volume of Bacon's "Essays," and from between the leaves draws out a sealed envelope.

"Here it is," she says, and hands Allen a telegram. "Oh, dear, I'm so frightened for fear it won't be all

right. Stop! Don't open it yet. Just wait a moment
till I get my breath."

Allen turns the brick-dust envelope over and over
in his fingers, not without a fast beating heart himself.

"Nonsense," he says, as steadily as he can. "Better know as soon as possible. It may be all right."

"May?" she cries. "Then *you* only think it *may?*
Oh, dear, what shall we do?"

"Do? Why read it, of course. But look here,"
suddenly. "Hadn't I better open it before your father
and mother? They will suspect something crooked if
I don't."

"No, no, no. Suppose your father won't consent?
I believe they'd tear you in pieces."

There is an earnest honesty in her voice that makes
Allen stare.

"Are you serious?" he asks.

"Serious?" she says, bitterly. "I should think I
was. I know them better than you do."

"I thought I knew them pretty well," Allen says;
"but I had no idea they were as bad as that."

"It's safer not to try. Come, you may open it
now," she says, putting both hands over her heart.
"I'm not overstrong here, the doctor says, but I am
quite ready."

"Poor child," Allen says, putting his arm about her.
"What have I been thinking of not to have noticed
how dreadfully you look. Come, dear, don't take it
so much to heart. We don't *know* that my father won't
give me the money. And even if he did refuse—"

"Oh, don't even suggest such a thing," she cries.
"I believe it would kill me."

"Why should it, dear? You could marry me all the same. You are of age. Wouldn't you?"

Lady Edith shakes her head slowly. "I couldn't go against their wishes."

"What?" A quick suspicion darts into his heart; he drops his arm from about her, and takes a step backward. "And are you, too—"

"No, no! You misunderstand me quite. Indeed, it is not that. In our class, in our rank, we never marry except as our parents wish. Oh, I see you do not believe me." Allen is silent. "What can I do to convince you?"

"Marry me at all hazards," he says, quickly. "Stay. I do not mean at once. I only ask your promise to do so; and that, only after I have tried every fair means to get your father and mother's consent. That is not so much. Will you promise?"

A gleam of sunlight comes into her face, like the sudden beam which darts forth from a dark and storm-riven cloud, and illumines for the nonce, what before was dark and desolate.

"I will! There! Are you satisfied?"

He takes her in his arms, and holds her to his heart.

"I am, darling—quite. And now, we can read the telegram with less fear and trembling. At worst it will be but a question of time."

His fingers do tremble, nevertheless, as he tears open the envelope, and unfolds the paper within:

Not by a jugful. Come home, is all it says, but it is enough for Allen.

"I don't understand," says Lady Edith, who reads the obscure sentence with him. "It is some joke, isn't it?"

"I wish it were," Allen says, with a sigh. "Oh, no, it is only too clear—to me. It means this : that I must go home without delay—not because I am ordered, but because I see it is the only thing to do. I am not disappointed. I knew he would answer so."

"He refuses, then," cries Lady Edith, bursting into tears. "And—and you must go away, all those miles? Oh, I can never let you do that."

"But, my darling," says Allen, "I must. Don't you see it is the only thing to do? I must do as he bids me if I wish to please him, and never fear but I shall be able to win him over. I must and I shall."

"But you won't stay long? You will come back? Oh, promise me you will. I did not know how much I loved you. I can not bear the thought of your going away from me."

"Say that again and again to me, dearest. It turns our misfortune into a happiness for me. But for this I should not have known your love. That makes up for every disappointment," and he holds her closer to him. "And now," he says, presently, "I suppose I must go and tell your father and mother."

"Oh, dear, what shall you tell them?" Lady Edith murmurs through her tears. "It seems all so hopeless when one thinks of them."

"No, darling. Remember what you have promised me. I shall tell them this : The reply is not so satisfactory as I hoped, but that I can make it all right by going back."

"I'm so afraid they will be rude to you."

"I shan't care if they are. The happiness of the future will make ample amends for any unhappiness in the present. Let us think of that."

When Allen tells Lord and Lady Oaktorrington of his father's answer, couched in the modified terms he has thought best to use, they are at first inclined to show their resentment to him in a manner more marked than by mere rudeness. After the first flash of ill-temper and chagrin fades away, they take a philosophic view of the situation, and see that Allen's return to America is the best, nay, the only, thing to be thought of.

"Even if he doesn't succeed, it will get him out of Edith's mind—for I really believe the child is silly enough to have feeling in the matter—and that is something to hope for, if he hasn't any money," Lady Oaktorrington says, complacently, as she and the marquis talk it over together. "I have sometimes thought," she adds in a whispered undertone, as if the walls had ears to hear the treason to her class principles, "that perhaps we are making a mistake in adhering so strongly to the settlement, if there is so much difficulty. One forgets the consul's telegram."

Lord Oaktorrington is already weary of the whole subject, and is only too willing to dispose of it as easily as possible.

"Yes, suppose we do relax our demands—give up the settlement," he says. "Have no more bother."

"And yet," says the marchioness, converted back again as much by her husband's ready acquiescence, as by the family considerations which arise in her mind, "what would our relations say?"

"Oh, bother them."

"It's easy to say that. But they have too much to leave to make us indifferent to them. Not a farthing should we get from anybody, if we broke through our family custom."

"Yes, I expect you are right," says Lord Oaktorrington, won over the instant money is suggested. "You generally are."

"I know I am," Lady Oaktorrington replies. "Yes, he must go."

And so on the following Saturday Allen sailed in the "Umbria" from Liverpool for New York.

CHAPTER XXV.

IT is the height of the London season. Town was never fuller; society never gayer; the summer sky never brighter; the season never better; Parliament never livelier.

"The Marquis and Marchioness of Oaktorrington and the Ladies Mary and Edith Vesey have arrived at 999 Eaton Square from Ashwynwick Park, Herts, for the season," announced the "Morning Post" in its columns of "Fashionable News," on the 1st of May, and at 999 they are still.

On this particular June afternoon the inmates of the said mansion are scattered. Lord Oaktorrington is either at the Carlton Club in Pall Mall, a Horse Show at Islington, Tattersall's, or (the odds on the last) smoking cigarettes and shipping shandygaff with Miss Valerie Trefusis of the Gaiety Theatre in the honeysuckle-covered summer-house of a neat villa near Lords' Cricket-Ground in St. John's Wood Road; Lord Frederick·Vesey, who is now M. P. for Bridgeleigh, is playing in a cricket-match, at Hunting-

ton Oval, for his county against the " Players " ; Lady
Mary and Lady Edith have gone to a garden-party at
Marlborough House under the chaperonage of their
aunt the Duchess of Kensington ; and Lady Oaktorrington, kept indoors by a slight cold (of her own
manufacture) caught at Ascot on the cup day last week,
is sitting at her writing table in the drawing-room.

"*My father has consented at last*," she reads aloud
to herself for the dozenth time from a letter she holds
open in her hand, "*to do all that you wish. I shall
leave at once for England, and take the first steamer
from New York I can get. At latest I should be with
you the end of this month, after which there need be no
further delay in the marriage. I am anxious it should
take place at once. I shall let you know by cable of my
sailing from New York.* It's curious we haven't
heard, for there are only two days of June left," she
says, putting down the letter to consult the framed
calendar before her. "I hope there can be no new
trouble." Even as she speaks the butler enters with a
telegram on a silver waiter. It is from Allen, dated
Queenstown.

Have just arrived here, it says, *Will be in London Thursday evening. No time to cable from New
York. Everything all right.*

"Thursday ? That's to-morrow. Dear me, what
a relief it is to have this business arranged at last ! "
Lady Oaktorrington says, leaning back in her chair,
and folding her hands in her lap. "And to get Edith
so comfortably settled, with Maud coming on so fast !
Fancy two *passée* girls for next season ! It is not
quite the match I should have chosen for her, but one
can't pick and choose in these days like our mothers

used. He's as good as Grubbings the brewer's son, or young Caper the pickle-maker's nephew, and they've each married a duke's daughter within the month. Dear me, no. He's most gentlemanlike and presentable, I'm sure. What a sell it will be for the Bouveries! How I wish I could let them know. Yes, I think I am quite safe in doing that now."

She reads the letter and telegram over again, putting special emphasis on *My father has consented at last to do everything you wish* and *everything all right*, to reassure herself, and then takes up her pen and writes :

A marriage is arranged and will shortly take place between Lady Edith Vesey, second daughter of the Marquis and Marchioness of Oaktorrington, and Mr. Philip Allen, of San Francisco, U. S. A.

She copies this, signs her name at the bottom of each, addresses one to the " Morning Post " and the other to the "Court Journal," rings the bell, and dispatches them to catch the afternoon post for the evening's delivery. She has barely done so when Lady Henry Tollemache is announced, followed shortly by Montie Vereker.

"Gone to Marlborough House, have they?" Lady Henry says. "I'm sorry now that I didn't go. But really Tummy's parties are such dreadful crushes that no one sees your frock however swell it is ; and then they are so awfully mixed, don't you know. Fancy Henry Irving and Toole were at the last I'm told. I think that is carrying things a trifle too far, don't you ? "

" I hope I'm not disloyal, dear, in saying so," says Lady Oaktorrington, "but I'm not surprised at any-

14

thing the prince does. It's a great pity he doesn't take a real interest in something useful. The army, for instance."

" He does. He's a field-marshal and I don't know how many colonels of regiments," says Montie Vereker.

" Is he really ? "

" Oh, by-the-bye, I hear that Beyndour is going out to the Soudan with the Camel Corps. Awful hard lines to be dragged away in the middle of the season like that, isn't it ? "

" It's a great shame, I think, the way men of rank who go into the army are expected to rough it like common people," says Lady Oaktorrington. " It's all Lord Wolseley's fault, of course. He is a Radical, and hates people whose titles are older than his. So he has got up this Camel Corps as a special thing for noblemen, and he's had it put into the papers in such a way that they can't refuse to go into it. It was his doing sending the Blues and Life Guards to Egypt. Just fancy ! Regiments that hadn't left London since Waterloo. I call it shameful. Don't you ? "

" Of course, I do. I'm sure he'll ruin the army if he goes on. He'll drive gentlemen out of it."

" That he will. I know Beyndour was on the point of sending in his papers a week or two ago, and, several of his brother officers, ás well as other men in the Household Cavalry, were going to do the same, when this Camel Corps was announced. Of course, they couldn't leave then without all sorts of things be-ing said about them, like what was said of the poor Duke of Cambridge in the Crimea."

" What was that ! " asks Lady Henry. " That was before my time."

"That he showed the white feather by coming home on sick-leave in the most important part of the campaign.   They said he shammed illness to get away."

"The beasts!   Because he was a royalty of course."

"Exactly."

"One can hardly blame them sometimes," says Vereker.   "Now look at Connaught.   The Queen wouldn't let him expose himself to any danger that time at Tel-el-Kebir.   He was kept safely in the line of reserves, by her orders."

"But mightn't the reserves have been called upon," suggests the marchioness, loyally.

"They weren't, as a matter of fact; and no doubt Lord Wolseley knew they wouldn't be.   Of course, as I say, you can't blame people after that for talking."

"But don't you think it's rather hard upon the Duke of Connaught?   He had to obey the Queen's orders."

"Oh, yes, it's very nice to put it in that way.   It's awfully jolly, though, to be a prince whose mother's a queen."

> "Betty's a lady and wears a gold ring,
>   And Johnny's a drummer and drums for the king,"

sings Lady Henry.   "By-the-by, talking of princes, reminds me.   They say Tummy had a most awful row with the princess the other night because he danced four times running with Miss Chancellor.   Their voices could be heard at the Marlborough Club having it out."

"How dreadful!" cries the marchioness.   "And who is Miss Chancellor, pray?   An actress?"

"Actress? No. You don't know who Miss Chancellor is? You can't mean it. Why, she's the new beauty."

"I thought the young person they call the Jersey Lily was," says Lady Oaktorrington.

"What, Mrs. Langtry? Oh, she's done for herself by going on the stage."

"Chancellor, did you say?" asks the marchioness. "Chancellor? I'm sure there is no peer with such a family name."

"Oh, dear, no. She's *not*

'English, you know,'

sings Lady Henry. She's an American."

"Oh, I say, Lady Oaktorrington!" Vereker calls out suddenly, keeping his eye on Lady Henry, who turns all sorts of colors. "Whatever became of that —hum—that American gentleman you had staying with you last year?"

"Do you mean Mr. Allen?" Lady Oaktorrington asks, drawing herself up.

"Yes. That was his name. Is he in England still, do you know?"

"No, he's not. But he soon will be. We expect him to-morrow night."

"I'm so awfully sorry," Lady Henry says, rising hurriedly, "but I've done a most awfully silly thing. I've actually forgotten an engagement. I promised to go to tea at Lady Darrell's, and I shall just be able to get there before it's too late, if I start at once. You'll forgive me for running away like this, I'm sure, dear Lady Oaktorrington. By-the-by, are you going to the Argenton's ball to-night? Yes? How awfully jolly.

They're dreadfully new, I know—coronet smells of paint, and all that, of course—but they give awfully swell balls, don't you know.   Good-by."

" Poor thing," says Montie Vereker, as Lady Henry's footsteps fade away down the broad staircase.   " She's irrevocably up a tree this time, I'm afraid.   What! You haven't heard?   Why, it's all over the clubs.   Even " Truth " had a very broad hint last week."

Lady Oaktorrington is as fond of a bit of scandal as any one, for all her straight-laced ways before the world's eyes.   She pricks up her ears immediately.

" Pray tell me what it is."

" I'm rather afraid it's an awkward tale to recite in a lady's hearing," Vereker goes on.   " But if you don't mind—"

" Oh, no, I shan't mind in the least, only hurry, for I expect Mary and Edith in every minute.   Pray go on."

" Well, then, they say that Lord Henry has begun proceedings for a divorce—that is, the papers are not filed in court, but they have been made out at his solicitor's for some time, waiting to find the where-abouts of one of the co-respondents."

" Then there are more than one?   How dreadful ! "

" Yes.   Harborough—"

" Oh, really," and there is a gleam of satisfaction in Lady Oaktorrington's eyes.   " One can't be surprised, can one ? "

" No one can't.   But you will be astonished when I tell you that the other is—just guess if you can—I'll give you three chances."

" Lord Swansdale ? "

" No."

" Sir Charles Chatfield ? "

" No. Once more."

" Colonel Delancy-Vere ? "

" No. It's your American friend—Mr. Allen."

Lady Oaktorrington starts forward in her chair and puts up both her hands, while the blood recedes slowly from her face and leaves her pale and wan.

" Impossible," she gasps.

" Not a bit of it. Only too true. And that's not the worst of it. But fancy your not having heard! Lord Oaktorrington and Beyndour must have known it ages ago."

" They never tell one anything. Oh, I can't believe it. She only met him that one day at Ashwynwick."

" It seems that that was quite enough. Lady Henry is no dawdler, you know, and I believe Americans are not given to being over slow on such occasions."

" You don't mean to say that she had the audacity while under our roof to—"

" I'm afraid I do."

Lady Oaktorrington falls back in her chair, her eyes close, and her hands drop limp on her lap. Were it not for the quivering eyelids Vereker would think she had fainted. He is about to ring, but waits a minute to make sure.

Lady Oaktorrington's eyes open again, slowly, and she whispers, " Go on."

" There isn't much more to tell. It's the usual thing—servants. Lady Henry quarreled with her maid, and then the maid went straight to Lord Henry. Harborough, it appears, he didn't mind so much. It's such an old story with him, and as a co-respondent he's rather threadbare. But he couldn't stand the American—that was too much for his sensitive nerves. The evidence, I believe, is pretty conclusive, one of the chief corroborating circumstances being that Lady Henry's pocket-handkerchief—an elaborate lace one—was found in the pocket of Allen's dress-coat by the footman who brushed his clothes. He bagged it at once, and gave it to Lady Henry's maid as a present from himself. She twigged it all in a moment, and has kept it ever since. Then, among Lady Henry's letters, which she received at Ashwynwick, and which her maid regularly opened, was one inclosing, in a blank sheet of paper, a check on Smith, Payne, and Smith's bank for two hundred pounds. He thought himself awfully sharp in not writing to her, but the check can always be proved at the bank."

"Of course, it will all come out in the papers," cries Lady Oaktorrington aghast, as she thinks of her two letters gone to the post. "What a fool I was," she thinks, "to be so hasty! But it may not be too late to stop them."

She makes a dash at the bell and rings it.

"I wonder what the deuce is up now?" thinks Vereker.

"Yes, m'lady, George posted them directly," the butler tells her.

She throws herself into a chair. "*What am* I to do? What *is* to be done?" she inwardly exclaims, twisting her fingers together. "Poor dear Edith! Oh, what a fool I was! I ought to have known better than to rely on a foreigner. How disgraceful of him!—Of course, it is not true?" she asks Vereker, who has been watching her narrowly, and thinks he can guess the cause of her perturbation.

"Ah, only too true, I'm afraid," he says, with a cruel glitter in his eyes. "Of course, that's the reason she wasn't asked to Tummy's garden-party. I could hardly help laughing outright when she said she didn't care to go."

"Oh, I don't mean about her. I mean about Mr. Allen."

"Didn't you see her confusion and haste to get away when you said he was coming to-morrow? She thinks it will all come out now."

"Yes—of course—of course," Lady Oaktorrington cries, in piteous tones.

"You seem to take your friend's difficulty a good deal to heart," Vereker says, carelessly.

"I do." A sudden thought brings salve to her wounds. "I wish we could get him out of it. Is Lord Henry in town?" She leans forward eagerly with the look of a drowning man, who thinks he sees a straw within reach.

"Yes. I saw him at the opera last night." Then, after a pause. "You are thinking of interceding with him in behalf of your friend? It will be quite useless, I assure you. Between you and I, his real object is to get money. He doesn't care a farthing about his wife's honor, and all that sort of thing. He's most awfully hard up, as everybody knows, and he thinks to get a lot of money out of this American, who is said to be very rich."

"All the better," thinks Lady Oaktorrington, smiling to herself. "I shall try, at all events," she tells Vereker.

"I'm sure I don't wish you joy of the effort," he says, getting up to go. "Believe me, it will be fruitless. I know Lord Henry better than you do. Goodby."   .

"What a fool that young man is, to be sure," Lady Oaktorrington observes, as she seats herself at her writing-table again. "I had no idea he was so dense."

"Of course, the old gal means to buy him off," Montie Vereker remarks, as he calls a hansom and drives to Lord Henry's chambers in Piccadilly. "It doesn't take more than half an eye to see that. I'll just go and give the poor chap the straight tip to make the figure as high as he can."

CHAPTER XXVI.

"Lord Henry Tollemache!" announces the butler next morning at 999 Eaton Square, and a fashionably dressed young man walks into the morning-room where Lady Oaktorrington is seated alone.

Lord Henry is tall, slight, and would be handsome but for the words dissipation and late hours written in big letters all over his face, from his dark-encircled eyes to his puffed-out, twitching under-lip. Lady Oaktorrington hardly knows him, except by sight, and has not exchanged a dozen consecutive words with him in her life.

"Pray be seated," she says, composedly. "I hope you will pardon my having taken the liberty of asking you to call here, but I knew of no other way of meeting you without delay, and time is of the utmost importance to consider."

Lord Henry's manners, like those of most of the young men of the day, are not satin-surfaced.

"Um," he grunts, putting down his hat, stick, and gloves on the table among Lady Oaktorrington's worsteds, and then lying back in an arm-chair and placing one leg over the other. "I hope you won't keep me long."

"Not five minutes if we can agree. You know, I dare say, or can imagine why I wished to see you."

"Haven't the ghost of an idea," he says, yawning, and putting up his hand, not to cover his mouth but to shield his left eye while he winks it.

"That's unfortunate. I shall only have to detain you longer."

"Worse luck for me."

"You won't mind my speaking plainly about your wife?"

"Not a bit. Say what you like."

"Well, then, I've heard you intend to—to—"

"Bring a suit for divorce? Yes, I do. I've put up with Georgina's little playful ways long enough. She's been playing the fool for five years, now."

"I hear—among others—you intend to make a friend of ours a co-respondent?"

"Who? Harborough?"

"No."

"Fitzwilliams?"

"No. Mr. Allen."

"Oh, the Yankee. Yes, I do. And by Jove, I mean to make him pay up. I like the fellow's cheek, truly."

"I suppose nothing would induce you to leave him

out," and Lady Oaktorrington puts the shadow of a stress upon " nothing."

Lord Henry looks quickly at her and then away.

" What! No fear. I expect to get more damages out of him than all the others put together."

" Then it's a mere matter of money with you? "

" Yes, of course. What else should it be? You don't suppose I'm doing it for fun. I hope I'm not such an ass as that."

" How much do you think you are likely to get? "

" Don't know. Depends on how many fellows there are, don't you know," and Lord Henry looks like a professor of mathematics elucidating a problem in algebraic equations. " The more there are the more there'll be."

" I mean from this Mr. Allen. The evidence is not positive against him."

" Not positive ! I only wish it was so sure against the others. The jury will give me two thousand pounds at least, so my lawyer tells me. He says juries are particularly down upon Americans nowadays."

Lady Oaktorrington elevates her eyebrows at the sum, but says nothing for a minute or two."

" You would be glad to get even one thousand, I dare say? "

" Um. Don't know." He looks at her to see how much further he'd better go, but only meets a placid, unreadable expression and a cold, indifferent eye !

" Why? "

" Because I thought, perhaps—" she stops and looks down at the floor.

" Perhaps, what? That half a loaf was better than no bread? Not when I'm sure of the whole loaf," and

Lord Henry slaps his glove across the palm of his hand to emphasize the two last words.

"I think it is rather a case of a bird in hand, et cetera," says Lady Oaktorrington, calmly. "Now, I'll tell you what, Lord Henry. Lord Oaktorrington and myself are most anxious that our names should not be drawn into a public controversey in the divorce court. We do not want Ashwynwick made the scene of your wife's indiscretions. She was our guest at the time, as was also this Mr. Allen. I suppose the fact that she was receiving our hospitality would have no weight with you in abstaining from—"

Lord Henry jumps up from his seat, and kicks down his trousers legs.

"Do I look daft?" he asks. "Am I going to chuck up a lot of money for any such rot as that? I didn't want you to ask her to stay with you. It's no obligation to me. A charming pair you asked to meet her, too! Harborough and this Yankee! I suppose I'm to blame for that."

"We won't discuss that," Lady Oaktorrington says, quietly. "Nor waste any more time beating about the bush. I will be plain. If you leave this Mr. Allen out of your divorce suit, and not bring us and our house before the public in such a disreputable light, I will give you a check for a thousand pounds."

Lord Henry's eyes sparkle.

"When?"

"Now—this minute—here is my check-book. Will you consent? Yes, or no?"

Lord Henry stops to wonder, just five seconds, if he can't do better, and then says:

"Ye—es. Give us the check."

She inserts the sum in a check already signed, tears it out of her book, and hands it to Lord Henry.

He takes it, turns it over and back again, examines it, and scrutinizes it in every part. " Hadn't you better cross it ? Ransom, Bouverie & Co. Thanks."

Lady Oaktorrington rings the bell.

" Show Lord Henry Tollemache out, please."

Lord Henry flushes red with anger. His eyes flash and glitter, and his lips mutter something that sounds only like a sullen hiss. He raises the check in both hands, and his fingers and thumbs clutch at the edges as if he were about to tear it in two. But he doesn't. He thinks of the piles of blue enveloped " midsummer " bills that lie upon his table ; he remembers how he has promised Dolly Vernon of the " Avenue " a Continental jaunt when the season is over—and he recollects the various and many things that can be done with a thousand pounds, and his rage cools with their contemplation.

" By-the-by, Lady Oaktorrington," he says, while he deposits the check in his waistcoat-pocket, and slowly draws on and buttons his glove. " Have you seen the " Morning Post " ? There are some odd marriage announcements worth reading. Ta-ta ! "

CHAPTER XXVII.

ALL London is at the Duchess of Kensington's ball. That is to say, all London west of Regent Street and south of Piccadilly, and of that, those only who are "in the swim " of the highest society.

Kensington House is one of the grandest residences

in Park Lane, and one of the finest town-houses in
London.   Yet the crowd is so vast that even the great
wide hall and broad staircase are thronged with people.
The ball-room is the immense picture-gallery of the
mansion, from whose walls the bewigged and beruffed,
the bepowdered, berouged, and bepatched ancestors of
the Molyneuxes (such being the family name of the
Kensington dukedom) in slashed doublets and armor,
short-waisted frocks and bust-displaying gowns, look
down in silence upon the equally *decolleté* dresses and
somber male evening attire of the present day.   Here,
crammed together in standing rows of three and four
deep round the walls, and in a mass of surging, jost-
ling, pushing, elbowing, hustling, and bumping, otherwise dancing, humanity in the center, are some of the
greatest people in the land.

It is long past twelve, and the Marquis and Marchioness of Oaktorrington and Lady Edith Vesey have
only just arrived from a reception at the Russian
Embassy.

Allen, who has been waiting and watching for them
for the last half-hour, feeling rather a fish out of water
during the tedious operation, meets them in the hall.

" How awfully late you are ! " he says.   " I thought
you would never come.   They are playing a waltz in
there, so don't waste a minute more out here than you
can help.   Let me see your card."

Lady Edith, unaccustomed to such enthusiasm, can
not help showing in her face and voice the irritation
it causes her.   People on all sides have stopped conversing, or turned their heads from looking elsewhere
to take note of them.

" I wish you wouldn't talk so loud," she says, irritably. "I suppose you mean my programme," and she gives it to him.

"I suppose I have the right to take you into the room, now?" and he offers his arm.

"Take me into the room? I don't know what you mean. Pray put your arm down at once. People don't go into ball-rooms arm-in-arm in England. At least, *we* don't. I must go with mother."

"Come, Edith," her mother says at that moment, giving Allen a slight bow and smile of recognition.

Lord Oaktorrington, having stopped to speak to some one in the crowd, the marchioness goes on alone, followed silently by Lady Edith, Allen making his way after them.

Lady Oaktorrington .formally introduces Allen to her sister, the Duchess of Kensington, whose sole remark is a stiff "How d'ye do?" and they pass on into the ball-room to make way for others pressing from behind. They stand among the crowd in silence for a time. Allen is the first to speak.

"Are we going to stick here like this all night?" he asks, with some impatience in his tone. "Don't you intend to dance?"

Before Lady Edith can answer, a small fat man with a bald head, short reddish beard, heavy droopcornered eyes, and a smirking smile, followed by a couple of other men with brass buttons on their coats, passes by through the crowd which makes obsequious way for him, the gentlemen bending their heads, and the ladies courtesying low.

Allen thinks he recognizes the human impersonation of dozens of photographs and woodcuts he has seen, but is not sure.

"Who is that swell!" he asks.

"How rude of you not to bow!" she says, crossly.
The aristocrat has grown strong within her in this in-
tensity of her own sphere, and she can't keep down a
sense of humiliation which creeps over her at the
thought of what seems to her at the moment her mis-
alliance. All about her are dukes and marquises and
earls, duchesses, marchionesses, and countesses by the
score, and lords and ladies by the gross, all of whom
have, as has she, each infinitesimal rule of aristocratic
form and ceremony at their fingers' ends, and with
whom not to be *au fait* of which would mean social
degradation. And here beside her stands her affianced
husband, a man who is as ignorant of these things as
is a chimney-sweep or a costermonger. She has never
realized before, as she does now, the downward step
she has taken. For the moment she is ashamed of
herself, ashamed of Allen, and her vexation grows as
she reflects upon her position. She almost hates him
for the instant as she looks at him, all unconscious of
her ire, poor fellow, and says, sharply:

"If you can't behave properly, I must beg of you
to leave us. It's fortunate mother didn't see you,
though dozens of others did."

Allen looks at her in amazement.

"I—I don't know what you mean," he stammers.

"Why didn't you bow to the prince? I'm so
awfully ashamed of you."

"Was that the Prince of Wales? How was I to
know?"

She groans inwardly.

"Fancy marrying a man who doesn't know the

Prince of Wales when he sees him!" she thinks. "How can I ever go on with it?"

"Ought I to have bowed to him?" he asks. "I didn't know."

"Of course you ought."

"O, come, there's no need to make such a fuss about it," he says, a trifle ruffled at her tone. "How can I be expected to know these things? I'm an American. You seem to forget that."

"I wish I *could* forget it," she answers, quickly. "Unfortunately, you give me no chance to do so."

The color comes to his face with a rush, and his lips compress tight.

"I wonder at myself standing this sort of thing so humbly," he says, hoarsely, in a low voice. "I wouldn't from any one else." She does not answer. "As I seem to annoy you so, perhaps I had better go. Goodnight," and before she can stay him by word or look he has vanished in the crowd. She would follow him if she dared, but the very "form" which she has been invoking for his condemnation forbids. No sooner is he gone than the inevitable reaction that ever attends unkindness to those we care for—self-reproach and unavailing regret—sets in with mighty force.

"What a fool I am!" she cries aloud to herself. "I'm so awfully sorry, now. What could have made me so unkind! I believe I have the most ungovernable, abominable temper on earth. And how good and patient he was! Can I ever make it up with him?"

"Can I have a glance at your programme, Lady Edith?" says Montie Vereker. "I hope you've something left for me. By Jove! What? I'm lucky. Mr. Allen has positively left one *valse* free. Oh, I beg your

15

pardon. I believe I must offer my congratulations, et cetera, et cetera. Eh?"

"Thanks very much," Lady Edith answers, looking down at her gloves.

"I'm sure I hope you'll be very happy," he goes on; "though to tell you the truth, I'm blessed if you look so at this moment. What is the matter?"

"Oh, nothing," she says, looking up and forcing a smile. "Nothing at all."

"I'll back there is, though," he says to himself. "No wonder, having to marry a cad like that. I'm surprised at her father and mother. Oh, the curse of gold! By-the-by, Lady Oaktorrington. Who do you think I saw a minute ago? Lady Henry."

"What—here?"

"Fact. Didn't you tell the duchess?"

"No. I wish I had. I thought every one knew. So you told me."

"I'm afraid I drew it a trifle too strong if I said that. You mustn't go too much by what I say. I sometimes make mistakes you know," and he grins, elfishly. "By-the-by, you've squared it with Lord Henry, I hear," he adds, in an undertone.

"Who told you?"

"She, herself, just now. She was in great glee over it, and said she'd like to come and thank you. She evidently thinks you did it for her sake."

"I hope she'll do nothing of the sort. I should be very rude to her. Why, Edith, where is Mr. Allen?"

"Gone home," says Lady Edith, shrugging her shoulders.

"Gone home?" echoes Lady Oaktorrington.

"At least, I suppose so. He said 'good-night,' and went away."

"I'll bet a fiver he's here still," Vereker whispers to Lady Oaktorrington. "And I'll back I could tell exactly where he is at this moment."

"Do you really think you could find him?" Lady Oaktorrington asks, anxiously. "Oh, would you, Mr. Vereker? And tell him I wish to see him. I should be so much obliged to you."

"All right," says Vereker, taking his leave. "I shall be only too glad," he adds to himself, "to show the fellow up, if I can. She'll have ten thousand pounds at least. Four hundred a year isn't a bad addition to one's income."

In a quarter of an hour he returns.

"Just as I expected," he tells Lady Oaktorrington, in a whisper. "He's with Lady Henry on the stairs. Did you ever know such brazen effrontery? I think you may safely give me this *valse*," he says, turning to Lady Edith. "He won't claim it, you know, if he's gone home."

CHAPTER XXVIII.

As Allen abruptly leaves the ball-room if his condition of mind and feeling is not quite, it is at least verging upon, that which he experienced on quitting the billiard-room at Ashwynwick on the night of his adventure with Lady Henry Tollemache in the ante-room. Although he may not be, as he was then, indignant and resentful, he is hurt to the quick, humiliated, and disappointed. He feels that it must be quite impossible that any woman who really cared for him could treat him so cruelly ; yet his regard for her to whom he has given the one love of his life has not abated one jot.   He still loves her as he has ever done since first he said to himself "She shall be my wife." But it is with a fixed conviction that she does not care for him in return.   The torture of unrequited love gnaws at his heart ; and with brows knit and eyes cast down he leaves her, never daring to look up lest he should see the old pleading expression in her face, and be brought to her feet again in unmanly submission to what he is now satisfied is nothing more than the heartless acting of a coquette, but which he knows will conquer him again as it has done before.   He has not taken a dozen paces before he begins to realize that he is behaving foolishly, if not unmanly.   She is only a woman after all, he argues, and it is unmanly for a man to take serious offense at what a woman says or does.   He should be above it.   Did he follow his impulse he would return at once.   With that intention he looks back and sees Montie Vereker at her side in earnest conversation, and she smiling upon him.   Manlike, he contrasts her ungracious treatment of himself with this, and all the old feelings return with redoubled force, a shade of resentment mixing itself with them.

"I'm a weak simpleton," he says to himself, as he pushes on again through the crowd.   "If she can smile upon others, why should not I do likewise?   But I know no one here.   That's where she has the advantage of me.   No doubt she knows this, and feels quite safe in letting me go from her without a word."

He reaches the grand staircase, and his onward path is checked for the moment by some new arrivals

coming in. While he stands waiting, he feels a sharp
tap on his shoulder from behind, and hears a woman's
voice say :

"Mr. Allen, aren't you going to speak to me?"

He turns, and sees Lady Henry Tollemache, sitting
on the stairs half a dozen steps up, in the act of drawing back her fan over the railing of the banisters.

Every recollection connected with her rushes into
his brain like the shock of an electric battery. His
first impulse is to pretend not to hear, and get away
as quickly as possible. But the incoming tide wedges
him in tight and immovable against the casing of the
stairway, and again her voice reaches him.

"Oh, come, now, I shan't let you treat me so shab-
bily. I insist upon your speaking to me."

His nearest neighbors regard him with looks of
blank surprise. It is becoming almost a scene. He
must answer her if only to avoid one.

"I beg your pardon," he says, with a serious face.
"How do you do?"

She thrusts out a little white-gloved hand through
the banisters for him to take.

"Do come up here and sit down a moment. There's
room beside me. I have something I particularly wish
to say to you."

The eyes of every one are upon him—a man refus-
ing to sit beside a woman at her own request! That
is how it appears in plain English. Can he, as a man,
as an American, allow such a stain to remain upon his
gallantry?

"I'll come as soon as I can," he says, and edges
round by slow degrees to the lowest step. When there,
for a moment the thought comes to him to dash out

through an opening before him left by the fat figure of an incoming dowager. He hesitates, and the space closes up again. It is too late.

"How slow you are!" comes the voice again to him, and the people still look. There is nothing else for him, so up he goes, receiving many ill glances and muttered imprecations from the couples he dislodges in his passage.

"I've been so anxious to see you," she says in a low, whispering voice, as he sits down beside her, "to thank you for—"

"Pray don't refer to that," he says, quickly, and he feels his temples grow hot. "I should like to forget about all that."

"*All?*" and she gives him a half-closed eyelid volley.

He would like to say, emphatically, "Yes," but he knows he will feel like a prig if he does, and certainly be thought one by her. He can't stand that. So he looks at her, and shakes his head. She is looking her best. Her gown of light blue satin fits her like a glove about her creamy shoulders and small waist; diamonds sparkle on her soft and undulating neck, on her white, rounded arms, and in her hair. One little blue satin foot, with an inch of open-work stocking over the arched instep, peeps out from beneath her short skirt, and a subtle perfume, as from a jasmine-covered bower on a moonlight night in June, exhales itself from her person, and lulls the senses into a delicious repose. Allen is conscious of the charm that takes possession of him, and, being only a man after all, he is glad he is here.

"Oh, by the by, I must con—"

Allen puts his fingers on his lips :

"Not now, please."

"What! Another forbidden subject? What *are* we to talk about?"

"Anything," he says. "Tell me who all these dreary people are. You know everybody."

"Dreary people?" she echoes. "Don't you know that those are some of the smartest people in the kingdom?"

"Are they? I shouldn't have thought it. They look so painfully unhappy, so stiff and formal and subdued. Are all balls in England so—so depressed as this?"

"Aren't American balls like this?" she asks.

"I should be sorry for them if they were," he tells her. "We may not have such grand people at them, but there is a life and spirit, a lightness and airiness, of jollity, geniality, and *bonhommie* about an American ball that I do not notice here. Your balls are like everything else that is aristocratic. They are suffused by such an atmosphere of repression and restraint that Nature can not draw breath at them."

"I like jolly, cheerful people," she says, brightening up. "I'm sure I should like America. Don't you think I should get on there?"

"I have no doubt about it. I should think you would get on anywhere."

"Thanks," she smiles. "It does one good to be appreciated sometimes."

"But tell me who all these people are," Allen says, thinking it safer to check the drift the conversation has taken at once. "I'm most anxious to know."

"Shall I? Very well, then, let us begin."

A second little blue satin foot joins the first, and, resting itself caressingly upon it, shows three inches more of stocking about a trim and slender ankle.

CHAPTER XXXIX.

"Do you see that tall, handsome, well-preserved, Frenchy woman?" Lady Henry begins. "The one in crimson satin and a tiara of diamonds. She was a beauty once though you'd hardly think so. She's the Duchess of Liverpool. I'll wager Marly is not far off. Yes, there he is going up to her now. Look! That thin, long-faced, man with a red beard and a funny straight nose. You must know who he is, surely, if you've been in the House of Commons."

"Do you mean Lord Marlington?"

"Yes, of course you know the scandal about him and the duchess?"

"No, I don't."

"Oh, no one ever thinks of inviting one without the other to stay anywhere. He won't go without her or she without him. Like love birds, isn't it?"

"Hasn't she got a husband?" asks Allen.

"Yes; I'll show him to you presently. I saw him not five minutes ago."

"Is that he near her?"

"Near her? No, indeed. That's the last place you'd find his Grace. Oh, there he is talking to Charlie Beresford. You know *his* curly brown hair and dancing eye, of course."

"Yes, I've seen him. Is that fat, red-faced man with the white hair and beard, the duke?"

"Yes; that's his Grace of Liverpool."

"He doesn't look as though he cared much."

"Nor does he. Funny, isn't it?"

"It's rather too serious to be funny," says Allen, thoughtfully. "There would be some shooting over it in California. The lowest man in America wouldn't put up with what one of your highest appears to enjoy in England. It's marvelous to me."

"But, you see, we don't go in for shooting about things as you do in America. We get damages in the divorce court. Make the other chap pay up, don't you know."

"Treat it as a mere matter of money," says Allen.

"Exactly. Those who dance must pay the piper. It's the best way."

"Then why doesn't the duke go for his lordship's pocket at once."

"I don't know, I'm sure. I expect he's waiting to let the damages accumulate," says Lady Henry, in the most matter of fact way. "But we are missing loads of people jawing like this. There! Look at that funny, thin, dried up, old lady with the odd fluffy white hair standing out round her head, near the ball-room door. Do you see? That's Sophia, Countess of Newberry."

"She is a queer-looking old creature, for a fact. But, what of her? Is she carrying on a game with—"

"Hardly," and Lady Henry gives him a pat with her fan. "She's over eighty. Yet, do you know, she's the most sought after guest in the kingdom, and goes everywhere. There's no one Tummy likes to have at Sandringham so much as her."

"Why, I wonder?"

"Oh, she's so bright, and witty, and says such amusing things in an old-fashioned quaint way. Tummy likes to be amused."

"Tummy is the Prince of Wales, isn't he?"

"Hush! Yes. You musn't talk so loud or you'll be up for high treason."

"Shall I? Why you all call him that? Yes, and the Queen 'Judy' and 'Mrs. Brown?'"

"I dare say we do. But we don't shout it out at the tops of our voices. I should hope we were too loyal for that sort of thing."

"Then your loyalty consists in keeping your disloyalty secret?"

"Eh? I don't understand."

"It doesn't matter. I know the meaning of 'Judy' and 'Mrs. Brown,' but 'Tummy'—what is it?"

"Do you mean to say you don't know?" and Lady Henry looks at him incredulously. "Nonsense."

"Haven't the faintest idea."

"Why, it's what children call their—their—do you know. It refers to his waist."

"Oh, I see," laughs Allen. "How stupid of me not to have guessed it! But I say," he hurries on as he sees a twinkle in her eye at the sound of his national word; "who is that little old weather-beaten man talking to old Sophia?"

"Old Sophia? Don't be disrespectful," and she raps his knuckles with her fan. "That's no less a personage than Sir Billy Buckle—odd name, isn't it? He's near eighty, if not quite. I believe he was in the navy with Nelson or somebody. He's an admiral now, and is another of Tummy's pals, and goes with him everywhere, from the Derby and Newmarket to

Cowes and the Engadine or the Riviera or Cannes or Homborg, or wherever he goes to recuperate every year after the season. He does all sorts of grotesque things to amuse the prince. Last year at Cowes he dressed himself up as an old French woman with short skirts and danced the can-can. Wonderful, isn't it, for an old man like that?"

"Rather undignified though, don't you think?"

"Oh, you Americans are so awfully goody-goody —on the surface."

"Are we?"

"Yes, and devils underneath."

"I'm glad there's some good in us even though it be but a skin. I don't think we, as a nation, hold a monopoly of one of the characteristics you mention. There, for instance, is an Englishman who isn't even goody-goody—as you call it—on the surface. He's bad all through."

"Who do you mean?" she asks, quickly.

"Does my description fit so many of these—these gentlemen, that you can not tell which I refer to? Ha ha! I am not surprised. I meant the Duke of Harborough."

"Is *he* here?" she asks, turning as pale as she can under her rouge.

"Where!"

"There, by the fireplace. I don't wonder you ask. He's hardly the sort of man one would look for in the highest society, is he?"

"He is a bad lot," she answers, dreamily. "But he's a duke."

"There's no shield like strawberry-leaves. But where is he? I don't see him."

"He's gone into the ball-room." Lady Henry gives a sigh of relief. "I'm so glad. I was afraid he was coming here."

"He had better keep out of my way," Allen says, fiercely. "I've determined to insult him as grossly as I can wherever I'm able to do so without infringing the rules of hospitality. I should just like to catch him in the street once."

Lady Henry smiles delightedly.

"This *is* a compliment," she says, to herself. "Of course, he knows." Then aloud to Allen. "You mustn't be so jealous. I'm sure I don't care a straw for him," and she half shuts her eyes again.

Allen opens his wide in wonder and looks at her.

"Jealous?" he says. "I don't know what you mean?"

"Don't you?" coyly. "I think you do. But never mind now, we'll talk about it another time. Dear me, we are missing a lot of swells. There's Lord Salisbury—that bald-headed man with the short neck, lumpy shoulders, and long, thick beard. He's stopped to speak to Lord Epsom—that big, smooth-faced man. They say he's seldom sober."

"Who? Lord Salisbury?"

"No, you silly! Lord Epsom. That's really the reason he left the Cabinet. The little pale chap with prominent eyes and curled-up mustache, is the brilliant but erratic Randy-Pandy."

"Yes, I know him."

"Oh, of course you must. He married a country-woman of yours. There she is beside him. How awfully pretty she is, so refined and intellectual. They say she's been the making of him."

"Do you know," says Allen, "that you are the first Englishwoman I've ever heard praise her. Why is it?"

"Jealousy, my dear. With all my faults, I hope I'm above such pettiness as that. How odd! Here comes Lady Sanduval, another American lady. You know her, of course?"

"No, I do not. I only know she was Miss Rodriguez, of New York. I never saw her before. I thought she was pretty."

"Ah, yes, poor thing, so she *was* once upon a time. But she has a brute of a husband. No wonder she's gone off in looks."

"Is that he with her? That big, coarse-looking fellow with red hair. He looks like a beast."

"Dear me, no. He goes nowhere. He's cut. That man with her is Lord Weston, the Duke of Grasmere's eldest son."

"Do you mean the man who married a—a—"

"*Femme du pavé?* Yes. When his father succeeded to the dukedom, he offered her a lot of money to let him get a divorce from her, but she was much too clever. She's the Countess of Weston, and will be Duchess of Grasmere some day. Charming, isn't it?"

"Yes, it does rather knock *noblesse oblige* into a cocked hat. Hello, here's a pretty woman. Who is she?"

"That pretty? You should see her close by. She's painted disgracefully, and she's only two or three and twenty. She's the Duchess of Ulster—Lady Irene Dunmore that was. That tall, awkward fellow, with the big mouth and funny eyebrows is Lord Swansdale. He's the manager of a traveling theatrical company."

"Yes, I know. He's been out to America with—what's her name?"

"Hyacinthe Dameron. Has he, really? I don't see any more. Oh, yes. That dark man with the shrewd face, and short, dark whiskers, is Mr. Chamberlaine."

"What? You don't mean Chamberlaine, the Radical member of Parliament? He here?"

"Yes. Why not?"

"When I was in England six months ago he was detested by the nobility, and looked on by them as the most wicked and dangerous man in England."

"Was he? He's a lion now in society. He has behaved so well on the Irish question and deserted Gladstone."

"I fancy his desertion of Gladstone is what really won you Conservatives over. How you hate that man! And yet I've never found one of you able to explain why."

"He's been the ruin of England."

"I'm sorry to hear England is ruined. I didn't know it before."

"Oh, you know what I mean. He would ruin England if he could."

"But why? What has he done?"

"Oh, lots of things. But don't bother about politics. You're an awful bore."

"Yes, that's what you all say. When you have no answer you call a man a bore."

"Never mind. There's Mr. Gladstone now. Talk of the D., etc."

"Where? Do you know I've never seen him."

"Not much loss. But there he is; and actually

bowing to Lord Salisbury and Lord Salisbury to him, as if they were the greatest friends."

"Do you mean that little man with the large head and tremendous shirt collars?"

"Yes, that's the old scoundrel. You can't mistake him."

"He looks different from his pictures when you see him in evening dress. I should hardly have known him."

"I don't think it signifies much what he has on. He's the same old villain still."

"How dreadfully severe you are. I suppose you learn all that from the Primrose League." Lady Henry sniffs and turns away her head. "And who is that smooth-faced man talking to him with the features of a low comedian?"

"Lord Rosemary. That's his wife behind him— that fat, coarse-looking Jewess. She was a Miss Oppenheimer, and had a couple of millions. It was a question of her or the bankruptcy court when he married her. He chose *her*."

"I think I should have preferred the bankruptcy court," Allen says, after a long look.

"I don't see any one else, Lady Henry says, presently. "If we were in the ball-room we could see a lot more. What a lovely *valse* they are playing now. It's 'Dorothy,' isn't it? Don't you like a *valse?*"

"Yes, I do," Allen says, studiously ignoring the gentle hint.

"Oh, by-the-by," Lady Henry says, after waiting a couple of minutes to see if he intends to ask her. "I quite forgot to ask. Is Edith here?"

"Yes, she is—or rather was," Allen replies, with a serious face. "Why?"—

"I thought I saw her through the ball-room door just now dancing with—with—er—with—" she stops to bow to some one in the crowd below.

"With whom?" demands Allen, quickly.

"Eh? Oh, with Jack Bouverie. I was wrong, wasn't I, in telling you she was engaged to him. But everybody thought so. It must be awfully nice to have a girl throw over another fellow for one, isn't it? Jack's awfully poor, you know."

"I thought you never went in for spiteful remarks," says Allen, warmly. "You know she was never engaged to Jack Bouverie."

"Oh, she has told you so, has she? Of course, it must be true, then."

"Hello!" exclaims Allen, looking at his watch. "Would you believe it? It's half-past two."

"Is it possible?" she answers, with a yawn. "I thought it was much later."

"Good-night," Allen says, getting up. "Thank you very much for telling me who all these people are," and without waiting for a reply he pushes on down the stairs, and in five minutes is out in the street looking for a hansom.

"It seems to me," he says to himself, as he lights a cigarette, and the cab rolls on up Piccadilly past the high iron railings of the Green Park, whose trees begin to stand out in the gray dawn. "It seems to me that I quarreled with every one I spoke to."

CHAPTER XXX.

LADY OAKTORRINGTON, after much deliberation and self-consultation, decides not to say anything to Lady Edith of Montie Vereker having seen Allen with Lady Henry on the stairs.

"It will only cause unnecessary trouble and delay, fending and proving," she argues. "It is not as if we wanted a ground for withdrawing from the marriage. On the contrary, it is our duty now to turn a deaf ear to everything. It has gone too far to retract now if we wished, which we don't. The marriage must take place, and as soon as possible."

Lady Edith, happy in her ignorance of any cause for quarrel between herself and Allen save what has been of her own sole capricious and self-willed manufacture, is ready and anxious to ask his forgiveness and be friends again as soon as he shall make his appearance. She has left a sleepless pillow, wet with many a self-reproachful tear, to scribble a little note to send him in case his coming should be tardy, and forgoes her regular morning's canter in the park that she may not miss him when he arrives.

The morning wears on ; the chimney-piece clock in the morning-room, where she and her mother are sitting, chimes the quarter-hours relentlessly from half-past ten to twelve o'clock, and still is there no sign of Allen. The birds have ceased their carolings in the square beneath the rays of the noonday sun, and the open window admits nothing but vertical heat and the scent of the boxed mignonette which decorates the sill, with an occasional rumble of wheels or *tock-tock* of

16

horses' hoofs upon the pavement below. Within, no
sound save the spasmodic scratching of Lady Oaktorrington's quill-pen, as she attends to her daily correspondence, and the monotonous ticking of the clock
breaks the silence which has reigned in the apartment
for an hour.

As the clock's muffled gongs chime the quarter-
past, Lady Edith, unable to restrain her feelings
longer, throws down the crewels with which she has
been pretending to work, and, with a long drawn sigh,
gets up and walks to the window.

"What a fidget you have grown, Edith!" Lady
Oaktorrington says, impatiently, looking up from a
polite and untruthful excuse she is endeavoring to
frame in answer to a dinner invitation which she does
not deem it advisable to accept. "It is impossible to
express one's ideas with you in the room."

"I'm sure I haven't moved before for over an
hour," Lady Edith answers. "I wish I had gone with
Mary, now. I forgot it was the meet of the Coaching
Club," and she thinks how she has wasted a whole
morning away.

"I'm sure I wish you had. Pray be quiet until I
get this tiresome thing written. Here, amuse yourself
reading these letters of congratulation," and Lady
Oaktorrington points to a large pile of letters.

"Thanks, I'm rather tired of them. They are all
alike. 'Hope she'll be happy,' and all that sort of thing."

"They ought all to be answered—at least, those
likely to give presents ought. I've marked them," and
Lady Oaktorrington goes on with her letter. "There!
that will do," she says, presently, putting down her
pen with a sigh, after first carefully wiping it. "Dear

me! it's just half-past twelve. By-the-by, dear, what can have become of Mr. Allen?".

"I can't imagine. I suppose he's huffy with me."

"Huffy with you, dear?" Lady Oaktorrington exclaims. "I think it is you—ahem—er—I think it is your way to imagine people are huffy with you. He surely has no reason to be huffy with you. You gave him none?"

"Yes, I did," and Lady Edith thereupon tells her mother of her behavior to Allen at the ball.

"How silly of you! Of course, that is why he doesn't come. We must send Freddy after him," and the marchioness rings the bell.

Before the bell can be answered, the door opens and Freddy walks in. He has an excited, flushed look in his face, and holds in his hand an open letter.

"I go after him!" he exclaims, in reply to his mother's request. "I don't think you'll want him here again when you hear this. It came by first post, but I've only just got up. It is from Fairfield. Listen:

"*My Lord: We have this moment received the inclosed letter, and deem it our duty to at once apprise you of its contents, being assured that you will communicate them to your family without delay.*

"*We have the honor to remain,*
"*Your lordship's obedient humble servants,*
"*Fairfield & Jenkinson.*

"Here is the inclosure:

"*H. B. M. Consulate,*
"*San Francisco, June 15th.*
"*Gentlemen: Referring to a short correspondence by cable between us of last November, in respect to the finan-*

cial condition of Mr. Samuel Allen of this city, I have thought proper to now advise you of the fact that there are at present serious rumors rife, and apparently with much solid foundation, that the monetary affairs of that gentleman are in a most unsatisfactory state. Owing to the failure of some gigantic mining-stock speculations in which he has of late been engaged, he is currently reported to be on the verge of bankruptcy.

"*Regretting that I am obliged to so soon negative the favorable statement previously made by me in regard to his finances, and trusting that it may not be too late to prevent any disagreeable consequences,*

"*I have the honor to be, gentlemen,*
     "*Faithfully yours,*
          "*Robert Heath, H. B. M. Consul.*

"There ! What do you think of that? Aren't we the most unfortunate people on earth?"

Lady Oaktorrington has stood silently clutching the back of a chair, her face working nervously, and her eyes moving rapidly from side to side, as if seeking for some spot on which to rest them.

"What *are* we to do?" she says in a strange, choking voice. "What *are* we to do? Oh, the dreadful disgrace! We shall be the laughing-stock of everybody. Fancy, the Bouveries! I could go down through the floor for very shame." She hides her face in her hands, and sobs pitifully. "It is our own fault for having anything to do with such a person—for descending from our rank and position."

"No, it is nobody's fault but mine," Freddy cries. "You have to thank me for introducing the blackguard into the house. I admit it. I was carried away by the infernal republican notions I got from living six months in that confounded country. But, never fear, I'll make it all right. I shall give him a piece of my mind that will bring him to his senses. It is not too late. The scoundrel!"

Lady Edith has been standing pale and motionless as a statue, her hands clasped before her, and her eyes closed.

At her brother's last words she opens her eyes and looks at him, her lips trembling with emotion, and a flush of indignation burns in each cheek.

"How dare you call him that!" she cries. "How dare you! What has he done to warrant or justify it? It is not his fault if his father should have been unfortunate in his speculations. Say that the marriage must not take place; say that I can not marry him, if you will! It is me, only me, on whom the blow will fall. If I can bear it, that is all you need consider. But don't abuse and vilify him, and call him outrageous names behind his back. You are a coward to do so."

" Hoity-toity! Did you ever? Who's calling names now, I should like to know?" Freddy exclaims. "Coward, indeed! I should tell him the same to his face, and I will. I wish he were here this minute."

The words are barely out of his mouth when the butler enters.

"Mr. Allen is in the drawing-room, my lady," he says.

"Now," cries Lady Edith, triumphantly, "we shall see if you will."

"Oh, of course," stammers Freddy, "you think it is devilish fine for you to say that. Why should I risk myself alone with the fellow? Those Yankees carry knives and pistols, and think nothing of stabbing or shooting a man."

" How dreadful ! " cries Lady Oaktorrington, running over and putting her arms about her son. " You shall not go near him, dear. I shan't let you."

" By Jove, no, I'll not see him alone, I'm not such an ass ; sneer away, as much as you like, Edith. Discretion is the better part of valor. I'll send a message to Beyndour to come at once and see fair play."

" Hadn't you better have father, too, and telegraph to Oxford for Bertie ? " sneers Lady Edith. " I dare say you could get Cecil up from Eton ; the more the better. But why not have in a couple of policemen to protect you ? Or, better still, get Beyndour to fetch up a troop of the Blues with him to stand guard in the street."

Lady Oaktorrington regards her daughter with blank amazement.

" Are you bereft of your senses, Edith ? " she asks. " I have never heard you talk so in my life."

" I know you haven't. But I am tired of holding my tongue and being kept down and repressed and restrained. I'm sick of this artificial, unreal life."

Lady Oaktorrington holds up her hands with a look of genuine consternation. " Oh—oh—oh ! " she cries.

" Yes," goes on Lady Edith, " and I mean to speak my mind in future. I'm no child to be kept in leading strings forever. And I'll stand up for the man I love—"

" How dreadfully vulgar ! " cries the marchioness. " Fancy a child of mine talking of love ! Faugh ! It is like maids with sweethearts."

" It strikes me you are deuced ungrateful," says

Freddy. " It's only for your own good, after all, that we care a farthing about it."

" It is so very good of you," Lady Edith answers, sarcastically. " I shall, however, act as I think best myself."

" What ! " exclaims Lady Oaktorrington. " Without considering your father's or my wishes ! "

Lady Edith makes no reply.

" I suppose you mean you'd marry him all the same whether he had money or not ? " says Freddy.

" Yes, I would—and I mean to."

" By Jove ! not with my consent."

" *Your* consent ? And pray, by what right do you assume to consider your consent at all necessary ? "

" By the right of a brother. Oh, you may sneer and shrug up your shoulders. It is natural I should wish you to be properly and comfortably married."

" Really ? " laughs Lady Edith. " Much you'd care whom I married, or what chances there were of my comfort if there was only plenty of money to be got."

" Well, I shan't agree to your marrying this fellow, at all events. That's flat."

" I really wish you had something of your own to think about," Lady Edith retorts. " Some occupation that would keep you from busying yourself about other people's affairs. Idle brothers are a curse to any girl."

" Go on ; insult me as much as you like," cries Freddy, goaded by her words. " It won't do you any good. Now, look here. If you don't get money to live on from him you must get it from—us."

" Oh, that's where the shoe pinches, is it ? I ought to have known as much. The more money I marry the less will have to be drawn from your share—or *vice versa.* Is that it?"

"Well, what of it?" asks Freddy, braving it out with a little bluster. "It's natural. Every one for himself."

"Then why say it is for my sake, when it is really for your own that you make all this trouble and difficulty? And now, just let me ask this question. Why shouldn't *I* expect *you* to marry a lot of money, so that I should have more coming to me in consequence? Answer me that."

"But you see, my dear child," explains Lady Oaktorrington, coming to Freddy's rescue. "It is different with Freddy and you. Freddy is a son, and you are only a daughter. Sons must always be thought of first. We can't alter the rules of our class to suit you."

"And why must sons be considered before daughters?" pursues Lady Edith, with the laconic directness of a skilled cross-examiner. She is almost surprised at herself as she goes on, and did she take time to realize her position, would strike her flag in ignominy before the shocked and haughty eye of her mother, and become the subservient slave of aristocratic rule and custom once more. But she does not let herself think. Impelled by a latent power within her, held in check for many a long year, but which has at last found vent, she hurries on, with flashing eye and commanding voice, as if inspired to her own emancipation from the shackles of custom and caste.

"Really, dear, your tone and bearing are most unseemly," her mother says, grandly. "I must really leave the room if you continue this."

"You evade my question! You can not tell me. I thought so."

"Can I not, indeed? It is because sons retain the family name, and daughters who marry don't. One's name must always be kept up," and the marchioness draws herself up proudly.

"And is it possible, mother, that you would let such a consideration as that govern or influence you in the disposition of any money you had to leave?" Lady Edith looks at her searchingly. "Would you treat me so?"

"Most assuredly," answers Lady Oaktorrington, with an unflinching mien, and an eye as cold as Wrangle Island. "Why should I care to what degradation and poverty the name of Allen sank? One must think of one's own."

"But I am your own!"

"Not when you marry."

"Without money," adds Lady Edith. "But suppose I married a duke or a millionaire, what then?"

"What? Oh, of course—er—you know—circumstances alter cases," and the marchioness smiles complacently as if she had said the cleverest, most original, and most consistent thing in the world. "But, my dear child," she goes on, with a serious face. "Pray stop this quarrelsome tone with your brother. Of course, you can not mean what you say. I know you must feel wounded and crushed at the news, so I forgive you. But we must now think seriously of the position we are in. It is very trying to be made a spectacle of before the world, but, of course, your marriage with this Mr. Allen must be broken off at once."

Lady Edith's decided reply is stopped by the entrance of the butler:

"If you please, my lord," he says, addressing Freddy. "Lord Beyndour has gone down to Twickenham on his coach, and won't be back till to-night."

"Confound it!" says Freddy. "I forgot the meet. Is Lord Oaktorrington in?"

"No, my lord."

As soon as the butler withdraws, Lady Edith laughs outright.

"What are you laughing at?" demands Freddy, with a savage voice and threatening action.

"At the opinion that blackguard, that scoundrel, up-stairs would have of you, if he knew how frightened you were of him."

"I don't care tuppence what he thinks."

"Evidently, or you would have at least offered to pay him what you owe him. Perhaps you had better now. He may need it."

Freddy does not answer, and the marchioness affects not to hear.

"Luncheon's on the table," announces the butler.

"What are we to do?" says Lady Oaktorrington. "I suppose we must ask him. It really won't signify.'

"Not with me, you don't," says Freddy. "I shall go and have luncheon at my club."

"He's not likely to fetch his knife or pistol to the table with him, is he?" asks Lady Oaktorrington, in innocent alarm. "Because if—"

Lady Edith laughs out again, and Freddy grinds his teeth.

A footman appears at the door with a letter. He passes it to the butler, who hands it to Freddy.

"What's this? another letter from Fairfield.   More about this—this—" he tears the letter open and reads:

"*My lord:*

"*We have this moment received the inclosed cable dispatch from the British Consul at San Francisco, and hasten to send it and its*—What's this?—*its welcome intelligence to you.*   Where's the inclosure?   Here it is:

"*Rumors false.   Allen has doubled his fortune.*"

"By Jove!   What an escape!"   He throws the papers to his mother, and sinks into an arm-chair. Then he jumps up quickly again.   "What must he think being kept alone so long?   What must the servants think?" he whispers to his mother.   "I must go up and apologize at once."

"Hadn't you better send for Beyndour?" is on the tip of Lady Edith's tongue, but she refrains.   All her ill feeling vanishes before the happiness which comes to her in the thought not only that her marriage can now be one of peace, but that Allen's position is reinstated in the eyes of the world.

"I wish he knew how I stood up for him," she thinks.   "But it does not matter, now."

"Come, Edith, let's make it up," Freddy says, stopping on his way to the door to kiss her cheek. "I've been in a beastly temper, and didn't mean what I said."

"Stay a minute, dear," Lady Oaktorrington says, in an undertone, putting her hand on Freddy's arm. Then aloud to no one in particular, though her eyes regard and her words are intended for the butler and footmen who stand in the hall: "Mr. Allen, did you say?   Is he here?   Oh, dear me yes.   I had quite forgotten him, poor fellow. I shall go myself and fetch him down. I am quite ashamed of what he must think."

"I should have been here earlier," Allen says with an apologetic glance at Lady Edith as he seats himself at the luncheon-table; "but I have been detained by a cablegram from my father which has been dodging me backward and forward, between my bankers in the city and the Metropole all the morning. I only got it ten minutes ago—that is, ten minutes before I came here," he adds with a smile.

"Nothing unpleasant, I hope," suggests Lady Oaktorrington, while a shade crosses her face. What if the rumors are true after all? Or, worse still, what if his father forbids the marriage now that he is so rich? Are her torments never to cease!

"No—not very," Allen answers, with a slight twinkle in his eye, as he hands the telegram to Lady Edith:

"Read it, please."

Prepared for any new misfortune which the ominous brown paper may have in store for her, Lady Oaktorrington sits with clasped hands before her, while Freddy tries to look as unconcerned as he can. Not without some misgivings herself Lady Edith unfolds the telegram and reads:

"*You can double the settlement, and draw on me for five thousand dollars for a present.*"

"So very good of him!" exclaims the marchioness, with a radiant smile, as soon as she gets her breath. "What a very charming person your father must be, Mr. Allen!"

"That's the proper sort of a guv'nor!" shouts

Freddy, in high glee, as he adds to himself, "we certainly shan't have to give her anything now."

   .   .   .   .

"Another small wedding at St. Peter's, Eaton
Square," says the many readers of the "Court Journal," as six weeks later they scan the "Marriages in
High Life," and immediately fall to reading the account of which the following is a full, true, and correct copy :

"On Thursday, by special license, at St. Peter's,
Eaton Square, Lady Edith Vesey, second daughter of
the Marquis and Marchioness of Oaktorrington, was
married to Mr. Philip Allen of San Francisco, U. S.

"Long before the hour named for the ceremony—
three o'clock—a large and distinguished congregation
of the relatives and friends of Lord and Lady Oaktorrington assembled in the church to witness the solem-
nization of the marriage rites. At three o'clock precisely the bridegroom arrived, accompanied by his best
man, Mr. Sanford Van Vleet, of New York, and took
his position at the chancel screen gate. Almost immediately afterward the bride with her father, attended
by six bridesmaids and preceded by the choir singing,
'The voice that breathed o'er Eden,' walked up the
central aisle to the altar-rails, and the service began. The bride was given away by her father. The
ceremony, which was choral, was performed by the
Lord Bishop of Hertford, assisted by the Very Rev.
Lord Basil Herbert, Dean of St. Boniface and the
Hon. and Rev. Harold Trefusis, Rector of Ashwynwick.

"The bridesmaids were Lady Mary and Lady Maud
Vesey (sisters of the bride), Lady Hilda Willoughby,

Lady Ethel Willoughby and Lady Mabel Talbot (cousins of the bride) and the Hon. Beatrix Fitzhardinge. They were dressed in short frocks of pink cashmere, with shoes, stockings, and bonnets to match, and each wore a gold medallion locket with the monogram V and A in brilliants, the gift of the bridegroom, and carried bouquets, also his gift. The bride was dressed in white satin profusely embroidered with seed pearls, and trimmed with old family lace lent by the Marchioness of Oaktorrington and the Duchess of Kensington for the occasion. She wore a *tulle* veil fastened with three diamond stars, the gift of the bridegroom's father.

"After the ceremony, the bridal party adjourned to the vestry where the marriage registry was signed, and then drove to Lord Oaktorrington's residence in Eaton Square where a magnificent wedding breakfast was served, by Messrs. Pirrini and D'Olier of South Audley Street. Only a few of the immediate relatives and intimate friends of the bride's parents were invited to the breakfast. At half past four, Mr. and Lady Edith Allen departed amid a shower of rice for St. Pancreas station, *en route* for Liverpool, from which port they sailed for New York on Saturday in the Cunard steamer 'Umbria.'

"The wedding-cake was supplied by Messrs. Izzard, of Bond Street, and the bridesmaids' frocks were made by Mlle. Eugenie Baissé of Regent Circus.

"The wedding presents were both numerous and costly, and—among many others—included the following:

"An India shawl, a copy of 'Some More Leaves from my Diary in the Highlands' and her photo-

graph (laughing) with autograph, from her Majesty the
Queen; a turquoise and gold bracelet from the Prince
and Princess of Wales; a pair of silver muffineers from
the Marquis of Salisbury; a silver-mounted riding-
whip from the Duke of Harborough; a silver-mounted
dressing- and traveling-bag from the Marquis of Oaktorrington; a point-lace handkerchief and ivory-han-
dled umbrella from the Marchioness of Oaktorrington;
a carriage-clock from Viscount Beyndour; a silver-
gilt paper-knife from Lord Frederick Vesey; a silver-
gilt inkstand from Lord Bertie Vesey; a brass-mounted
plush blotting-book and envelope-case from Lord Cecil
and Lady Maud Vesey; a tea-cosy from Lady Mary
Vesey; a pair of silver napkin-rings from the Duchess
of Kensington; an oxydized silver paper-weight from
the Duke of Kensington; a pair of oxydized silver
spill-holders from the Ladies Hilda and Ethel Willoughby; a hand-painted photograph-frame from Lady
Mabel Talbot; a pair of antique brass snuffers from
the Hon. Beatrix Fitzhardinge; a silver-topped smell-
ing-bottle from Lady Henry Tollemache; a China
plaque from Lord and Lady Bouverie; a carved oak
wall-bracket from the Hon. John Bouverie; a hand-
painted fan from the Hon. Emily Bouverie; a *robe-de-
nuit* case from the Hon. Augusta Bouverie; Tenny-
son's poems from the Hon. Montague Vereker; a
diamond necklace and three diamond stars from Mr.
Samuel Allen (father of the bridegroom); a diamond
and sapphire bracelet, diamond locket, and solitaire
diamond earrings from the bridegroom; a set of gold
and diamond bangles from Mr. Sanford Van Vleet;
a diamond and ruby gypsy ring from Mrs. Leonard
P. Norris; opal and diamond bracelet from General

Simon Jackson; a complete set of household silver from Senator James D. Smith; a half-hunter keyless lady's repeater, with monogram and crest on the back in brilliants from Colonel Livingston, United States Army; a hall-clock and aneroid combined from the servants at Ashwynwick and Eton Square; a silver tea-service from the tenants of the Ashwynwick estates; a set of silver side-dishes from the tenants of the Campsottin estates; and a set of silver teaspoons from the tenants of the Tewtorlock estates."

.   .   .   .

As the steamer " Umbria " drops slowly down the Mersey, crosses the bar, and then with full speed heads down channel, Philip Allen and his bride stand on the hurricane deck and watch the fast-receding shores of England.

"It all seems like a happy dream," Allen says, "from which I fear every minute to awake."

"And I shall not feel quite secure," Edith replies, "until we pass Queenstown. Father or mother or Freddy may be there to take me back again."

"They can't do that now, dear. They couldn't if they would. No earthly power can take you from me, now."

"Are you quite sure?"

"Quite."

"Then I am perfectly happy," and she nestles her face against his shoulder.

As the good ship rounds Holyhead, and the bold and rocky Anglesean promontory gradually shuts out from view the low line of British coast beyond,

Allen, in the silence of his heart, speaks his valedictory :

"Farewell, O great and glorious land ! on the vast and far-reaching dominions of whose sovereign the sun never sets ; on whose national escutcheon history has left no stain ; whose victorious flag has never known defeat ; whose record among the nations of the earth is one long unbroken story of integrity, morality, courage, religion, civilization, liberty, and progress ; whose watchwords are magnanimity to the weak and helpless and resistance to the defiant and strong ; whose guiding star is freedom, farewell ! And, O grand and mighty kingdom, where rank means worth and nobility merit, to whom do you owe all your greatness, all you have done, achieved, gained, won, become, and are to-day, in science, literature, art, commerce, manufactures, and trade, either in peace or in war—your lords or your commons, your people or your aristocracy ? "

THE END.

www.ingramcontent.com/pod-product-compliance
Lightning Source LLC
Chambersburg PA
CBHW031427020726
47499CB00005B/1625